The Daisy Dalrymple Mysteries

Cornish Mysteries

BURIED
IN THE
COUNTRY

A Cornish Mystery

CAROLA DUNN

CONSTABLE • LONDON

CONSTABLE

First published in the US in 2016 by Minotaur Books,
an imprint of St. Martin's Press, New York

First published in Great Britain in 2016 by Constable

A CIP catalogue record for this book
is available from the British Library.

ISBN: 978-1-47211-547-8

Printed and bound in Great Britain by CPI Group (UK) Ltd, Croydon CR0 4YY

Papers used by Constable are from well-managed forests
and other responsible sources.

MIX
Paper from
responsible sources
FSC® C104740

Constable
An imprint of
Little, Brown Book Group
Carmelite House
50 Victoria Embankment
London EC4Y 0DZ

An Hachette UK Company
www.hachette.co.uk

www.littlebrown.co.uk

ACKNOWLEDGEMENTS

Thanks again to Beth Franzese for help with Aikido, and to The Cornish Fishmonger for information about the catch of the day (and month). Especially, gratitude to my sister Helen for once more chauffeuring me from her home on the Tamar to refresh my memories of Tintagel and Bodmin Moor, thus saving me from the horrors of driving in the UK.

BURIED
IN THE
COUNTRY

ONE

Cornwall, February

Eleanor was halfway down the stairs when she heard the phone ring in her flat above. She hesitated for a moment. Teazle, already at the bottom, gave a sharp yip of impatience, but the little Westie had been out once today so she wasn't desperate. Eleanor had a few minutes to spare. The lawyer's office was less than five minutes' walk.

As she turned to go back up, Eleanor was sure the ringing would stop before she reached the phone, especially when she discovered that, for once, she had remembered to lock her door. But the *brrr-brrr* continued, even while she searched her pockets for the key, opened the door, and crossed her small sitting room to the counter that separated it from the tiny kitchen.

Brrr-brrr: Someone really wanted to talk to her. She lifted the receiver and gave her number.

"Mrs. Trewynn? Eleanor Trewynn?" A woman's voice, crisply impersonal, exuding patient determination.

"Yes," Eleanor admitted cautiously. "Who's speaking?"

"Sir Edward Bellowe's personal secretary, Mrs. Trewynn. At

the Commonwealth Relations Office. Just a moment, I'll put you through."

Before her husband's death and her retirement to her little cottage in Cornwall, Eleanor had been ambassador-at-large for an international charity, the London Save the Starving Council. In that capacity she had travelled the world, persuading local officials from village chieftains to national leaders that LonStar was not an imperialist plot.

Her success was not regarded with universal approbation at the CRO, jealous of their turf, but Sir Edward had long been one of her supporters. He had even called on her services, unofficially, at one of the peace conferences that had ended the Nigerian civil war.

"Eleanor?"

"Good morning, Sir Edward. What can I do for you?"

"Good morning. Before I forget, Gina sends her love."

His wife, Georgina, was a dear friend. *Softening me up*, Eleanor thought. "Please give her mine."

"Of course, of course. Er, I wondered whether you might have a few days free at the beginning of next month?"

"I might. I'd have to check my diary. What did you have in mind?"

"If you're available, I'd rather explain that by letter. We want to keep the business quiet, if possible. We're rather sensitive to the possibility of spies."

"Spies?" Eleanor's mind wandered to some of the current Commonwealth trouble spots: Sri Lanka—Sinhalese Buddhists against the Hindu Tamils? Pakistan—East versus West? Northern Rhodesia—blacks repressed by minority whites? Cyprus—Greeks against Turks? There were all too many.

She caught the tail end of what Sir Edward was saying: ". . . on the Friday?"

"This coming Friday? No, you said early March?"

"The first weekend."

"Oh yes. Are we talking about London, or your place in the Scillies?"

"I'll let you know in the letter. If you're free?"

"Hold on a mo. Let me find my diary." She looked round the sitting room and spotted her handbag on one of the chairs by the fireplace. A few days in London at the government's expense would make a nice change, she thought, setting down the receiver and fetching the bag.

As she picked it up, Teazle gave an approving, hopeful *whuff*, but when she returned to the telephone, the little dog sent her a reproachful look, curled up in a fluffy white ball, and went to sleep.

"Sorry, girl."

"I beg your pardon?"

"Sorry, I was talking to the dog. Just a minute." One-handed, she dug through the contents of the handbag. "Here it is. March. First weekend . . . Nothing that can't be postponed." On the other hand, though the Bellowes' house was extremely comfortable and March was a beautiful time of year to visit the Scillies, spring storms sometimes cut off the islands from the mainland, by both sea and air, for days. One might find oneself stuck amid antagonists at daggers drawn. . . .

". . . get it tomorrow or the next day. Give me a ring, reverse charges, of course, when you make up your mind."

Eleanor promised to do so and they said their good-byes. At the click of the receiver being set down, Teazle instantly awoke and trotted to the door.

"All right, we're going." Now where had she put her shopping basket?

She found it on the landing outside the door, where she had dropped it while fumbling for the key. Teazle scampered ahead as she set off down the stairs again.

The ground floor had been converted into a LonStar charity shop when Eleanor bought the cottage, so she wasn't taken aback to see a complete stranger in the passage. Teazle startled the woman, though. She scuttled into the volunteers' lavatory under the stairs before Eleanor could introduce herself.

It was probably just as well. The phone call had taken longer than expected and had already made her late for her appointment with Mr. Freeth. The dog leashed, she hurried past the loo and through the door to the street.

As if to contradict her misgivings about early March in the Scillies, the sun was shining and no trace of a breeze stirred the mild air, full of the smells of seaweed, tar, and the bakery on the opposite side of the narrow road. They turned right, downhill past the front of the LonStar shop. Nick was in the window of his gallery next door, arranging a couple of paintings. Teazle headed for his shop door, but Eleanor had no time for a chat. She and Nick waved to each other.

On the way down the street, she exchanged brief greetings with several people without slowing her footsteps. As she crossed the old stone bridge over the stream, an ancient mariner, sunning himself on the low parapet, stopped her to warn her—his Cornish accent as thick as clotted cream—not to be taken in by the day's warmth.

Gazing out over the small, cliff-sheltered harbour with its stone quay to the blue sea and sky beyond, he said, "There do be a storm a-brewin' out yonder, my lover. Gales afore mornin', you mark my words. Don't 'ee go to sea."

Eleanor promised not to go to sea, thanked him for his advice, and walked on, once again reflecting uneasily on the Scilly Islands in March. A pair of supercilious herring gulls perched on the opposite parapet eyed her, then noticed Teazle and flew off screaming imprecations.

Halfway up the opposite slope stood one of Port Mabyn's largest structures. Built into the hill, on three levels, it had originally been a pair of houses with two front doors. Now it was split horizontally, the lower door leading to the offices of Freeth and Bulwer, Solicitors. Upstairs was the partners' residence. Eleanor had been there for drinks several times, and for a couple of dinner parties. She remembered the sitting and dining rooms as comfortable but unremarkable except for one of Nick's abstract paintings in the place of honour over the fireplace.

Eleanor was acquainted with Freeth and Bulwer's secretary, a large, cheerful woman with improbably red hair. They had met now and then, here and there about the village, including in the LonStar shop.

"Hello, Mrs. Trewynn. Lovely day for the time of year."

"Isn't it? I'm going to take the dog for a walk on the cliffs when I'm finished here."

"Seize your chance before the storms roll in. Mr. Freeth is ready for you now."

"He won't mind if Teazle—?"

"You know he won't. Go right in."

"Thank you, Mrs. Raleigh."

Mr. Freeth came towards the door to greet her with a welcoming smile and an outstretched hand. A slight man of middling age and height, wearing a grey tweed suit, a white shirt, and a grey-and-black-striped tie, his most distinctive features were heavy-framed glasses and sandy hair thinning into a pronounced widow's peak. His smile was friendly and cheerful, though in repose his face had a melancholy cast.

He and Eleanor shook hands. He seated her, bent to tousle Teazle for a moment, then returned behind his desk.

"I just need your signature on a couple of papers, Mrs. Trewynn. It's the same business as last year, regarding the use of part of your house as a charitable enterprise. The government changes the regulations by a few words now and then, and we want to make sure everything is up-to-date. Would you like to read them? Or I can summarise for you."

Peter would have said she ought to read every word, fine print included. But Peter was gone, killed by a rioting mob in a far corner of the world, and Alan Freeth had a sterling reputation. Not that sterling was what it used to be.

"Please, I forgot to bring my reading glasses. If you don't mind?"

"Not a bit. This one just affirms that you receive no rent nor other valuable consideration for LonStar's occupation of the ground floor of your premises."

Eleanor signed. The whole business was finished in ten minutes.

"You'll send your account?"

"Consider it a donation to LonStar, Mrs. Trewynn."

"That's very kind of you. Come on, Teazle, walkies."

"Enjoy yourselves. It's a pity to waste such a beautiful day, especially at this time of year. I wish I could go with you."

Eleanor commiserated. Having more than once met him out on the cliffs, she knew him for a vigorous hiker. He ought to get a dog, she thought. He was rarely accompanied by Mr. Bulwer's tall, stooped figure, his partner being of a more intellectual and con-templative nature.

As she toiled after Teazle up the steep, stony path, helped here and there by steps cut into the rock, Eleanor took off her wind-breaker and tied it round her waist. The February day was turn-ing out almost hot!

Misleadingly hot. Storms could blow up with little or no notice. She really didn't fancy the Scillies in March. She could always decline Sir Edward's invitation, but then, supposing negotiations failed and war ensued, she would always wonder guiltily whether her presence might have tipped the balance.

The ground levelled off into a sward of low, wiry green grass with stretches of taller hay-coloured tufts and frequent outcrops of rock. The lie of the land concealed the harbour below; on the far side of the inlet, Crookmoyle Head sloped up to the lighthouse at the tip.

Eleanor turned in the opposite direction. The curve of the ho-rizon was a distinct line separating dark blue sea from pale blue sky. She walked on till she could look directly down the cliff, a sheer fall to wet rocks and frothing breakers. Beyond, a steady procession of waves rolled into Port Isaac Bay. Teazle stayed a prudent distance from the edge, sniffing after rabbits in the long grass.

A mile or so farther on, they came to one of Eleanor's favourite spots for Aikido practice. Flat and smooth, it was hidden from the path by a granite outcrop taller than she was.

She disliked being watched, not that many walkers were to be expected in February. People were either fascinated or embarrassed to see a small woman with curly white hair apparently disco-dancing without music, in the middle of nowhere, all alone but for an equally small dog with equally curly white fur. It was an embarrassment she didn't want to inflict on her friends, so she had told no one that she was a practitioner of one of the martial arts.

At her husband's insistence, she had learned when she started travelling in some of the most dangerous parts of the world. They had chosen Aikido because of its emphasis on protecting oneself without hurting one's attacker.

Though not expecting ever to have to use it in peaceful Cornwall, she continued to practise as often as possible for the benefits to body and mind. In fact, Aikido had come in useful a couple of times, not in far-off places but right here in Cornwall. Each time, her swift moves had taken no more than a few seconds, so brief a duration as to leave those present slightly puzzled at the outcome and still oblivious of her unusual skills.

Accustomed to her mistress's antics, and uninterested, Teazle wandered off. She never went far. When Eleanor finished her practice, the Westie was lying nearby, nose on paws, ready to continue the walk.

Eleanor glanced at her watch. "Sorry, we'll have to go back or the shops will be shut." Did other people apologise and explain to their dogs? "I've had beans on toast for lunch two days running."

Not that Teazle would understand the desire for a change, even if she understood the words. She happily ate the same tinned food almost every day.

Emerging from behind the sheltering rock, Eleanor felt a breeze on her face, stirring her hair. At the horizon, sea and sky merged into a milky haze. Old Mr. Penmadden's prophesied storm was on the way. They retraced their steps down to the village.

As they passed the lawyers' building, Mrs. Raleigh popped out, holding Eleanor's shopping basket. "I've been watching for you. You left this behind."

"Thank you! I hadn't even missed it yet."

"There's a fishing boat just come in." The secretary was noted for keeping a finger on Port Mabyn's pulse. "If you like fish, it doesn't come any fresher. Back to work. Bye-ee." She retired to her desk in its vantage point at the window.

Eleanor made her way to the quay, where a smack was unloading dripping crates. A deck-hand rapidly filleted a couple of Dover sole for her. He threw the remains to the circling gulls, who caught the pieces in midair and squabbled over them. Teazle gave him a reproachful look.

Outside the greengrocer, they met Jocelyn. The vicar's wife ran the LonStar shop, but she alternated days on duty with her second in command—and bitter rival—the wife of the minister of the Nonconformist Chapel.

"Good morning, Eleanor. I saw you down on the quay."

"I bought some sole."

"I was just going to get some."

"It seemed like a good idea at the time. I'm never sure how to cook it, though." Eleanor's wandering life had not been conducive to the mastery of culinary skills. "Last time I grilled it, and it came out rather like shoe leather."

"You'd better come up to the vicarage for lunch and I'll cook it with ours to show you how."

"Thank you, Joce, but I was going to invite Nick to—"

"Bring him with you. Are you going in here? They have some excellent leeks, but the lettuce is *not* fresh today."

"I'll get leeks," Eleanor promised. She was very fond of Jocelyn, but her friend did tend to be bossy. It was usually easiest to follow her suggestions. "If you'll show me how to cook them so that they don't go mushy."

"All right. You'd better come at one o'clock. I'll pop in and invite Nicholas for half past."

Eleanor hurried through her shopping so as to have time to change into a skirt. Joce had long since given up hinting that slacks were unbecoming to a woman of mature years, but she wouldn't be seen dead in them herself. With a budget as meagre as Eleanor's, she had an enviable knack amounting almost to genius for finding smart and suitable clothes among the donations to the shop.

Nick, as usual, turned up generously bedaubed with paint. He was abstracted throughout the meal. Though he roused himself to say how delicious it was, that was more innate politeness than real appreciation. Tim, the vicar, was, as always, gentle and vague. His occasional comments and questions concerned either his parishes and parishioners or some internal theological debate obscure to Eleanor. She and Jocelyn were left at liberty to discuss cooking, the shop, and the weather.

When Eleanor and Nick left the vicarage, storm clouds were building up in the southwest.

"Damn," said Nick, "it looks as if we're in for a drenching. I'd better move the car up the hill. Is the Incorruptible down by the stream?"

"Do you think it'll flood?"

"Better safe than sorry. What a nuisance! I want to get back to the studio. It was nice of Mrs. Stearns to invite me, but the interruption—"

"You had to eat."

He grinned. "Not necessarily. When things are flowing."

"What are you painting?"

"Nielsen's *Four Temperaments* Symphony."

"Sorry I asked. Why don't you give me the car key and I'll drive yours up to the top parking? Teazle will enjoy riding up and walking down twice."

"When you put it like that . . . Are you sure?"

"Of course," said Eleanor. "After a lunch like that, I need the exercise."

Since finding a market for his serious pictures in London, Nick had splurged on a Morris Minor Traveller, a "Woodie." Though secondhand, it was considerably younger than Eleanor's pea green Morris Minor "Moggie." She enjoyed driving a car that didn't rattle and groan going uphill, as the Incorruptible did.

The space in the back was big enough to lay flat even Nick's largest canvases. It would hold much larger donations when she went on her foraging expeditions, she mused. Could she justify—or afford—a newer, larger car?

Not really, she decided with a sigh as she parked the Traveller in the lot at the upper end of the village.

She and Teazle walked down through the opes, the maze of steps and passageways that gave access to all the houses not fronting the single street. In the tiny sheltered gardens, early daffodils swayed in the freshening breeze, often surrounded by a carpet of purple, yellow, and white crocuses.

The dog was perfectly happy to climb into the Incorruptible and repeat the trip. On the way down, a gust of wind threw a spatter of rain at them.

The next morning, it was still raining, a determined drizzle that seemed set in for the day. The meadow by the stream was underwater, but the bridge was unaffected and the post arrived at the usual time. With it came the expected letter from Sir Edward.

It was in an unofficial envelope, addressed by hand. Only the initials on the back flap told Eleanor whom it was from. He was serious about secrecy, she realised. She mustn't tell even Jocelyn, who had brought up her post after noticing it on the floor inside the street door in the passage below.

"Something interesting?" she asked.

"What? Oh, sorry! No, not particularly."

Joce gave her a sceptical look. "I must get back to the shop. I'll leave you to read it in peace. You won't be out collecting today, I imagine. There'll be water all over the roads. I wondered if you could lend a hand in the stockroom for a while? Miss Macy sent word she has a cold and won't be in."

"Yes, of course." She wasn't permitted to serve in the shop, as she had only to look at the cash register for it to stop functioning. "I'll be down in half an hour or so."

As the door closed behind the vicar's wife, Eleanor tore open the envelope. Tintagel! They were to meet just a few miles up the coast, at the King Arthur Hotel, a massive Victorian excrescence about half a mile from the centre of the village. Perched on the cliffs overlooking the castle ruins, it was generally regarded as a blot on the landscape. These days it would certainly not have got planning permission.

Though exposed to the weather, it was at least accessible. Sir Edward confessed that he had wanted to go to the Scillies, but in view of the stormy long-term weather forecasts, Gina had put her foot down. She would act as hostess.

If Eleanor would arrange to arrive on Friday afternoon, in time for tea, it would be much appreciated.

That was all. No hint as to which particular conflict was to be the object of their efforts at reconciliation. Even Sir Edward, it appeared, considered Eleanor's function to be nothing more than spreading sweetness and light, as Gina's was to make sure the accommodations were in order and everyone was comfortable.

Eleanor would have liked a chance to prepare her thoughts in advance for whatever knotty situation she was about to plunge into. She was annoyed.

London, February
"Hello, Freddy."

"Sandman!"

"Ssshh, don't use that name."

"Sorry. You'd better come on in."

"What a dump. Sunk in the world, haven't you."

"It's not my fault."

"How much a week are you blowing on the Devil's wheel, mate?"

"Not that much. It's hard to find a straight wheel in London, and I can't afford to go back to the Riviera. When did you get out?"

"Couple of days ago. I've been looking for your sister."

"She moved."

"That's bloody obvious, innit. You always were a fool. Dunno why your old man wasted his money sending you to that fancy school. Heard he died while I was inside?"

"Ages ago."

"That's a shame. Smartest man in the business, and not flashy. Never once suspected, was he? Must have put away a packet. So how come you're living in this dump?"

"I went down for another stretch. Just a few months, but he said if I couldn't make a go of it straight or crooked, he washed his hands of me."

"Don't whine. It's pathetic. Gets on my nerves."

"Sorry, S—Vic."

"Does this mean you can't pay what your old man owed me for

CAROLA DUNN

the last haul before I was sent down? The interest's been mounting up while I've been on the Moor, you know."

"Not my problem. My father left the lot to my sister. She sends me an allowance, barely enough to scrape by."

"Ah, now that makes me even keener to talk to her. Where is she?"

"I don't know."

"Pull the other one."

"She moved while I was inside and she never told me. Buried herself in the country somewhere. Said she didn't want me hanging about."

"I don't blame her. But you must have some idea where she is, if she's sending money."

"I get cheques in the post."

"What's the postmark? Where's the bank?"

"I never looked."

"God, don't you have any initiative?"

"There didn't seem much point. She wouldn't give me an extra penny if I went on bended knee."

"We'll see about that. Meantime, I hope that couch is comfortable, because you'll be sleeping on it till the next cheque arrives. Got any smokes? And a beer would go down a fair treat."

"You know I only drink vodka."

"That's right, keep your breath clean for the ladies. Have to step out for some Guinness, then, won't you, mate?"

TWO

Cornwall, March

"The DCI wants to see you, Pencarrow," announced the desk sergeant as Megan entered the Launceston police station. "Pronto. As in an hour ago."

"Oh hell! I knew I should have taken the time to stop for lunch on the way back. Do you know what for?"

He shrugged. "Been a naughty girl, have you?"

She glared at him. He put his hands up in front of him in a gesture of surrender.

"Don't bite my head off! D'you rather I asked if you'd been a naughty boy?"

"No, sorry. It's just that bloody Inspector Bruton in Bude. . . . Never mind. Is Scumble in a bate?"

"Not more than usual. Good luck."

"Thanks."

Megan hurried up the stairs. The headquarters for the northern region of the Constabulary of the Royal Duchy of Cornwall was a three-story building on the Town Square—actually a triangle.

It would not house CaRaDoC much longer. The local force would soon move to a boring modern structure on the outskirts of the small town.

For now, Detective Chief Inspector Scumble had a pleasant view from his office window, a glimpse over the buildings opposite the castle ruins and the green hills beyond. However, responding to his "Come in," Megan had eyes only for her guv'nor.

"Sir?"

"What took you so long, Pencarrow?" The irritable question was for form's sake. "You get it sorted?"

"Yes, sir. There wasn't much to it, just a bit of a kerfuffle in a caravan park. They'll rent to anyone at this time of year, Gypsies, 'travellers,' hippies, you name it. The beat bobby could have dealt with it, but Inspector—"

"Never mind that now. Get your report to me as soon as you can. No hurry."

Megan looked at him in surprise. Usually he wanted a typed report yesterday. "Something's up?" she ventured.

"A lot of tomfoolery," he growled. "First, we have a report of a missing solicitor."

"How long?" She took out her notebook.

"Left four days ago after saying he'd be away overnight."

"But, sir, if we chased after every adult male who—"

"*You* know that, Pencarrow. *I* know that. Superintendent Bentinct knows that. Do you want to explain the facts of life to the chief constable? This bloke's partner rang up Major Amboyne direct. They're on some committee together. And the CC is very particular about staying on the right side of lawyers. *Bleak House* syndrome, the super calls it."

"We did *Bleak House* at school. It's about a family beggared by lawsuits."

"So I'm told. The CC doesn't seem to be doing too badly. Doubtless there are different levels of beggardom. Anyway, the result is we have to at least make a show of taking it seriously, which means you go and get the details."

"What's the name, sir? And where?"

Scumble glanced at his memo pad. "Freeth, Alan Freeth, has gone AWOL. A very sober, responsible, reliable individual, according to Mr. Bulwer, who has had to placate a number of clients who had appointments with him."

"Freeth and Bulwer? Sounds vaguely familiar."

"Port Mabyn. Friends of your auntie, I daresay. Maybe she can give you the lowdown on this Freeth character."

"Is that permission to stop in and see Aunt Nell, sir?"

The chief inspector sighed gustily. "I suppose so. Briefly. Then, unless you have some idea where to look for the missing lawyer and barring an emergency, you can take the rest of the afternoon off—"

"Thank you, sir!"

"Let me finish my sentence, Pencarrow. At half six, you'll meet the southbound train at the station here. Unmarked car. You'll drive a couple of passengers to Tintagel. A young chap and his minder."

"Minder? A child? A witness?"

"An Oxford undergraduate student and a civil servant." Scumble shrugged. "Don't ask me."

"Two men. How will I recognise them?"

"Not that many people this early in the year. Two blokes getting off together."

"That should help," said Megan ironically.

"I'll be giving you an envelope—sealed—with official instructions. I imagine they'll tell you how to recognise the pair. Bowler hat, red carnation in the buttonhole, and *Times* in hand, for all I know. Tight-furled umbrella goes without saying."

"I take these two to Tintagel? It's just up the road from Port Mabyn. It would make more sense to see Bulwer after I drop them off."

"Ah, but you won't be dropping them off. You're to stay on as security detail."

"That's a job for a uniform, sir!"

"Undercover. The CC wants to send a female detective officer, and you're still the only one in CaRaDoC."

"What? I don't understand, sir."

"I'm not sure I do. They've got a complicated situation on their hands. Sit down. This is it, as far as I can make it out from what little I'm authorised to know. What matters is that some bigwig at the Commonwealth Office decided to hold some sort of secret conference at the hotel this weekend. They're pretty sure the people attending are being watched by an adversary."

"Who—?"

"Don't ask me. The CC may know, or even the super, though I fancy not. You and I are too low on the totem. Whoever it is wants someone to watch out for suspicious strangers. Your average detective constable can disappear in a crowd, but without one, he sticks out like a sore thumb. So someone had the bright idea of swiping my sergeant. No one will suspect you of being a copper."

"That would depend what I do, wouldn't it. Trouble is, it's a small village. If they want me to go round watching people and asking questions—"

"No, no, nothing like that. You'll be staying at the hotel."

"On expenses, I trust."

"Of course. Paid for by the Commonwealth Office, not CaRa-

DoC. They're staying in a set of rooms in a wing often reserved for small groups, with a private sitting room and dining room. You'll be in the main hotel, nearby. There won't be many guests at this time of year. All you have to do is keep an eye on them and see if anyone is nosing about: other guests, staff, or drop-ins to the bar or restaurant. They don't get many of those, as it's half a mile from the village."

"And what do I do if someone's prying? Warning them off would just confirm that there's something to be warned off."

"Patience, Pencarrow, patience." He was a fine one to preach, Megan thought. "You'll inform the bigwig in charge. The suite has a private phone. You'll have help, too. Scotland Yard is sending a man to escort another student down, one of those rabble-rousers at London University. He'll work with you, spell you if necessary."

Megan's heart sank. Her ex-boyfriend, Ken Faraday, had somehow become the Met's Cornwall expert. She had no wish to see him, far less to work with him. "Did they give you his name?"

"No, but I expect it'll be the Boy Wonder, don't you think?"

"Probably."

"Don't look so down in the mouth. You're quite capable of fending him off if he gets frisky."

"Yes, sir." But she'd rather not have to. It would complicate a job that already sounded both complicated and boring. Perhaps— she touched wood—her partner would be a complete stranger, maybe even a WPC. After all, she had been sent because the brass reckoned being female was as good as a disguise.

"It's just the weekend." The DCI slid an envelope across the desk to her. "Here's all the gen, including the phone number of the Commonwealth Office bloke you report to. Name of Sir Edward Bellowe."

Uneasily, Megan recalled Aunt Nell mentioning her friends the Bellowes. Sir Edward and . . . Gina, that was it. But Aunt Nell couldn't possibly have anything to do with whatever was going on in Tintagel. Could she?

Megan decided she didn't need to disclose such a vague connection to the guv'nor. "Right, sir."

"Keep me up to date. In case of emergency, radio the nick before informing the bigwig. You'd better take a hand-held—"

"And a spare for the bloke from the Met? He won't have the local frequency."

"Good thought. Yes, one for the Boy Wonder. I don't want him mucking up my airwaves, though. Just take a two-way for the pair of you. And a mini-camera, if we have such a thing. You know how to use 'em?"

"Of course, sir."

"A mug shot of any nosy-parkers might turn out useful." Scumble looked her up and down with disfavour. "And find something else to wear. You look like a plainclothes copper. Or would if you weren't female."

She knew better than to say that was why she was wearing the middling-grey trouser suit from Marks and Sparks, neat and plain but allowing freedom of movement. For the caravan park job, it was right. As she was going to pretend she wasn't an officer, it was wrong. For the solicitor, though . . .

"Well, what you waiting for, Pencarrow? Get a move on, or you won't be there till midnight."

Megan wasn't actually in any hurry. She decided to take an hour of her afternoon off before she went to Port Mabyn. Lunch was imperative. It was half past two, so all the cafés would have stopped serving, but she could make a sandwich at home. She wouldn't even have to bike up the hill to her tiny bed-sitter as she had to pick up a police car to get to the coast.

"Nick!" The studio door was open so Eleanor dashed straight through from the gallery in front, Teazle at her heels. "Oh, Nick, I'm awfully sorry to interrupt, but the car won't start and I absolutely have to get to Tintagel this afternoon. Could you possibly come and have a look?"

"It's all right; I haven't actually got beyond standing at the easel, staring and wondering whether I'm going in the right direction."

"May I take a peek? Is it your . . . um . . . *Four Temperaments* painting?" She studied the picture. "I can't say I understand it, but I like it. Which, given my ignorance and lack of aesthetic appreciation, probably means you're going in the wrong direction."

Nick laughed. "I'll play the LP for you sometime. If you still like the painting when you've heard it, all well and good. Let's go and see what's up with the Incorruptible."

The car was back in the meadow by the stream, in the small wooden shed Eleanor rented for it, because being prone to rust was one of its defects. It was a tight fit. Nick, tall and lean, sidled in and managed to open the driver's door just wide enough to squeeze inside. Peering through the back window—not as clean as it might have been, Eleanor admitted to herself—she saw his elbow move.

Nothing happened.

He stuck his head out of the window and said indignantly, "You didn't tell me it won't even turn over!"

"It doesn't turn over? Is that bad?"

"It's dead. Either the battery or the starter, I expect. I'm no expert."

"Mechanic?"

" 'Fraid so."

"Botheration! It will have to wait. Nick, can you possibly give us a lift to the King Arthur Hotel?"

"Of course. I welcome an excuse to postpone thinking about this picture. I'll just dash home and get my keys and my camera. A mackerel sky like this often makes for a spectacular sunset."

Eleanor retrieved her suitcase from the Incorruptible's boot, gave the car a consoling pat, and closed the shed's doors. The Traveller was parked right next to it, the rear seat folded flat to accommodate an easel, among other odds and ends. She found the back doors unlocked, put the case in, and gave Teazle a boost up beside it.

Waiting beside the car, she gazed up at the sky. Hazy sunshine filtered through the high, thin clouds, which reminded her more of a ploughed field than a mackerel's scales. Whatever image they evoked, they presaged rain, perhaps another storm. She was glad not to be on her way to the Scillies.

As Nick drove up the hill out of the village, slowly but without the Incorruptible's rattles and squeaks, he asked, "You're meeting someone at the hotel? Should I stick about to bring you home?"

"Thanks, but I'll be staying the weekend. Till Monday at least."

"Teazle too?" He glanced over his shoulder as the dog yipped in answer to her name. "Living the high life! You're meeting friends there?"

"Sort of. I'll be . . . Well, it's all very hush-hush. I'm not supposed to talk about it, and my host has made sure I won't by not telling me just what it's all about."

"Who's your host?"

"Oh dear, I wonder if I'm allowed to mention his name?"

"This is beginning to sound very mysterious and sinister, Eleanor."

"Not sinister!"

"No? Well, all the same, I'm going to turn up every day and ask for you."

"Honestly, Nick, that's not necessary. Sir—my host *is* a friend, and in any case, it's a big hotel. There's bound to be other people staying, even at this time of year."

"All the same . . . I'll tell you what. You'll have to walk Teazle. Let's arrange to meet somewhere. You know the parish church, out on the cliffs south of the village?"

"St. Materiana's, yes. Did you know the name probably originated from Matrona, the Mother Goddess?"

"No, really? But that's beside the point. I'll be nearby from, say, ten tomorrow morning. That should give you plenty of time to walk over after breakfast."

"Nick, look at the sky!"

They had reached a high point of the road, with a clear view to the west. The mackerel sky had already passed to the east. Heavy black clouds were building up in the west, and in the distance the slanting columns of rain squalls marched across the sea.

"It's moving in fast. So much for my sunset."

"So much for walking to the church tomorrow. I'm more likely to bung Teazle out with instructions to walk herself."

A sudden gust buffeted the car. "It may blow over in the night," Nick said hopefully. "Not the car, the storm. We can always shelter in the porch if there's just a light rain."

"But you won't be able to pretend you're painting."

"I'll take some photos of the interior. If you don't come, I'll go to the hotel and insist on speaking to you."

"Oh, Nick, honestly! I'm not walking blindfolded into danger.

At worst, the company may be a bit sticky, but that's what I'll be there for, to help smooth over the sticky patches."

"All right, then, if it gets too sticky for your liking, give me a buzz and we'll meet in the village for a drink or a cuppa or lunch, or whatever you fancy to cheer you up."

"Weather permitting, I'll try to make it to the church. If I don't, for goodness' sake don't kick up a fuss. You can be sure they have a very good reason for the secrecy."

"Can't you just tell me who 'they' are?"

Eleanor considered. "I can't see how it could hurt to tell you that two of them are friends I've known for years."

"That does make quite a difference," Nick admitted.

"I did say you had no need to worry about me."

"Yes, you did." He laughed. "I'll be there in the morning anyway. Now I come to think of it, I bet paintings of the inside of the church would sell well if I can get the light right. It's very old. And then, there's your Mother Goddess. . . ." His eyes took on a faraway look.

Eleanor hoped he could see the bends in the road through whatever visions loomed in his head.

THREE

From the top of the hill down into Port Mabyn, Megan saw the storm clouds piling up on the horizon. What a relief that her job in Tintagel was to be in the hotel, not the village!

As she drove slowly down towards the bridge and the harbour, she glanced up at the window above the LonStar shop and wondered whether Aunt Nell was at home, or at least downstairs helping to sort donations. Nick Gresham's shop next door looked deserted—yes, there was a CLOSED sign in the window. She went on, past the lawyers' building and up to the car park to leave the car, then walked back down.

She introduced herself to the secretary and showed her warrant card. "I understand Mr. Bulmer reported his partner missing. I'm here to get the details."

"He's with a client at present, Miss . . . Should I call you Detective Sergeant?"

"Miss is fine. Perhaps you could tell me what you know, while I'm waiting. Has Mr. Freeth ever gone off for a few days without explanation before?"

"Never," the woman said vehemently. "He's very considerate

and ever so proper in his ways. The one thing I did wonder . . ." She hesitated.

"Yes? Oh, may I have your name? Just for the record."

"Florence Raleigh. Don't tell Mr. Bulwer I said this. I don't want him worrying. It's just that Mr. Freeth is a great rambler. You know, he likes to go on long walks? So I did just wonder if he saw some-where nice to walk as he was driving and decided to stretch his legs and had an accident. There's places on the moors—he's told me himself—where old mine workings and such aren't properly fenced off. Or the cliffs, or even by a river and he slipped and fell in."

"It's possible, of course. There aren't many hikers at this time of year, so he might not have been found. But I'm afraid there's not much we can do about it."

"No, I do see that. I just thought I ought to mention it."

"I'm glad you did, Mrs. Raleigh. We never know what scrap of information might help. Even knowing that you share Mr. Bulwer's concern is helpful."

"I s'pose you wouldn't know whether to take it seriously, if—" She broke off as footsteps sounded in the entrance hall outside the open door of her room.

A couple passed, followed by a tall, thin man, slightly stoop-shouldered. His greying hair, thick and wavy, was on the long side, adding to his scholarly air. He ushered out his clients and came into the secretary's room, with a questioning glance at Megan.

"Mr. Bulwer, this is Detective Sergeant Pencarrow, about Mr. Freeth."

His expression brightened. "Thank you for coming, Sergeant. If you'll excuse me just a moment, I'll tell Mrs. Raleigh what needs doing with these papers; then we'll go to my office."

Megan was prepared for a wait of several minutes, but his in-

BURIED IN THE COUNTRY

structions to his secretary were as concise as he'd promised. He led the way to a room that gave an impression of prosperity. Megan mentally noted the fact but concentrated on the man. He offered her a seat in a comfortable leather chair and took the second one in front of his desk, as if his concern for the missing man was more personal than professional. Or was she reading too much into a simple action?

"I rather thought the police weren't going to take Alan's disappearance seriously," he said.

"We take all missing persons reports seriously, sir. I'm afraid that doesn't always mean we can do anything about them. Do you have reason to suspect he may have run off with funds entrusted to him?"

"No! Absolutely not. Alan is absolutely honest and trustworthy."

Did the gentleman protest too much? "So Mr. Freeth is not suspected of wrongdoing, and he's a competent adult. Does he have any serious medical condition?"

"No. Healthy as a horse."

"Would you mind explaining to me why you are concerned enough about his absence to report it?"

"He's never before gone away without . . . without discussion beforehand. He's very reliable, conscientious. He wouldn't deliberately miss appointments with clients."

"Were any of them urgent?"

"Well, no, not really, though people tend to believe their own concerns are urgent."

"He'd know he could rely on you to cope, sir."

"I suppose so. Yes, of course."

"How long have you been in practice together, if that's the right term?"

"Seventeen years, give or take. Before that, we took articles at the same firm in London. Then I bought a partnership down here. A couple of years later, Alan joined me."

"You know each other very well, then."

"Obviously. That's why I'm . . . anxious. It's just not like him. His note said he'd be gone overnight. And he didn't take enough clothes for longer."

"When, exactly, and where did you receive the note?"

"Midday Monday. He went out to call on a client, by appointment, at eleven o'clock. To be precise, the appointment was at eleven. Mrs. Raleigh says Alan left about quarter to."

"I assume he drove?"

"Certainly. We keep our cars just up the hill, in the car park." Megan nodded. "And the note?"

"Mrs. Raleigh went into his office a little before one. Not having seen or heard him come in, she wasn't sure if he had but went to see if he wanted anything done before she went out for her lunch hour. She found the envelope on his desk, propped up to face the door. It had my name on it, so she brought it straight to me. It said—"

"Did you by any chance keep it?"

"Ye-es." Bulwer sounded wary. "It's . . . upstairs. We live 'over the shop,' you see. Do you *have* to read it?"

"No, not at this point, sir. But please don't dispose of it. Would you tell me what it said, please?"

"Just that he'd been called away urgently and would be gone overnight."

"Nothing about whether it was business, or family, or a friend in need?"

"Nothing but what I've told you."

"No hint of where he was going. You must see, sir, that even if we had your sense of urgency—"

"Which you don't. Don't worry, Sergeant, I understand."

"Even if, there really isn't much we could do."

"I'm sorry I wasted your time."

"I just go where I'm told, sir. I'll report to my superiors and they'll make the decision as to whether to act. I'd better have the make, model, and licence plate of his car." Megan wrote them down, then stood up. "If he doesn't return and you haven't heard from him by Monday, I expect they'd reconsider. By the way, do you happen to have a photo?"

"Yes. I've kept a recent print handy in case you wanted it." Bulwer opened a desk drawer and handed her a snap.

"Mr. Freeth wears glasses."

"He's always been shortsighted. He can't see much without them. Another reason for worry." The lawyer rose and shook her hand. "Thank you, Sergeant. I . . . I can only hope he'll be home by then."

As Megan walked down the road, she realised she hadn't asked whether he had got in touch with family and friends to see if anyone knew where Freeth was. But, in spite of Bulwer's excessive reaction to his partner's absence, the solicitor was too intelligent to have omitted such an obvious first step.

She was sure Bulwer had not been entirely straight with her. He had hesitated a couple of times in a way that sounded evasive, though it might be the vestiges of a stammer overcome. He was genuinely worried about Alan Freeth; that much was obvious. After more than twenty years of friendship, they were close. They both lived "above the shop," and Bulwer knew what clothes were missing. . . .

Aunt Nell would tell her what was what.

Megan went through the side door and up the stairs to knock on her aunt's door. No response. She tried the door. For once it was locked, so she took out her key and let herself in.

"Aunt Nell?"

Silence. Teazle would have responded even if Aunt Nell was in the loo.

Nick would have been her second choice as a source of information. His absence left only the local copper, who was probably out on his beat, driving around the nearby villages, or the vicar's wife. The prospect of tackling Mrs. Stearns on such a touchy subject made her quail, but Scumble wanted reliable local information about Freeth and Bulwer. Jocelyn Stearns, if she was willing to talk about them at all, would be accurate and discreet.

In Aunt Nell's flat, Megan changed into the slacks and peach-coloured pullover she had brought with her. The door locked behind her, she went downstairs, outside, and in through the shop door. A volunteer was ringing up a sale. She and the customer both nodded to Megan.

"Good afternoon. Do look round. If you need help, I'll be with you in a moment." The volunteer returned to the complexities of the ancient cash register.

"Excuse me, is Mrs. Stearns in today?" Megan asked.

"Yes, she's in the stockroom. Just knock on the door at the back."

She did as she was bid. Another volunteer was helping Mrs. Stearns to arrange clothes on a rolling rack. Megan asked for a word in private.

"Dolly, would you take those through now, please? What is it, Megan?"

"Do you know where my aunt is, Mrs. Stearns?"

The vicar's wife frowned. "No, I don't. Not just out and about; she said she'd be away for a few days. She didn't tell you?"

"No. I've been very busy. She may have rung several times and missed me."

"You just missed her. She left an hour or so ago. Sorry I can't help."

"Maybe you can. I hoped you could tell me a bit about Freeth and Bulwer."

"They are excellent solicitors."

"Perhaps I should have said Alan Freeth and Roland Bulwer."

"I do not approve of gossip."

"I'm a police officer, Mrs. Stearns. I need information, not gossip."

"I suppose I'd better not ask why. What do you want to know?"

"Are they . . . a couple?"

"My dear Megan! The law is surely no longer concerned with—"

"Not with their . . . relationship." Megan picked her words with care. "However, if they . . . have an emotional attachment beyond friendship, it could explain Mr. Bulwer's anxiety over Mr. Freeth's unexpectedly prolonged absence. Without, that is, postulating awareness of some hazard that he's unwilling to divulge."

Mrs. Stearns was obviously dying of curiosity, but after her condemnation of gossip, she couldn't very well try to ferret out details. "Yes, they're a 'couple,' with considerable emotional attachment, I presume."

"What is the attitude of the village people in general?"

"They ignore it."

"They never gossip about it?"

"Did I not make myself clear, Megan? I do not listen to that kind of talk."

"Sorry. The Church's attitude hasn't changed, though, has it?" Pure curiosity prompted the question.

"All Timothy—my husband—will say is, 'Judge not, that ye be not judged.' Or he talks about the woman taken in adultery."

"'He that is without sin among you, let him cast the first stone,'" Megan dredged up from memory.

"'Let him first cast a stone.' And after all, adultery is one of the commandments, whereas . . . the other matter is part of all that tedious stuff about shellfish and pork and mixed fabrics. Jesus said nothing on the subject. Though Paul . . . but he also said women must be silent in church," Mrs. Stearns added in an outraged tone.

"I expect the vicar likes a slice of bacon for breakfast."

"He never notices what he's putting in his mouth, but I cannot suppose eating bacon to be sinful."

From which Megan gathered that the vicar's wife liked bacon and was as willing as the villagers to overlook Bulwer and Freeth's relationship. Probably it had dawned on everyone only gradually as the two partners' bachelorhood prolonged itself to unlikely lengths. "I'm glad to hear it, Mrs. Stearns. I must be on my way. Thanks for your help."

As she departed, via the door to the passage and so to the street, Megan decided she would write up a report on Freeth and Bulwer once she was settled in the King Arthur Hotel, which sounded like a deadly dull assignment. It would give her an excuse to avoid Ken's company. Scumble might be impressed by her conscientiousness. Though probably not.

As she passed Nick's shop again, she noted that it was still closed. Stepping closer, she saw a paper Sellotaped to the window above the CLOSED sign, advising the public that the gallery would reopen the following week.

At this time of year, sales of his work were slow, so it wasn't surprising if he'd taken a few days off, perhaps for a painting trip. All the same, she was annoyed that he hadn't let her know. She had gone out with him a few times, and even stayed in with him more than once. Her irregular schedule—as well as living twenty miles apart—made it difficult to arrange meetings.

He had no duty to notify her, she reminded herself. Besides, as she'd told Mrs. Stearns, she hadn't been easy to get in touch with for the past week or so. Maybe he'd tried without success.

Reassuring herself didn't help. She drove back to Launceston feeling altogether fed up.

FOUR

When Eleanor and Nick reached Tintagel, rain had not yet started falling, but the clouds had moved in with amazing speed, bringing early twilight. The wind had risen, too, blowing steadily from the southwest.

"The Weather God's reminding me to be grateful I'm not on my way to the Scilly Isles," said Eleanor.

"Huh? Your friends wanted to go to the Scillies in March?"

"No, they didn't. That's why I'm grateful."

"So these are the people you visited—"

"Nick, don't. I shouldn't have said that."

"'Loose lips sink ships.' Now what was their name?" he teased.

"Nick!"

"Don't worry, I won't tell the villains. I don't even know who they are or what they want."

"Nor do I. Don't try to find out."

"I wouldn't have a clue how to begin. So you *are* expecting trouble!"

"Not the sort of trouble you want to protect me from. Just someone trying to find out what's going on. As far as I know."

"As far as you know."

"I don't actually know anything," said Eleanor, exasperated. "Just that it—whatever 'it' is—is so hush-hush, I won't be told till I get there. You're leading me on to imagine all sorts of nonsense."

"You'll get the answers soon enough."

They had to drive through the village to reach the hotel. Apart from its legendary association with the legendary King Arthur, Tintagel was a typical Cornish village, the cottages built of Cornish granite, some whitewashed, with lichened slate roofs. Many had window boxes already bright with daffodils and crocuses, even a few hyacinths.

The street forked. The left-hand branch led down towards Tintagel Haven, a rocky inlet too narrow and dangerous for a harbour, the tiny beach accessible only by steep steps at low tide. Also down there was the hazardous isthmus connecting the mainland to King Arthur's island, with its ancient ruins. Nick took the right-hand branch, going up to the hotel.

Looming darkly through the gathering gloom, the towers at each corner added to the impression of a sinister mansion in a gothic novel.

"I'll come in with you." Nick pulled up in front of the portico.

"You don't need to—"

"If only to make sure you don't blow away. The wind is something fierce."

Since Eleanor was having trouble opening the car door against the blast, she couldn't deny it. While Nick came round to help, Teazle scrambled between the seats, over the gear lever, and hopped onto her lap, ready to spring out. Eleanor hugged her tight against her shoulder.

Nick opened the door. Eleanor got out. Half-sheltered from the gale by the car door, she hesitated for a moment. The hotel's front door was as yet unlit and under the porch it was dark as night.

A white blob resolved into a shirt-front as a man in black stepped forward.

"Good evening, madam."

"Oh, it's you, Norton!" The Bellowes' butler. Teazle yipped a welcome that suggested memories of treats slipped to her on the sly. "Good evening. Were you waiting for me?"

"Yes, madam. Sir Edward realised he had omitted to inform you that our party is accommodated in the northwest tower. Perhaps the gentleman wouldn't mind driving you to the side entrance, in view of the inclement weather. You will see the entrance at the rear, sir. There is a light above the door."

"Sorry I can't give you a lift, old chap, but as you see, I've got the back laid flat."

"Thank you, sir. I shall proceed on foot, as it is undesirable that I should be observed entering the tower from the lobby. It is a very short distance."

Restarting the Traveller, Nick observed, "And I bet his hair arrives unruffled."

"Of course. He's a very superior butler."

"It looks as if your host has brought his staff with him. In the service of secrecy, I suppose." He drove round the corner and stopped in front of the door to the northwest tower. "You stay in the car till the superior butler arrives. I'll get your case out."

Norton rejoined them a moment later. He opened the passenger door. Eleanor stepped out, Teazle still clutched to her, and was practically blown into his arms. He steadied her as she leaned down to shout against the roar of the wind, "Thanks, Nick, and for pity's sake, be careful driving home."

He waved. She had no free hand to wave back, so she nodded,

then turned to go with Norton. However superior, he was more manservant than butler, really, for in these servantless days his duties weren't limited to traditional butlerian pursuits, though he played that part on occasion. Pre-war, he would have had a minion to carry her suitcase, but he picked it up without any lessening of his air of dignity.

"If you will please come this way, madam." Unlocking and opening the door, he managed not to let it crash back against the wall, quite a feat. Eleanor let the wind blow her inside. With some difficulty, Norton closed the door behind them, relocked it, and presented her with the key. "And here is the key for your room, madam. I expect you will wish to go up before joining her ladyship in the drawing room."

Knowing she must look as if she'd been dragged backwards through a bush, Eleanor gratefully accepted the suggestion.

The narrow entrance hall and the stairs were haphazardly updated Victorian, clean and well polished, but somewhat oppressive. Most of the walls had been painted cream, but one in an unobtrusive corner still had crimson-flocked wallpaper. The overhead light was an elaborate electrified chandelier. Norton pointed out a nook containing a telephone, and two doors. One led to the rest of the hotel, the other to a small service courtyard, "where you can take the little dog, madam," he said delicately, "while the rain continues."

"She prefers a bit of grass, but any port in a storm."

"Both doors use the same key as the door through which madam entered."

Two keys fewer to remember, Eleanor thought thankfully, but she mustn't forget to lock the doors after her. "This is a bit of a change for you from the Bellowes' London house or the Scillies. Did they bring all their staff?"

"Not all, madam, but enough. Sir Edward trusts us not to talk about his business. The hotel staff are mostly foreigners, but a few are local people so gossip would be inevitable. We are, perhaps, a trifle understaffed for the number of guests expected, but you will not notice any deficiency in service, I hope."

"I'm sure I shan't." Eleanor nearly asked him whether he knew who else was expected, but she'd find out soon enough.

Her bedroom on the second floor was the same uneasy mixture of Victorian and modern. A gas fire took the edge off the chill, though the room could not be described as warm. Norton intercepted her gaze at the four-poster bed and hastened to assure her, "Interior spring mattress, madam."

Not that she hadn't slept in everything from grass huts on stilts to mud huts with a smoke hole in the roof, but still . . . "Good."

He set her suitcase on a low table and bowed slightly. "Shall I send Lady Bellowe's maid, madam?"

"No. No, thanks."

"The . . . ah . . . conveniences are just opposite. This being a hotel, they have signs on the doors." Norton did not approve.

"I'll be down in a few minutes."

He bowed again and withdrew. The moment she was alone, she heard the wind whistling round the building and noticed the curtains stirring in draughts from the window. Why on earth would anyone build a hotel on a bare height exposed to everything the Atlantic could throw at it?

She went to the window, parted the drawn curtains, and found it open half an inch at the top. Closing it, she peered out. It was over an hour before sunset, but the low black clouds had brought premature darkness. Eleanor couldn't see much. She wasn't even sure which way her room faced until raindrops suddenly splattered against the glass. The way they hit and spread suggested she was looking out into the face of the storm as it blasted in over the invisible sea. She should have a marvellous view in daylight if the weather cleared.

The rain started to hammer on the windowpanes. Worrying about Nick's homeward drive through the storm, she closed the curtains and prepared herself for afternoon tea with Sir Edward and Lady Bellowe.

Norton appeared the moment Eleanor set foot on the landing below. He led her to the first-floor sitting room and ushered her in. She barely had time to register an eclectic combination of every style since the 1890s before she was enveloped in the large tweed-costumed embrace of Georgina, Lady Bellowe.

"Eleanor, I'm so glad you're here. I do dislike being the only woman in the party, even if it's not really a party, just politics."

"*Just* politics!" exclaimed Sir Edward, a man of middling height, whose spare build was dwarfed by his wife's generous bulk. "My dear Gina, it's neither love nor money that makes the world go round; it's politics. I'm very grateful that you've come, Eleanor." He shook hands with her. They sat down, and he leaned forward earnestly. "I do hope your stay will be comfortable as well as interesting and of great service to the Crown."

"Let her settle in, Edward, before you start on the 'service to the Crown' part. Tea, Eleanor? Or would you prefer a little drinkie?"

"Tea would be perfect," Eleanor assured her, and on cue Norton, assisted by a maid, appeared with a tea tray.

Tea featured splits with strawberry jam and clotted cream. Having poured tea for all, Gina helped herself liberally, absently feeding a scrap of the soft roll to Teazle. "I shouldn't go near the cream, I know, but I've been dashing up and down three flights of stairs, trying to make the hotel—our part of it—feel homely. I'm sure that used up an immense number of calories."

"Unquestionably."

"As for dinner tonight, my poor cook is trying to cope in a kitchen the size of a galley. I'm told the groups that rent the tower in summer don't expect much in the way of cooking facilities, but at this time of year we can't take a picnic out on the cliffs! Thank goodness you didn't have far to come, Eleanor; I hope the drive wasn't too dreadful in this weather?"

"The wind didn't come up till we were nearly here. In any case, I wasn't driving." Eleanor explained about her poor dead Incorruptible. Then she had to explain the nickname, which amused Sir Edward no end.

"Robespierre, eh?" he chortled. "The sea-green incorruptible. And now your car is as dead as its namesake. I'm sorry to hear that. I should have sent a car for you; I knew it. You'll be reimbursed for car hire, of course."

"It's all right. A friend was quite happy to bring me."

"You didn't tell him what we're here for!" Sir Edward yelped in alarm.

"I don't *know* what we're here for. And I think it's about time you told me."

"Ah, yes. In a word, Rhodesia. Or Zimbabwe, if you prefer."

"Rhodesia! Don't tell me you've got Ian Smith to—"

"No, no, no. He's nowhere near ready to admit that a couple of hundred thousand whites can't continue indefinitely to lord it over millions of blacks in this day and age."

"Except in South Africa."

"Sanctions may work there, too, in the end, if everyone stands firm, but they look like they're taking a long time."

"If not Smith, then who?"

"How much do you know about the situation?"

"Only what anyone can read in the paper or hear on the six

o'clock news. LonStar never had much to do with Southern Rhodesia. The colonial government, whatever its faults, was one of the best at famine relief. I did meet Joshua Nkomo and Ndabaningi Sithole." Eleanor might forget her keys, but she never forgot people. "They're both in prison, aren't they? Or has Smith released them?"

"Not much chance of that," Sir Edward said despondently, "as long as their ZANU and ZAPU colleagues who got away to Zambia are waging guerrilla warfare across the border. As well as fighting with one another. We're constantly trying to talk sense into *them*, of course, but it's China and the Soviets they turn to for help and advice."

"So who's left? Whom are you wooing now?"

"More tea, Eleanor? And may I give the dog some cream?"

"The merest smidgeon. I'd hate her to be sick on the hotel's carpet. And yes, thanks, Gina, I'd love another cup."

Sir Edward also passed his cup, and helped himself to a second split, piling on jam and cream before he answered Eleanor's question. "We're taking a shot—bad choice of words!—at the next generation. Quite a few are in exile in Britain, many on student visas. We're hoping they may be more amenable to reason. If we can persuade the younger people to unite and to pursue nonviolent means to achieve their aims, we can help them to support Bishop Muzorewa's party rather than ZANU or ZAPU. Perhaps by the time sanctions start really biting and Smith is willing to come to the table, they'll be in charge of his flock, or at least influential."

"You've invited students? You're expecting slow progress!"

"Only to sound them out. Besides, they're older than the general run of undergrads. In their mid-twenties, I believe, having taken their A-level exams after arriving in Britain."

"How many are coming?"

"Just two," Gina put in.

"One from LSE—"

"The London School of Economics? Aren't they the most turbulent students in the nation?"

"Probably," Sir Edward agreed gloomily.

"And wasn't there some sort of fuss about Marxist lecturers?"

"Er . . . yes."

"And you expect me to talk sense into—"

"Not at all. The political part is mine. If you can just keep peace between the two of them—"

"Who is the other?"

"He's up at Oxford. Brasenose."

"Oxford must be more conservative, surely."

"All young people are revolting these days, even at Oxbridge. If they're not intellectual revolutionaries, they're National Front louts."

Looking amused at this sweeping condemnation of a generation, Gina said, "I don't recall hearing of Oxford students rioting in the streets, dear." She added hot water to the silver teapot.

"Less turbulent than LSE, perhaps. They vent their unrest in debates instead of in the street, and provide the pseudo-intellectual justifications for the rioting elsewhere."

"Don't Oxbridge people tend to look down on the rest of the academic world?" Eleanor asked. "London University included?"

"Well, yes."

"Oh dear! And I suppose, just to help matters along, one of your guests is Shona and the other Matabele?"

"Ndebele they call themselves now. But yes, I'm afraid so. ZAPU and ZANU aren't strictly tribal, though, and that's the division we need to overcome."

"You're so good at smoothing ruffled feathers," said Gina.

Eleanor sighed. "It would be easier if they weren't adversaries in so many respects. What are their names?" She passed her cup to Gina for another refill and helped herself to a second split.

"Tariro and Nontando. We're using first names only, for security."

"What is all this fuss about security? What are you afraid of?"

"We don't want Smith to catch wind of this latest undertaking. The Rhodesian settlers have many sympathisers in this country. That's why the two of them will arrive at night and stay out of sight. My private secretary—"

"Is that different from your personal secretary? Civil-service language is so confusing."

"Yes, Payne is my assistant. The other is a receptionist-stenographer type. Payne took the train from London to meet Tariro at Reading, off the train from Oxford, to travel the rest of the way together. A local plainclothes policeman will pick them up from Launceston and drive them here. A Scotland Yard plainclothesman will drive the other down from London. We didn't want the two travelling together."

"Paranoia," said Gina, smiling at Eleanor. "Pure paranoia."

"It seems to me," Eleanor pointed out, "that of all the places where a couple of Africans would be bound to attract attention, Cornwall is probably near the top of the list. They'd be much less conspicuous in one of the big industrial cities."

"But so would snoopers," Sir Edward retorted irritably.

"Very true." Eleanor reminded herself that her role was peace-keeper, not devil's advocate. So far, she wasn't doing much of a job. She could only hope to do better when face-to-face with the intellectual debater and the turbulent rioter.

FIVE

Nick had watched with a frown as Eleanor went off cheerfully with the butler. He wished she had explained her reasons for coming to Tintagel. She had a tendency to involve herself in dangerous situations, and the fact that so far she had come to no harm was no guarantee that she would come through safely this time.

The door closed behind them. Nick set off homeward, shrugging. There was nothing he could do about it except turn up tomorrow as promised and hope she remembered he'd told her he would. Weather permitting.

He'd feel responsible, though, if anything happened to her. And Megan would no doubt consider him responsible. He wished he hadn't offered her beloved Aunt Nell a lift. But dammit, he was very fond of the old girl, too. He hadn't known when they set out that there was anything fishy about her destination. Megan could hardly expect him to have turned back as soon as Eleanor started talking about spies.

Spies! What on earth had Eleanor got herself mixed up in? Perhaps he'd find out tomorrow.

Or perhaps not, given the weather. While he drove through

the village, the wind wasn't too bad, but beyond shelter of the houses it shook the car, the steering wheel juddering in his hands. As usual, the heater didn't work.

When he reached the spot where the B3263 made a sharp left turn, he noticed a bed-and-breakfast sign pointing the other way. Unlike the others he had passed, it had neither a CLOSED nor a NO VACANCY sign swinging below it. On impulse he turned right, towards the sea, just in time to catch a downpour flung by the wind directly at his windscreen.

The wipers couldn't cope with it. Half-blind, he drove on cautiously along a narrow but straight lane with low drystone walls on each side. He passed a farm track on his left, and shortly he came to a nameless hamlet.

Dimly, through sluicing rain and the semidark, he spotted another B and B sign. He found himself in a still narrower lane, with grass and weeds growing down the centre. He would have given up if there had been anywhere to turn. What might be a delightful solitude with sea views in the height of summer seemed likely to be a desolate, windswept isolation in a raging storm.

At the back of beyond, just as the lane petered out into a cart track, a low building appeared on the right. Built of the local grey stone, its rectangularity blurred by the rain, it merged into the landscape like an outcrop of granite.

All Nick cared about was the B and B sign fastened to the zigzag slate wall round the front garden and the lit window in the side wall, near the back.

Between the wall and the lane was a gravelled area, half-occupied by a bright blue Range Rover. Nick drove past and backed in ahead of it. He pulled up the hood of his anorak and made a dash for the front door.

His vigorous knocking brought no immediate response. Then

a slight movement of the curtain in the large window next to the door made him conscious of being observed. While he appreciated the need for caution in this lonely spot, the jutting lintel gave next to no protection and he was rapidly getting soaked through. He knocked again, wishing he'd taken the time to change out of his paint-stained jeans. Dammit, he hadn't known he'd need to look respectable!

The door opened a few inches, on the chain. The face that appeared was obviously a woman's, though he couldn't make out much of the visible strip, with the light behind her. He thought he heard footsteps in the hall, receding, but the noise of wind and rain made him uncertain.

"Yes?"

"I saw your sign out by the main road—"

"Sorry, I forgot to take it down. I'm not really open at this time of year."

Nick seized on the "not really." "Look, I'm soaked to the skin and chilled to the bone. The wind is shaking my car to pieces and it's only going to get worse as I reach higher ground, if I try to drive home. I'm willing to pay whatever you ask for a room." He crossed his fingers in his pockets, not sure how much he had in his wallet. "I'm throwing myself on your mercy. If you really can't accommodate me for the night, at least let me come in to get warm and dry off a bit."

The one blue eye he could see looked him up and down, lingering on the sodden, bedaubed denim. "Oh, all right. I wouldn't want your death on my conscience, for sure. Half a tick."

The door closed. Through it, the rattle of the chain was audible. As it started to open again, Nick thought he heard a man's voice at some distance.

The woman's head was turned to look back down the hall. "It's up to you," she said, and turned back to Nick. "Come in. Goodness, you *are* wet!"

"This is just from three minutes on your doorstep. Thanks. I'm Nick Gresham."

"Mrs. Mason."

She was a plump woman in her forties, with rosy cheeks and smile lines around her eyes and mouth, though at present she looked troubled. Her dark red wool dress, pink cashmere cardigan, and pearls suggested a certain degree of affluence, as did the modernised farmhouse. The hall retained the old slate paving, but the walls were painted pale blue, with a white picture rail and doors. A well-polished antique half-moon table held a registration book and a bowl of pink hyacinths in bloom, their fragrance heavy in the air. Above hung a mirror in an ornate gilt frame. It reflected a picture hanging on the opposite wall: one of Nick's landscapes of the North Coast.

"Mr. Gresham?" Her eyes flicked from jeans to painting. "The artist?"

"Yes. I hope you have no objection to housing the artist as well as the art."

"It's an honour. And when the weather clears, you'll have a hundred-yard walk to the most wonderful views."

"Sounds terrific, but I wasn't intending to stay. Benighted by the storm. I haven't any luggage." Nick grinned at her. "Would you like payment in advance?"

"No, that's all right." She gave him another dubious up-and-down look. "You ought to get out of those wet things. I can lend you a dressing gown. I keep a spare for people who forget to bring one. I haven't put in en suite bathrooms yet, I'm afraid."

"Beggars can't be choosers. It's very kind of you to take me in."

"Why don't you take off your shoes while I fetch the dressing gown and some slippers. I'll dry everything over the Aga." She bustled off towards a narrow staircase, carpeted in haircord, at the back of the hall.

Nick sat on the straw-bottomed chair beside the table. As he untied his sodden plimsolls, he wondered whether Mrs. Mason would expect him to strip off his clothes in the hall, too. He took off his wet socks. The slate floor felt icy.

Returning with a white towelling dressing gown and a pair of carpet slippers, she pointed to the second door on the right. "That's the cloakroom. It's all yours. The next door is the kitchen. Bring the wet stuff in there."

The first part of the cloakroom had a washbasin—next to a door to a lavatory—and a row of pegs for coats. Nick noticed several plastic rain capes, and on the floor were gumboots in various sizes, as well as a well-stocked umbrella stand. Apparently a good many of Mrs. Mason's guests arrived ill-prepared for Cornish weather.

Nick's anorak hadn't actually soaked through—he had exaggerated a little. He hung it on one of the pegs. His T-shirt was dry, his pullover a bit damp at the front where the rain had blown in at the neck of the anorak. His jeans were wet from mid-thigh down. He took them off and put on the dressing gown. With the aid of the mirror over the basin, he attempted to smooth down his hair, making himself as respectable as possible for someone in slippers an inch too short and a fluffy garment halfway down his bare shins.

He didn't mind so much being seen by the kindly Mrs. Mason, but the man she had spoken to, presumably her husband, was bound to laugh himself silly.

Jeans, socks, and shoes in hand, shuffling so as not to lose the slippers, Nick went out to the hall. The kitchen door was slightly ajar. From within came a man's voice, an educated voice with nothing of Cornwall.

". . . All very well, Rosie, but if he's staying the night, he's sure to see me and he'd wonder why I haven't spoken to him."

Who? Not to mention *Why?*

Nick coughed and cleared his throat. "Hello?"

"Too late," said Mrs. Mason softly, then in a louder voice: "In here, Mr. Gresham. I hope you haven't taken a chill. I've made you a cup of tea."

He went in, saying, "Thanks, that's very—" and stopped abruptly as he recognised the man sitting at the table, cradling a cup of tea in his hands.

"Hello, Gresham. Caught by the storm, eh?"

"Freeth!" They were pub acquaintances. "What a coincidence." On the point of explaining that he'd driven Eleanor to Tintagel, Nick hastily reassessed the position.

Whatever Eleanor was doing apparently required a degree of secrecy. She had mentioned spies. The lawyer had been in confab with Mrs. Mason as to the wisdom of concealment of his presence, though he had decided against. He hadn't been stranded out here in the middle of nowhere by the storm: His Range Rover was more than capable of coping with wind and rain.

However unlikely it seemed, for all Nick knew, Freeth was a spy.

"Rosie is . . . a friend of my youth." Freeth was obviously considering each word carefully. It was a lawyerly trait, and Nick didn't know him well enough to be sure it wasn't his usual manner. Or perhaps he was just avoiding the word trap of "old friends," an expression that women on the whole did not appreciate. "I came over to give her a hand with some legal matters. It's taken longer than expected, so she kindly offered me a room."

With most men, Nick would have made certain assumptions

that didn't apply in this case—unless a good number of people had been mistaken for a good number of years. Freeth was as gay as the Gay Gordons.

During this brief exchange, Mrs. Mason had taken Nick's wet clothes, draped jeans and socks over the Aga rail, and placed his shoes on a tin tray on top of the lid of the slow oven.

"Sit down, do," she said. "Milk? Sugar? Here you go. And help yourself to a piece of cake." She seemed nervous. The old friends avoided each other's eyes, even when she offered him more tea and another slice of cake.

The cake was homemade, chocolate, and delicious. Nick, who had somehow missed lunch, was also happy to accept a second helping.

"I'll have to walk this off tomorrow," said Freeth. "The storm is so violent, I should think it'll blow itself out by morning." He paused, and they all listened for a moment to the whistle of the wind and the hammering of the rain. "It's just as well you're not driving home tonight. But what brought you to this out-of-the-way spot? There are plenty of guest houses in Tintagel."

"All the signs I noticed said 'closed,' but I wasn't really looking until I left the village and the wind tried to blow my car off the road. I spotted Mrs. Mason's sign and thought I'd chance it."

Now he was here, it seemed an ideal spot for keeping an eye on Eleanor. By footpath along the cliffs to her hotel couldn't be more than a couple of miles, an easy walk—depending on the weather—or, by road, a ten-minute drive. If he stayed a day or two—depending on Mrs. Mason's consent—he might also be able to find out whether Freeth's business here was as innocent as he claimed.

He always had painting and sketching equipment in the back of the car, so he had a ready-made excuse for staying. In fact, just remembering previous visits to the ruins on the island brought visions—a phantom castle rising from the broken walls; ghostly knights riding out through the surviving archway, its solidity supporting insubstantial walls and turrets. . . .

Freeth and Mrs. Mason were staring at him.

"Sorry, occupational hazard. Sometimes the pictures I want to paint are more real to me than what's in front of my eyes. I'd rather not go out to the car to get my sketchbook. I don't suppose you have such a thing, Mrs. Mason?"

"As a matter of fact, I do. One of my guests left it last summer. When I wrote to her, she said not to bother to post the whole thing to her, just the used pages. It's a very nice one, just half a dozen sheets missing, so I kept it. It's in the cabinet in the front room. There's a packet of drawing charcoal, too. Is that what you need?"

"Mrs. Mason, you're an angel!"

"I'll fetch them."

Before Freeth had a chance to intervene, Nick hurried after her out to the hall. He was sure he wouldn't be able to winkle any information out of a canny lawyer, but Mrs. Mason might respond to carefully phrased questions.

She turned to the door beyond the cloakroom, near the front door. It was marked PRIVATE. As she opened it, she heard the shuffle of Nick's slippers close behind her. Startled, she swung round with a look of alarm.

"Oh, it's you! You made me jump. This is my private sitting room and office, where I do my accounts. The income tax rules for B and B's seem to get more complicated every year."

"For artists, too."

He followed her into a comfortably furnished room. The windows, facing the front and side of the house, had venetian blinds for privacy as well as green velvet curtains for warmth. A driftwood fire flickered in the slate fireplace. Mrs. Mason had a good record player, a wireless, and a small television, Nick saw at a glance.

Her desk was more evidence of prosperity, a very nice walnut writing cabinet, eighteenth-century, its glass-doored shelves crammed with books. It would have brought a good price had she needed the money. She knelt on the superb Oriental rug— Persian?—and unlocked the bottom drawer. A sharp tug brought it out a couple of inches, but it was obviously heavy.

Sitting back on her heels, she clutched her hand to her chest. "Would you mind opening it, Mr. Gresham?" She spoke breathlessly, and, to Nick's dismay, her lips had taken on a bluish tinge. "My heart's a bit wonky," she said apologetically. "I'll be quite all right in a minute." From the pocket of her cardigan she took an enamelled gold pill-box.

Nick stooped over her. "Let me help you to a chair."

"Just a moment." She slipped a tiny pill under her tongue.

Angina. Nick's grandmother had had the same trouble. Nitroglycerine worked remarkably quickly. The colour was already returning to her lips, though she kept her hand pressed to her chest.

He helped her to stand up and move to a comfortable chair by the fire. "I'll fetch you a glass of water. Or brandy?"

She gave him a faint smile. "Water. Would you call Alan?"

"Yes, of course." He couldn't help glancing at the bureau, its lowest drawer protruding an inch.

"Get the sketchbook first. I'm sure I noticed it in that drawer a day or two ago. On the left."

With some effort, Nick pulled out the drawer. It was heavy and stuck a bit. The contents formed three piles, the middle and right-hand stacks consisting of five or six ledgers each. The top one in the middle was marked with the previous year's date.

The heap on the left was more heterogeneous, and therefore less neat: a couple of photo albums, some folders of loose papers, several worn, faded manila envelopes, bursting at the seams. Nick saw the edge of a sketchpad near the bottom. Trying not to disturb the stuff on top, he pulled it out.

With it he'd accidentally caught up the item beneath, another manila envelope, this one obviously new. As Nick separated the two, he saw that the envelope was labelled "Last Will and Testament." He looked at Mrs. Mason, an apology on his lips, but she was leaning back in the chair, her eyes closed.

Hastily, but careful not to crease it, he returned it to the bottom of the pile.

So that explained Freeth's visit. Or did it? Nick frowned. He had a feeling he was missing some obscure factor that spoiled the neat explanation. Not that it was any of his business. He returned to the kitchen.

"I'm afraid Mrs. Mason isn't feeling well. She asked for you, and for a glass of water."

Freeth leaped to his feet. "How bad is she?" he asked, filling a glass at the sink. "Should I call her doctor?"

"Not too bad, I think. She took a pill and it seems to have helped."

The lawyer hurried out. Nick poured himself another cup of tea from the pot keeping warm on the range and sat down at the table with the sketchpad in front of him. Damnation, he hadn't got the charcoal.

He looked around. A shopping list with a pencil laid on top caught his eye.

HB, of course, but better than nothing. He started to draw.

SIX

Five minutes before the London train was due, Megan drove into the Launceston station car park. She parked the dark blue Morris 1100 police car at the far end from the only two vehicles already there.

A light rain was beginning to fall, so she flipped up the hood of her green parka and reached for the umbrella on the floor behind her seat. The people she was meeting might need it, though during her years in London she had never seen a civil servant without one. They were carried, tightly furled, like a badge of office, and seldom actually used.

Considering all the secrecy, perhaps he wouldn't want to be identified as a civil servant. He might even have abandoned his pinstriped trousers, waistcoat, and college or regimental tie.

A fourth car pulled into the car park. Megan scrutinised it suspiciously. The inside light went on and she recognised the wife of a local man who often had business in Plymouth. He—or she, for that matter—could be a spy, but it seemed highly unlikely.

As Megan crossed the car park, she glanced at the two vehicles that had arrived before her. One was an empty car; the other,

CAROLA DUNN

an anonymous van, with no lettering on the side panels. The latter looked pale blue in the bluish light of the mercury-vapour lamp, though it was probably plain white. Backed into its space, it had two silhouetted figures in the front, heads together studying an unfolded map by the light of a torch. Definitely fishy. If a spy had found out that Payne and the student had taken tickets to Launceston, it would make sense to drive down, so as to have transport available to trail them to their final destination. The local train from Plymouth was slow, with many stops, so it wouldn't have been difficult to get here ahead of it.

If following Sir Edward's guests was what they were up to, they'd have a bloody hard time of it on a rainy night. Lacking sufficient information to judge whether the prevailing paranoia was justi-fied, she had her doubts.

She went onto the platform. Except in the tourist season, Launceston was a sleepy country station that never bothered with platform tickets. The stationmaster was the sole employee. He lived in a cottage nearby and put in an appearance only when a train was expected. He was standing under the awning, gazing along the line. Seeing Megan, he waved.

"Hello, Mr. Lobcot."

"Evening, Sergeant. No trouble, I hope?"

"Not this time." Last year, at the busiest time of year, she had had to make him rack his memory with a description of a villain who might or might not have caught a train to London. "I'm just meeting passengers."

"Good luck to 'em," he riposted with a grin. "Got your cuffs ready? Here she comes."

The blinding cyclops eye of the diesel engine pierced the night. With the usual clanks and bangs, the two-carriage train drew up at the station. Three doors opened and out stepped the business-man whose wife was waiting for him and a woman laden with Marks & Spencer shopping bags. From the third door, two men descended, one wearing a yellow bobble hat, with a duffel bag slung over his shoulder; the other in a tweed cap, carrying a small suit-case and a tightly furled umbrella.

They spoke to each other, then turned towards the exit. As Megan went to meet them, she saw that beneath the bobble hat was a black face. She hadn't been given his name, so she addressed the civil servant.

"Mr. Payne?"

"Yes?" Cautiously questioning.

"I'm your chauffeur, Detective Sergeant Pencarrow." Megan kept her voice low, in deference to the man's suspicious demeanour. "If you and Mr. . . ."

"Tariro."

". . . Mr. Tariro—"

"Just Tariro." The black student grinned at her. "My surname is an Official Secret, I'm told."

She smiled. "Then I'm Megan."

They went out to the car. Megan unlocked the boot, and as they deposited their bags, she opened the back door. Payne got in.

"May I sit in front?" Tariro asked.

"You won't see much, what with the dark and the rain. And the weather's only going to get worse as we approach the coast, according to the forecast."

Tariro slewed his eyes sideways at Henry Payne and said firmly, "I'd still prefer to sit in front, if it's all right with you. I have a tendency to feel car-sick in the back," he added in sudden inspiration.

Megan gathered that the student and the civil servant had not taken to each other on the train journey. "Just as you like," she said, unlocking the front passenger door.

As she went round to the driver's side, she saw the van's headlights switch on. The offside lamp was the yellowish colour usually confined to fog lights in the UK, though in general use in France. Happily, minor motoring offences were none of her business nowadays.

When she turned out of the car park, the mismatched lights were close behind. They trailed her to the A30 roundabout, where she lost sight of them for a minute, but they soon showed up again. Not that she could call it significant, since the alternative routes were few.

Glancing at the rearview mirror from time to time to see if they were still there, she asked Tariro the obvious questions: how he liked Oxford, which college he belonged to, what course he was taking.

His answer to the last question baffled her. "PPE?" She hazarded a guess, "Education? Or economics?"

"Philosophy, politics, and economics. Harold Wilson and Edward Heath both read PPE. Philosophy is interesting but not terribly practical. Economics has obvious uses. Politics is my favourite."

"Would you like to follow in Heath's and Wilson's footsteps? Become prime minister?"

"Of my own country, who knows?"

"Which country—"

Payne coughed meaningfully, but Tariro said, "Zimbabwe. Southern Rhodesia."

Megan racked her brains for what she knew about Southern Rhodesia.

The road forked, the A30 continuing southward, the A395 branching off towards the North Coast. The van was still behind them when they reached the highest point on the way to the coast and the wind slammed the car. She was thankful to be driving an 1100, not a Mini.

Despite the heavier car, she had to grip the steering wheel tightly to counter the buffeting. It took all her concentration to keep the vehicle on the road; she could barely make it out through the swishing windscreen wipers. The headlights illuminated little but diagonal shafts of water. The hammering of rain on the roof made talk impossible.

She couldn't have seen the van unless it had been bumper-to-bumper on her tail. Nevertheless, once they crossed the A39, she drove on down the narrowest and most tortuous side lanes. She knew them well, but any stranger was sure to get lost in the maze. Besides, they had the advantage of high hedge-banks that gave some protection against the wind's violence.

They reached the hotel at last. Lights shone in front of and under the portico. A few lit windows showed as dim squares. Megan's orders said to deliver her passengers to the northwest corner of the building. She drove round the massive structure.

Peering upward, Tariro said uneasily, "It looks like a prison."

"Does rather, doesn't it?"

"My dear chap, nothing of the sort," Payne chipped in hastily. "An excellent hotel, I'm told."

The door at the back had a light over it but no portico. "Hang on half a tick," said Megan, "while I make sure we can get in this way."

"Let me." Tariro reached for the door handle.

"No." Megan put her hand on his arm. "You're guests; I'm staff. If anyone has to appear drenched and tousled, it's me."

The wind whipped the car door from her hand. She managed to shut it behind her. Blown forward, she lurched to the door and tried the handle.

It was locked. Hotels did not commonly lock their entrances in the middle of the evening. Someone was taking security very seriously. She found a bell button and pushed twice.

After waiting what seemed like forever but was no more than a minute by Megan's count, she was about to ring again, when the door opened a crack, spilling light, then slammed back a few inches against the chain. Rather than try to make herself heard above the storm, Megan held out her warrant card through the gap. It was plucked from her fingers and, after a moment, returned to her.

She leaned forward and shouted, "Two passengers, Payne and Tariro."

"Please bring your passengers and their baggage to the doorstep, Sergeant." The voice didn't seem to Megan to be raised; rather, perfectly modulated, as though to cut through the babble of a drawing room to announce dinner without shouting. "I shall now shut the door and wait here. Ring again when they are ready to enter immediately. I shall await your return. Your car can be parked just across the drive, opposite this door." Which he closed.

"Oh, wonderful!" Megan muttered. She had hoped to attain shelter along with her passengers.

She turned back to the car. A pale face observed her anxiously through the back window; in the front, only the yellow hat was visible. She fought her way to the boot and took out the duffel bag and suitcase. The extra weight anchored her a bit as she carried them to the doorstep, but opening the driver's door without letting it escape her grasp again was another battle. She got in and managed to yank it closed.

"Someone's waiting to let you in. The butler, I think. Ring the bell. I've got to park the car."

She waited to see them enter before she moved the car. Then, her own holdall in hand, tacking like a yacht sailing against the wind, she made it back to the door.

Without much hope, she tried it before ringing the bell. The butler—compassionate or careless—had left it unlocked. Megan got herself inside and slumped for a moment against the wall before snibbing the lock. Of all the crazy places to build a hotel, the top of a cliff overlooking the North Atlantic just about took the biscuit.

Wondering how to find Sir Edward, to whom she was supposed to report, she glanced round the hall. It was more of a corridor than a hotel lobby, with a staircase and four doors besides the one by which she had entered.

She decided she ought to know her way about. She tapped on the nearest door, listened for a moment, then looked in. It was a dining room, the oval table set for six, with curtained windows at one end and all along the far side. Presumably it overlooked the cove and the castle ruins to the southwest and the sea to the northwest. Perhaps, to a hotelier, the views made up for the exposed location.

On the opposite side of the passage, one door opened to a small kitchen, where a harried woman stirring a pan on the stove barely glanced up when Megan said, "Police. Just checking." The other was labelled as a cloakroom.

The door at the far end also bore a legend: TO MAIN LOBBY. It was locked. Megan assumed hopefully that she would be provided with a key. She and her Scotland Yard counterpart couldn't be expected to battle their way round the building to reach the main hotel, where they were to be put up.

"Sergeant?"

Megan whirled round. The butler had come with silent tread down the stairs. She ought to have been more alert. "Yes?"

"I beg your pardon for startling you." His bland face showed neither amusement nor apology. Megan hadn't had much to do with butlers, but they were supposed to be imperturbable, and this one passed with flying colours. "Here is the key to the door you have just examined. It will be snibbed shut between eleven and seven. This one is for the tower entrance door."

"I locked it when I came in."

"Thank you, Sergeant. You might as well leave your bag here. Sir Edward wishes to speak to you upstairs, if you'd be kind enough to follow me."

Assuming consent, he started back up the stairs, a trifle wearily, Megan thought. Perhaps he was human after all.

She went after him. He opened a door on the first floor corresponding to that of the dining room below, stood aside to let her enter, followed her, and announced, "Detective Sergeant—"

"*Yip!*" A small white dog scampered across the floor, yipping all the way.

"—Pencarrow, sir."

"Teazle?" Megan bent down and picked her up. "Aunt Nell?"

SEVEN

"Megan, dear, what a lovely surprise." Eleanor jumped up from her seat by the fireplace and went to meet her niece.

"You can't possibly be half as surprised as I am. I was looking for you this morning and no one knew where you were. Not even Mrs. Stearns."

Though realising that Megan was here in an official capacity, Eleanor had no idea how much she knew, or was permitted to know. She cast a questioning look at Sir Edward as he joined them, very natty in a dark blue blazer and striped tie which Eleanor was sure had some significance that escaped her.

There had been a bit of a scene earlier, when Gina told Eleanor they wouldn't dress for dinner. Not having packed her one and only, rarely worn, evening dress, Eleanor was relieved. It was quite smart enough for the occasional local dinner party—Jocelyn, who had impeccable taste in clothes, had chosen it for her from a particularly fruitful donation to the shop—but not for the Bellowes. Eleanor had decided she'd rather be gauche in her good wool than shabby in her secondhand silk.

Sir Edward always dressed for dinner, he had spluttered. Gina reminded him that their guests were students and exiles, unlikely to possess dinner jackets. In his day, he had retorted, undergrads at Oxford all had dinner jackets, though for all he knew, LSE students might have worn boiler suits.

Gina had put her foot down.

Now Sir Edward once again exuded annoyance, though he smiled. "So, Detective Sergeant Pencarrow is your niece, Mrs. Trewynn? What a coincidence. I wasn't aware that you had a relative on the local force."

Eleanor failed to see any reason for his irritation. However, she had suffered through enough clashes with civil servants to know they were sometimes touchy over the most unexpected trifles. Often it was best to pretend one hadn't noticed. "Megan transferred from the Metropolitan Police several years ago," she explained. "Sir Edward Bellowe, dear."

Gina came up beside him, beaming. "How delightful, Eleanor! You'll dine with us, of course, Miss Pencarrow."

"Gina, really!"

"That's very kind of you, Lady Bellowe," said Megan, "but I'm afraid I'm on duty. My orders are to report to you, Sir Edward."

"Exactly." He gave his wife a repressive look. She wasn't going to win this bout.

"Another time." She had a twinkle in her eye. "Eleanor, we must arrange something, but for now, we'd better leave them to their business."

"I'll see you later, Megan." Eleanor retrieved Teazle from Megan's arms and she and Gina retreated to the sofa and their drinks.

Megan left a couple of minutes later. Teazle, who was just settling down, jumped up and went to sniff and whine at the door, then gave up. Sir Edward returned to stand with his back to the fire.

"Sorry if I was a bit abrupt, Eleanor. I was disconcerted, first by the police officer's being a woman—"

"You are an old fuddy-duddy," Gina said fondly.

"And then by her being your niece."

"I was surprised to see her. What's she doing here, or is it a secret?"

"Not from you, I suppose. Not to be spoken of in public. DS Pencarrow has accomplished the first part of her job: bringing my secretary, Payne, and the Oxford student from the nearest station. You must have heard Norton tell me that they went up to their rooms and will be down shortly. The sergeant and her counterpart from Scotland Yard, who should arrive any moment . . ." He frowned at his watch. "They're staying in the main hotel, to watch for anyone showing undue interest in us."

"What happens if someone does?"

Sir Edward frowned again. "We can't do much, to tell the truth, but at least we'll be forewarned. If we know about them, we can do our best to thwart them, whatever their designs. With luck, the officers will be able to discover how much they know, and what their intentions are. That's why I asked for two men who wouldn't appear to be police."

"No doubt that's why one of them is a woman," Gina proposed. "Protective colouring."

"Yes, I daresay. Good point, my dear."

"Darling, give me a bit more gin and It. I'm used to entertaining grave diplomats of all shapes, sizes, and colours, but I find I'm quite nervous about these young people."

"Nonsense," said Eleanor. "I'm sure they'll be charming. On the whole, I've found young Africans to be far more respectful of their elders than the youth of Britain."

Sir Edward laughed. "She's got you there, Gina."

"The young people," Eleanor added anxiously, "the students, they won't be in danger, will they? If Ian Smith finds out you're talking to them?"

"I hardly think so. He's a blind fool to imagine he can hold back the tide of history, but he's not— Yes, Norton?"

"The second party has arrived, sir. As you instructed, I directed the officer to the front entrance, to receive your orders from Sergeant Pencarrow—"

"Not another policewoman?"

"No, sir." The butler came as near to a smirk as a good butler would allow himself. "The student he conveyed here, Miss . . . er . . . Nontando, went up to her room to tidy herself."

"Miss! *Miss?* Are you sure, Norton?"

The butler's lips twitched. "Positive, sir."

Sir Edward sank his head in his hands with a groan.

"This is a great opportunity, Sir Edward," Eleanor pointed out. "One thing Africa needs badly is more educated women, more women involved in governance."

Gina consulted her watch. "Only if they don't spend too much time doing their hair. Norton, once they're both down, and Mr. Payne, of course, we'll give them ten minutes for a drink and then you can serve dinner."

"Certainly, madam. I will inform Cook." With a slight bow, Norton turned to the door. It opened as he reached for the handle. He stood aside to let a young African enter. "Mr. Tariro, my lady. I hope I have pronounced your name correctly, sir."

Tariro smiled. "Spot on, old boy."

Gina and Sir Edward converged on him. Eleanor sipped her Scotch and soda and observed. Tariro's clothes were very similar to Sir Edward's, though his trousers had an up-to-date flare. Only his Afro mop of hair—a style Eleanor had rarely seen in Africa—

suggested revolutionary tendencies. His manners were excellent. His speech, though influenced by the clipped accent of Southern African colonial English, was mostly Oxford, like Sir Edward's. It was odd, she mused, that Oxford University had somehow, sometime, developed its own distinctive brand of the Queen's English.

Sir Edward asked what he'd like to drink and went to pour him a sherry, while Gina brought him over to be introduced to Eleanor.

"A dear friend of mine," Gina explained to him, "who has spent a good deal of time in Africa, including your country."

They shook hands and Eleanor asked, "Did you have a good journey down?"

"Oh yes, Mrs. Trewynn. The trains were more or less on time." The young man grinned. "And I don't get a police chauffeur picking me up every day."

"What a treat!"

"Your chauffeur was Mrs. Trewynn's niece," Gina told him.

"She's a whizz of a driver. Conditions were horrible."

"It wasn't too bad when I arrived," Eleanor said, "but I was quite glad not to be driving. My car broke down just as I was about to leave. I had to beg a friend for a lift."

"What kind of car have you got?"

Eleanor found herself involved in a discussion of the faults and merits of the Morris Minor. It was not a subject she would ever have guessed would come up at a meeting of this sort.

While they were chatting, another man came in, a white man, unannounced by the butler. He looked every inch a junior civil servant in mufti—a discreet grey tweed instead of pinstripes. Sir Edward brought him over to say hello to Gina, whom he knew, and introduced him to Eleanor as his secretary, Payne, then drew him over to the window, where they talked in low voices.

The door opened and Norton, holding an ice bucket, announced, "Miss Nontando, my lady."

"Nontando!" Tariro exclaimed softly as Gina surged to her feet and went with Sir Edward to welcome the latest arrival.

A striking figure in a sleeveless scarlet trouser suit over a sunshine yellow blouse, she was almost as tall as her fellow countryman, even with her short-clipped hair contending with his bushy head. Fashionable platform shoes accounted for several inches of her height, Eleanor realised. Despite this impediment, she bore herself with the queenly carriage that enabled African women to walk with astounding loads balanced on their heads. The effect was elegant and self-confident.

Tariro was watching, too, frowning. When Gina turned and, a hand on Nontando's arm, started to bring her over to meet Eleanor, he drifted away without a word. Eleanor wondered whether they had met upstairs and developed an instant mutual antipathy . . . No, her entrance had taken him by surprise. They had met previously, and either disliked each other or had crossed swords over politics. Or both.

The number of Zimbabwean exiles in Britain was probably not large. Large enough to keep their factionalism alive, though; otherwise Sir Edward would not propose to exercise his diplomatic skills on this pair.

Eleanor decided she'd better start earning her keep by trying to find out what exactly was amiss between the two Zimbabweans. She invited Nontando to sit beside her. "I hope you don't mind my dog."

Nontando hesitated a moment. "No, of course not."

Teazle, dozing at Eleanor's feet, opened her eyes to study the newcomer but did not move.

Gina went after Tariro. Sir Edward brought Nontando a glass of lager and waved the whisky decanter. "A drop more, Eleanor?"

"No, thanks. This will do me nicely." She still had half her drink left.

He took the decanter back to the tray and stopped to talk to Tariro and Gina, who had parted the curtains to look out at the storm. Meanwhile, Norton popped in again to beg for a word with her ladyship. Payne started towards Eleanor and Nontando, but Eleanor gave him a look that he correctly interpreted as "Stay away."

"Have you met Tariro before, Miss Nontando?" she asked. "Something gave me that impression."

"Something like his walking away before we could be introduced?" Nontando said drily. "Yes, we met in Oxford. We both did our A-levels at Oxford Tech, so we could hardly help getting to know each other."

"I imagine it was a relief, in a strange country, to know some-one from home."

"It was. In fact, we . . . went out together."

Lived together? Eleanor wondered. "Then he stayed in Oxford and you went to London."

"He was offered places at both Oxford and LSE. He could have chosen London," Nontando said resentfully. "He wanted me to give up my education, marry him, and get a job. To support him. Typical Shona. Though, to be fair, Ndebele men are just as bad. If you know Zimbabwe, you know women count for nothing."

So much for Sir Edward's peace conference!

Gina returned. With a sigh, she flumped into a chair.

"Just a little domestic contretemps. Cook really does not have adequate facilities for a dinner party."

Nontando laughed. "Remember I'm a starving student, Lady Bellowe. I, at least, won't be a critical audience."

"How kind of you to say so, my dear."

"Though I daresay they have higher standards at Brasenose College," Nontando added snidely.

Gina sent a questioning glance Eleanor's way. Eleanor shrugged slightly. It was not for her to explain the root of Gina's guests' dissension.

EIGHT

As instructed, Megan had driven round to the front of the hotel and parked the car there. Checking in at reception, she noted that the large, comfortably furnished lobby had plenty of nooks perfect for lurking. Damp and chilled, she didn't stop to look about but went straight up to her room. It was not the draughty garret she had expected, but warm and much larger and more comfortable than anything she could have afforded for herself.

The reason for this unwonted expenditure of the taxpayers' money (by the CRO, not the chronically underfunded CaRaDoC) was clear when she leaned against the radiator to part the closed curtains.

Despite the night and the still-pouring rain, she could tell that she was just to one side of the well-lit front entrance portico, facing southeast. In daylight, she would have a view over the main car park and down the drive to the village, perfect for watching comings and goings. Inside, she was right opposite the main staircase and not too high up. If anyone approaching looked worthy of investigation, she could run down to the lobby in no time.

She was about to close the curtains, when the twin beams of

headlights showed hazily through the downpour. One was yellow. A white van—the same white van?—pulled up to the portico and stopped.

Megan managed to pull off her damp socks and shoes while watching the van. A man got out on the driver's side. At least she assumed it was a man, because he wore a trilby. As he circled the vehicle and disappeared under the portico, she dashed across the room to her bag to retrieve dry shoes, tights, a skirt, and a pocket torch. She turned off the overhead light and returned to the window. She could see out better now, and in the unlikely event of anyone looking up, they wouldn't see her.

Still peering down, she put on dry clothes, draping the wet ones over the radiator and shoving the toes of her shoes under it. Not good for the leather, but otherwise they'd take forever to dry.

The man came out again. He stooped to the van's window, shouting or just nodding to someone inside. Then he went round to the back, opened one door, and took out a couple of suitcases. Meanwhile, a man in headgear reminiscent of Andy Capp's climbed out on the passenger side and darted for shelter.

The first man went after him with the cases, then emerged a minute later without them. He got back in and drove off to park, backing into a space as if ready for a quick departure. The mismatched headlights went off.

Megan let the curtains fall together, crossed by torchlight to the door, and turned the light back on. Hastily, she dug her sponge bag out of her holdall. At the mirror over the washbasin, she ran a comb through her hair and applied peachy lipstick.

Nothing to do with the possibility of Ken's turning up, she told herself as she hurried downstairs. Her role as a holidaying visitor called for lipstick.

When she was far enough down to see the reception desk, two

men were standing in front of it. Both wore fawn raincoats. The shoulders of the tall, thin one were dark with rain. Trilby in one hand, he kept shifting his weight from foot to foot, impatient or nervous. His sleeked-back hair was unnaturally black, thinning. His companion had kept his cap on, as well as a green muffler, hiding his hair. He was shorter, burly. His hands stayed in his pockets while the other signed the register.

There was something furtive in their stance.

All this Megan observed as she came down the last few steps, treading lightly. She was sure these were the pair she had seen sitting in the van at Launceston station, but their arrival puzzled her.

She was as good as certain they hadn't followed her in the lanes; apart from the near impossibility, they would have arrived much sooner. Yet here they were. If they had known already where she was going, why draw attention to themselves by waiting in the station car park and driving out immediately behind her?

More likely, it had just been a convenient place to stop and consult the map to work out how to get here.

The receptionist, a middle-aged woman, handed over two keys, the tall man taking possession of both. Not wanting to be caught snooping, Megan took the last two steps more heavily. She still made very little sound, but both men swung round instantly.

At the same moment, the front door opened, letting in a blast of cold, damp air. The men continued turning till they faced it. Megan and the receptionist also looked that way.

"Ken!"

"Hello, darling."

Unwillingly following his cue, Megan went to meet him and accepted a kiss on the cheek. "I was beginning to wonder whether you'd decided to wait out the storm somewhere and I'd have to dine alone."

"Whatever happened to the blue skies and sunny beaches in the posters?" DS Kenneth Faraday, always referred to by DCI Scumble as the Boy Wonder, was as tall and broad-shouldered as Megan's boss, considerably less bulky, twenty years younger, and much better looking. In black jeans and a damp down jacket, his hair dripping, he didn't look at all like a policeman. At that moment, his expression was not the usual cocksure arrogance, but an unaccountable mixture of smugness and sheepishness, to which was added curiosity as he stared at the backs of the two raincoated men now hurrying to the stairs. "Trouble?" he asked softly.

"I'll tell you. You'd better check in first."

"Right. Give me ten minutes and I'll meet you in the bar."

Playing up to the image he had chosen to project, Megan tucked her hand into his arm and went with him to the desk.

"I'm afraid both rooms adjacent to Miss Pencarrow's are already occupied," the receptionist said, her accent Cornish, her tone chilly.

"I believe you have a room reserved for me. The name's Faraday."

"Oh yes, Mr. Faraday. Let's see now. Yes, your room is on the first floor, southwest side. When the storm passes, you'll enjoy the view over the Haven to the castle ruins. If you'd just sign the register, please, and I'll get your key." She pushed the ledger across the counter and turned to the key board.

Megan read the names scrawled on the two lines above Ken's: Victor Jones and Adrian Arbuthnot, both of London.

Ken signed, took his key, refused help with his baggage, and thanked the receptionist. She disappeared through a door behind the desk as he and Megan turned away,.

"Victor Jones, Adrian Arbuthnot," said Ken.

"'Victor,' probably his real name, or one he often uses," said Megan. "'Jones,' one step above Smith. 'Adrian Arbuthnot,' pure fiction."

"You're pretty certain they're villains, then?"

"Pretty certain. Though they may have nothing to do with our job here. I'll explain when you come down."

"See you in the bar. I'll have a pint of bitter, local draught if they have it."

"All right. Hold on, here's the key Sir Edward gave me for you."

"To . . . ?"

"When you come down."

He nodded and, pigskin suitcase in one hand, he took the stairs two at a time.

Showing off as usual, Megan thought. That moment of sheepishness, though—what had brought the expression to his face? In the past, it had generally signified the arrival in his life of yet another long-legged blonde, but he couldn't have picked one up yet, nor brought one with him.

Megan strolled round the lobby, noting in particular a couple of cosy nooks with a good view of both the entrance and the stairs. Then she went through to the bar. In the far corner was a door to the exterior, making the bar accessible to nonresidents—while also providing an escape route for anyone hoping to evade surveillance. On her right were curtained windows that in daylight would have the same view as her bedroom just above.

The room was thinly populated. A group of eight or nine Americans were complaining about the weather to a harassed English guide. Another joined them as Megan watched, saying, "Aw, come on, folks, give the guy a break. It's prob'ly ten degrees and snowing in Minneapolis."

A few middle-aged couples were scattered about the large room, talking quietly or silent and glum. The only person who looked content was a man of about sixty sitting at the bar with a bleached blonde thirty-five years his junior. The bar stool pose and her mini-skirt contrived to display the girl's long, shapely legs.

Megan asked the barman for Ken's pint and a half of cider for herself. "Quiet tonight," she remarked as she paid, boggling at the total, adding a tip, and wondering whether she could put it on expenses. "The storm must have kept a lot of people away."

"We don't aim for the pub trade, miss. There's not many local people come in, though we do get a few tourists that's staying in the village, and them with summer cottages."

"I nearly didn't make it myself this evening. It was a beastly drive."

"I did hear some people that booked for tonight rang up to say they'd stop the night somewhere else and come on in the morning. But we got a few the other way round, wasn't planning to stay here but didn't want to drive any farther. Six of one and half a dozen of the other, if you take my meaning, miss, and it all comes out in the wash. Excuse me, miss." He went to refill the glass of the smug man at the bar.

Feeling she had made a good start at establishing a gossipy relationship with the barman, Megan settled in a corner with a clear view of both doors. If Jones and Arbuthnot came in, she couldn't miss them, but she had to allow for their villainy being of a different stamp.

A Rhodesian spy might stay in the village, drive up to the hotel, and enter through the exterior door. In fact, since the village had several perfectly good pubs, any nonresident who braved the storm to get to the hotel bar was more than likely up to no good.

Ken came in. His gaze took in the entire bar and those in it, without lingering for even a moment on those long legs. Megan wondered whether his self-restraint presaged yet another attempt to persuade her to return to London, now that women were at last to be allowed the rank of Detective.

He wound his way between the tables to join her. As he sat down, he reached for his beer and took a big gulp. "Ah, that's better. Thanks."

"Tough drive?"

"Not bad till the last twenty miles. But my passenger was determined to do some sightseeing en route. Stonehenge, Winchester Cathedral—thanks to the Beatles, Salisbury Cathedral, Dartmoor."

"I'm surprised you ever got here. You weren't followed?"

"No, I'm sure of that. You were? By those two in the lobby?"

"By them if by anyone." Megan frowned. "I just don't know." She described the van as she had seen it in the station car park and how the mismatched lights had followed along the main roads. "Up to that point, I was wondering why anyone would have chosen such a distinctive vehicle for the purpose."

"Assuming they stole it, they might simply not have noticed."

"True. Presumably, they'd have been in a hurry to get away. Do you think I ought to check whether it's been reported stolen?"

"Not if it means going out into the storm in the dark to get the licence number! You didn't note it down at the station?"

"I couldn't read it. The light was rotten. Besides, I had no reason to suspect anything then. What makes you think it was stolen, anyway? Surely the Rhodesian white settlers aren't the sort to drive small stolen vans. Don't they all live on huge estates with dozens of servants and hundreds of workers?"

Ken grinned. "That's certainly the impression you get from the press. Perhaps sanctions are beginning to bite? More likely, Smith's government employed a couple of crooks to do the dirty work for them."

"Could be. Or could be hired by a sympathiser over here who wants to keep his nose clean. But whoever they are, I don't believe they could have followed me through the lanes."

"I must admit I had a hard time just finding my way here tonight, without trying to follow taillights."

"And you were following the signs, weren't you? The lanes I took are half as wide and have no fingerposts except to farms. Besides, they arrived fifteen or twenty minutes after I did. Either they already knew where my passengers were going or they're nothing to do with us and just happened to be coming here."

"Bit of a coincidence!"

"Coincidences happen. On the other hand, if they *are* spying on this Zimbabwe business, they already knew quite a lot, or they wouldn't have been waiting at the station at the right time. But why wait at all if they knew we were coming here?"

"My brain's spinning." Ken groaned. "Let's go and get something to eat."

"Hang on, I've got a two-way hand-held for you." She glanced round. No one was paying them the slightest attention, so she took the small radio from her shoulder bag and handed it to him under the table.

"Thanks."

"And here's the key Sir Edward gave me for you, for the connecting door to the northwest tower, where he is staying."

Pocketing it with a nod, he gulped the last of his beer, and they headed for the dining room.

The menu was pricy, like the bar drinks, but Sir Edward's department was paying the bill for their meals. Ken still had the irritating—though useful—ability to summon a waiter without

BURIED IN THE COUNTRY

raising a finger. They ordered scallops, landed that morning before the storm blew in, with local spring lamb jardinière to follow.

The waiter was a washout as a source of information. He was Spanish and his command of English seemed to be strictly reserved for food. He took their orders; then Ken asked whether they often had nonresidents coming to dine. "Not in this weather, of course," he added.

The man looked baffled. Uncertainly he said, "Huether better *mañana*, sir," and went off with a puzzled face.

"Bad luck." Megan sat back. "Of course, our pair could even be quite innocent tourists. Only, the tall one looked to me like a con man. The sort who preys on lonely, well-off widows. And the other looked like a thug."

"He did indeed. Prison pallor, I shouldn't be surprised. Not long out. I could swear I've seen a photo of his ugly mug."

"Along with 'Wanted for . . . ,' or his fingerprints?"

"Undoubtedly. But not under the name of Jones. Not a case I was on, or I'd remember. I can't pin him down."

"Victor something?"

Ken shook his head. "Doesn't help."

"We could be wrong. It doesn't do to judge by looks."

"'There is no art to find the mind's construction in the face.'"

"What?"

"*Macbeth*."

"Oh. We did *Romeo and Juliet*."

"There's no way to tell a man's character by his face."

After a moment's thought, Megan said, "It could be the opposite. 'There is no art,' meaning it's simple."

"But it's not simple, or con men wouldn't exist."

"And Lombroso's head bumps have been thoroughly debunked, too. Besides, I was judging by their furtive behaviour as much or more than by their faces. Do you think they might have recognised you?"

"If they're London crooks, it's always possible they've seen me before, at the Yard, or in court, or perhaps investigating their mates. And some petty criminals develop a nose for a copper, though I must have looked more like a drowned rat than a policeman."

"You did," said Megan, laughing.

"Oh well, if they did guess, maybe they'll give up whatever their little scheme is."

"They must have some sort of scheme, don't you think? They're Londoners, or so they wrote in the hotel register. What are they doing here buried in the country on the North Coast in early March? A holiday seems highly unlikely."

"I might believe in a holiday if they'd brought the missus and the kiddies! I'd say they must have a specific target in mind, not just a vague hope of a good haul at a comparatively pricy hotel, especially in the off-season."

"One way or the other, we'll just have to keep tabs on them. The barman seems to be a bit of a gossip."

"He does, does he? Have you been chatting him up?"

"Just chatting. Cultivating a promising source."

"Sounds much better that way. It'll impress Sir Edward."

"I wasn't going to bother him with it. Surely he'll only want to know if we find out something definite."

"I was told to report this evening."

"He never said anything to me."

"No?" Ken sighed. "A gentleman of the old school, I daresay."

"You mean he believes a woman's only use as a detective is that she doesn't look like one?"

"I was trying to put it tactfully."

"Bloody cheek! Who's done all the detecting that's been done so far, I'd like to know?"

"You have, and I'll make sure you get the credit, so don't blame me. Come to think of it, the instructions may well have come from my guv'nor, not Sir Edward, so don't blame him. After all, he did leave it to you to brief me, though I've pretty well got the picture. We're to watch out for nosy strangers, right? Here's our food," he added with obvious relief. "Calm down, Megan. Could we possibly have a truce while we eat?"

NINE

Whatever Gina's cook's difficulties, Eleanor found nothing amiss
with the dinner she provided. The company was pleasant, too.
Gina carefully steered the conversation to uncontroversial topics, allowing everyone to enjoy the meal in peace, barring a few
missteps.

The name of the hotel and King Arthur's mythical connection
to Tintagel interested both the students. Eleanor described the ruins on the island.

"It was probably a monastery," she explained, "with a possible
lookout fort going back to Roman times."

"I'd love to see it," said Nontando eagerly.

"Sorry." Sir Edward was firm. "Even if the storm abates, showing yourself outdoors would completely breach security."

Nontando didn't protest, but she looked defiant.

"It's a terrific climb across to the island and up to the ruins,"
Eleanor pointed out quickly. "Quite daunting."

"Did you ever visit the ruins of Great Zimbabwe, Mrs. Trewynn?"
Tariro asked.

"No, I never had an opportunity. From what I heard, they dwarf King Arthur's castle. Have you been there?"

"No. The settlers claim it was constructed by Europeans, but archaeologists say the city was built a thousand years ago, half a millennium before Brasenose was founded in 1509. There were no whites in my country then."

Gina returned to safer ground with a question about the history of his college, and thence gently to college sports, in which he was active.

Eleanor noticed that Nontando and Tariro never spoke directly to each other. Sir Edward appeared to be aware of the coolness between them, at one point glancing from one to the other with a slight frown. No doubt he put it down to their tribal and political differences. Eleanor decided she could warn him of their personal antagonism without betraying Nontando's confidence.

Whether she could lessen the tension was another matter. She would need time to talk to each of them, time to discover whether the breach could be mended, and if so, how to tackle it.

She was given no time that evening. After dinner, Sir Edward "suggested" that his wife and Eleanor would be more comfortable taking their coffee upstairs. He was going to hold a short preliminary meeting with the two students, with Payne taking notes.

"Discussing what to discuss tomorrow," Gina said with a touch of acid as she followed Eleanor up. "Talk, talk, talk. Eleanor, would you mind frightfully if I deserted you for half an hour? I feel a headache coming on and perhaps I can stave it off if I lie down for a while. There's a shelf of books in the sitting room, quite a varied collection that I expect people have left over the years."

"Why don't you go straight to bed? I'll make your excuses to the others."

"Would you? I'm sure I'll feel right as rain in the morning."

"You'd better be. I'd be bound to make a mess of giving orders to Cook and Norton."

"Now that I doubt, but I think I'll take your advice. Good night." Gina went on up the next flight of stairs.

"Sleep well."

Eleanor went into the sitting room. She gave the bookshelf a desultory look, not taking in the titles. Norton brought her coffee. She sipped, and decided a decent coffeepot was one thing the tower's kitchen lacked.

What she really wanted was to talk to Megan. Surely no one would be suspicious of a little old lady having a chat with another guest at the hotel? She would just pop through the connecting door and see whether Megan was in one of the public rooms. She wouldn't go so far as to ask for her room number. It would look like a casual meeting.

Eleanor made sure she had the key and enough money on her to buy a drink, or a cup of coffee. Perhaps the main hotel had a better coffee maker.

"Stay!" she said sternly to Teazle, who gave her an injured look, sighed, and stretched out on the hearthrug. Eleanor went back downstairs and through the connecting door, careful to lock it behind her.

The main lobby wasn't the functional hall with a desk that she'd expected. It was a large room with a confusion of arches and a bewilderment of comfortable furniture set out in small groups round low tables. Tired and feeling her age, Eleanor peered round, hoping to spot Megan. She saw signs to the bar lounge and the dining room. Her niece might be tucked away in either, or up in her room.

But no, here she came, threading her way between the tables, looking very pretty in a peach-coloured jersey and chocolate brown skirt.

"Aunt Nell, is everything all right? Did you manage to escape Sir Edward's toils? Where's Teazle?"

"Asleep by the fire, I hope."

"We're having coffee. Come and join us." She took Eleanor's arm.

"Oh dear, I forgot you have a colleague with you. Are you sure he won't mind?"

"He'd better not, if he knows what's good for him. Anyway, you know him."

"Your friend Ken Faraday? How nice!"

"That's one way of looking at it," Megan said wryly. "His boss has annointed him expert on this remote corner of the realm."

Faraday stood as they approached. "Mrs. Trewynn, delighted to see you again. Will you have coffee?"

"Yes, please."

A waiter appeared at his elbow, and a moment later a second pot of coffee appeared on the table. Megan poured a cup for Eleanor. It was a vast improvement on the Bellowes' cook's concoction.

"You're staying here, Mrs. Trewynn? You live just down the road, don't you?"

"Yes, not far. Sir Edward invited me to . . . join his party. I'm staying in the tower."

"May I ask what your part is in this gallimaufrey?"

Eleanor consulted Megan with a glance.

"It's all right, Aunt Nell. Ken is part of the 'gallimaufrey.' I'm curious, too. I didn't expect to find you here!"

"It's because of my experience all over the world." She tried to explain her role. Put into words, it sounded muddled and nebulous, but then, she thought, Sir Edward's purpose was also pretty nebulous. After what Nontando had told her, she wouldn't give much for his chance of success.

Naturally, she didn't mention Nontando's story to Megan and Ken.

"You two brought Nontando and Tariro here, I gather?"

"Glorified chauffeurs, that's us," Ken joked.

"And would-be spy catchers," Megan added. "We're here to watch out for nosy strangers."

"Though we haven't been told what to do with them if we find them. What do you think, Mrs. Trewynn, is it likely that someone from the . . . opposition, I suppose we can call them, will turn up, trying to discover what's going on?"

Eleanor was in a quandary. Though she didn't really believe Ian Smith's sympathisers were dogging Sir Edward's footsteps, it wasn't for her to say so. And suppose he was right? Well, suppose he was right, would it matter? He himself doubted that Nontando and Tariro would be endangered.

"I have no idea," she said. "Have you seen any suspicious characters?"

"Yes," they said in unison.

"You have? Oh dear!"

"They're in the restaurant at present," said Ken.

"But they look more like common crooks than international agents." Megan described the two men. "At least we have more idea of what we're looking for, now that you've clarified things, Aunt Nell."

"Oh dear, have I said more than I ought? I assumed the situation had been explained to you."

"Don't worry." Ken grinned. "We won't give you away."

"I'm sure I didn't mention Z—the country involved."

"Tariro told me that much in the car," said Megan. "I expect it was an oversight that we didn't get the whole story. We're police officers, after all. If he didn't trust us, he could have had his own people do the job, or a couple of spooks."

"Spooks?"

"American slang, Mrs. Trewynn. The *real* spies."

"In this case, *anti*-spies. Special Branch, or even MI5. Not that MI5 would be interested without a Cold War connection."

But there *was* a Cold War connection, Eleanor thought. Sir Edward said ZANU and ZAPU were supported by the Soviets and the Chinese. She had best not mention it to these two, however. "That reminds me, dear, was there a particular reason you were looking for me earlier? At home, I mean?"

"Yes, as a matter of fact." Megan hesitated, glancing at Ken.

"I can take a hint as well as the next man," he said genially. "I'll make myself scarce."

"Just a few minutes."

"I expect Sir Edward will send for me soon."

"Oh, all right. Thanks. Always the gentleman," she said sotto voce as he went off towards the bar, "even when he was being a right sod."

Eleanor was a little anxious by that time. "What is it, Megan? What on earth did you want to see me for, so badly that you even tackled Jocelyn?"

"Mrs. Stearns was actually very helpful, apart from not knowing where you were. She was quite worried about you. Shouldn't you phone her and at least assure her you're all right, even if you can't say where you are or why?"

"I ought to have told her I was going to be away for the weekend. Sir Edward had me in such a tiswas over security. . . . I'll ring her when I go back to the tower. Now, for pity's sake—"

"As it happens I was looking for information about a missing person. He probably has just as good a reason for being missing as you do, and normally we—the police, that is—we wouldn't be interested unless there was something fishy about his absence. We looked into it only because it was reported by a solicitor."

"In Port Mabyn? Roland or Alan?"

"I knew they'd be friends of yours."

"I talked to Alan Freeth just the other day. Such a nice, helpful man. One of their clients disappeared?"

"Not a client, one of the lawyers. Mr. Freeth, in fact. Did you notice anything odd about him when you saw him?"

"No, not at all," said Eleanor, puzzled. "But it was business, not a friendly chat. He's vanished? Poor Roland must be distraught."

"He is. That's why I decided I'd better talk to you and make sure I hadn't . . . imagined things."

"Joce clarified things for you?"

"Yes, and pretty much confirmed my impression that Bulwer reported Freeth's absence for emotional reasons, not because he was seriously concerned that he was in danger. I covered the financial side of things with him. No money missing, according to Bulwer, though if Freeth doesn't turn up reasonably soon, their clients' accounts will have to be audited, I imagine."

"Alan Freeth wouldn't steal!" Eleanor said indignantly. "He's not that sort of person at all."

"Aunt Nell, there isn't a 'sort' of person who steals. Anyway, I wasn't accusing him. We'd be hunting for him in earnest if he was suspected of theft."

"You're not— Your colleagues aren't hunting for him?"

"When a grown man walks out of his own volition, we can't—" She stopped as Ken came up to them.

"Sorry to interrupt. I just wanted to let you know, Megan, that I'm off to see Sir Edward. I don't suppose he'll keep me long."

"All right."

"I'd better go back with you," said Eleanor. "Gina—Lady Bellowe—went to bed early, and if Sir Edward is occupied with you, I ought to be there to keep Nontando and Tariro from each other's throats."

"Like that, is it?" Ken asked. "It doesn't augur well for the peace talks, or whatever he has in mind. Megan, our pair are in the bar now."

"Well, I'd be too conspicuous going in there alone, so—"

"Yeah, it's not the sort of bar that cares for lone females hanging about."

"Oh, shut up! My friendly barman wouldn't mind, but the crooks might take note. I'll see them if they come out."

"Perhaps I should take a peek at them," Eleanor suggested. "I'd like to know who I'm watching out for."

"No!" they said as one.

"The last thing we need is for them to realise they're being watched," Ken added.

"Let alone for them to be aware of your interest, Aunt Nell," said Megan. "Whatever they're after, we don't want them after you, too."

TEN

Nick, meanwhile, had been invited to have supper with Freeth. Even if the other options had not been to plunge back out into the storm or to go hungry, he would have accepted. Though he couldn't seriously suspect the lawyer of spying on Bellowe, he was curious about his relationship with Mrs. Mason.

"It won't be much of a meal," Freeth apologised. "Rosie—Mrs. Mason—is a good cook, but she's not feeling at all well. I made her go to bed. Cooking is not my forte, but I can open a tin of soup and make some sandwiches, if that will do you."

Nick offered to help, so he stirred the cream of mushroom soup while Freeth rummaged in fridge and larder for sandwich ingredients and sliced a loaf. Then Nick put sandwiches together while Freeth took a tray with soup and crustless bread and butter up to Mrs. Mason.

The men ate in the kitchen, between the crumbs and smears of preparation at one end and Nick's sketchpad at the other. After an exchange of inconsequential remarks about the storm and the likelihood of flooding in Port Mabyn, Nick said tentatively, "I hope my unceremonious arrival didn't upset Mrs. Mason. I'd hate to think I'm responsible for her . . . attack."

"Good lord, no, not at all. I'm afraid her condition is serious, even though it's not always apparent." Freeth looked at his sandwich with unseeing eyes. "There's nothing to be done, it seems, except try to relieve the symptoms."

"I'm sorry." Chest pain and breathlessness, he remembered. However, his grandmother had survived in that condition for many years, long enough to cut him out of her will for disgracing the family by becoming a professional artist. "You've known Mrs. Mason for a long time, you said?"

"More precisely, we knew each other a long time ago, in London. We were both Londoners. We'd lost touch, but when she needed a lawyer, she wrote to me. It's not hard to find a particular solicitor, as long as he's in active practice."

"You're all on official lists, I suppose. The Law Society and all that. A good, solid, respectable profession. Does it run in your family?"

"No. My forebears were for the most part good respectable clergymen, but far from solid in the financial sense. My father pinched and scraped to pay for my articles."

"Which world did Mrs. Mason come from?" Nick asked idly, more to keep Freeth talking than because he cared. The man had an interesting face. Nick pushed aside his dishes—empty—and reached for the sketchbook. "Law or religion?"

"Neither." Freeth was amused. "Or rather, the wrong side of the law. Not that I knew it at the time, not to begin with. Nor did Rosie, in all the time I knew her. I'd swear to that. Her mother died when she was in her teens and she kept house for the old man." He stood up. "I'll go and get her tray." He glanced at Nick's sketch in passing but didn't comment.

After all, what could one do with a face using a hard pencil? Nick hadn't liked to return to Mrs. Mason's desk for charcoal when she was ill upstairs. Dissatisfied, he turned back to the almost architectural drawing he had been doing of the kitchen. Its stark simplicity had a certain pleasing quality, but he couldn't take it much further. He might as well start on the washing up.

"Doing all right, then, are you, Pencarrow?" DCI Scumble's call had come through just after Aunt Nell and Ken went off to the tower. "Nasty bit of weather for the drive?"

"Very nasty, sir. I managed."

"The forecast says it'll blow over by morning. Should be dry by the time you go down the village to see if there's any gossip about nosy strangers."

"I think Sir Edward expects us to stick around, sir."

"Rubbish! I bet all the hotel workers are foreigners, aren't they?"

"Well, yes."

"So what do you expect to get out of them? Talk to the locals. By the way, did the Boy Wonder turn up?"

"Yes, sir."

"Bright eyed and bushy-tailed as ever, I suppose. Is he being a pain in the . . . neck?" The guv'nor no longer guarded his tongue as carefully as when Megan first joined his team, but he still sometimes came over mealy-mouthed.

"Not too bad. Just occasionally annoying."

"And what about the pinstripes and bowler brigade that requisitioned your services?"

"I've only spoken to the top man for a couple of minutes, sir. His assistant is one of the two I picked up, but he barely said a word. The other passenger sat beside me. He was quite chatty."

"He's not a bureaucrat. They're a cagey tribe. Beware of bureaucrats, Pencarrow. I've always found it a sound maxim."

"Yes, sir."

"This was the student? Did he let on what's going on?"

"Not exactly, sir, but I learned a bit from who he is and where he comes from. I'd better not tell you—"

"Dammit, Pencarrow, those pen-pushers have infected you!"

"—on an open line, sir. I'll give you a full report when I get back, of course." Megan hesitated. "I . . . um . . . perhaps I ought to mention that my aunt has turned up, too. As well as DS Faraday."

"Mrs. Trewynn? Now why does that make me think this is going to end in chaos?"

"I can't imagine," Megan said crossly. "Sir Edward wouldn't keep asking for her help if she wasn't helpful."

"Doubtless international intrigue is already so complicated, your auntie can't make it any worse. As long as she stays out of CaRaDoC business—"

"There's something else I'd better tell you, sir. . . ."

The response was a loud groan. "Don't tell me Auntie's already on the trail of a murderer!"

Megan was tempted to tell him not to be ridiculous, but in spite of its irritations, she wanted to keep her job. "Nothing to do with Aunt Nell, sir." She told him about being followed—possibly—from Launceston and the arrival of the two unprepossessing men at the King Arthur Hotel. "Ken—DS Faraday and I agree that they look fishy, but not the type to go in for espionage."

"Can't arrest people for looking fishy, more's the pity."

"We can keep an eye on them, though, and I was thinking I ought to notify the local man. PC Yarrow—he was very helpful with that fraudulent medium. I'll go out in the morning and get their licence plate number."

"Call it in to the nick and we'll run it, but leave it to me to get in touch with Yarrow. On second thoughts, you'd better get that number now and ring me back, in case they're planning to rob the hotel and scarper in the small hours."

"Sir, it's—"

"Raining. Yes, I know. And you're a police officer, Pencarrow, not a Victorian debutante."

Raining! If it was just the rain! But Launceston, in its sheltered valley, probably hadn't felt the full power of the gale-force wind. "Yes, sir."

"Mind you don't blow off the cliff." He hung up, fortunately, so Megan's retort was uttered to a dead receiver.

Though she had a pocket torch in the shoulder bag that accompanied her everywhere, she'd have to go up to her room to get her parka. How much longer would Ken be gone? She didn't like leaving the suspects unguarded, even if she hadn't a clue what their goal was.

The guv'nor didn't take kindly to being made to wait. Megan went upstairs and changed into her wet slacks and shoes, wishing she had brought more clothes with her. A few minutes later, she trudged across the car park towards the glimmer of the white van. The wind had abated somewhat. It still blew rain at her and reduced visibility, but it didn't seriously impede her progress.

No wonder she hadn't read the number at the station. The plate was filthy. The sides of the van were splattered with road dirt, but the plate was even dirtier than the filthy weather could account for. Crouching, she examined it in the beam of her torch.

Beneath the overlying grime, smears of mud obscured the figures—deliberately, she was sure. Even staring from a couple of feet away, she could only just make them out. The middle letter was O. She was pretty sure most O's were Birmingham-issued. The men claimed to be Londoners . . . but the registration was C, so the van was a few years old and could have changed hands more than once.

She wondered for a moment whether she ought to clean off at least some of the muck to make it legible, in case the van had to be followed later. The men would probably notice, though. The rear plate would be less obvious—but still risky. One of them, at least, was bound to go and open the doors to put their luggage in, not to mention swag, if any. Besides, she was reluctant to sacrifice her handkerchief.

Of course, the plates could have been stolen. Come to that, the van was quite likely stolen, and might even have plates from a different vehicle. Nonetheless, Megan memorised the numbers and letters, then went round to the rear to make sure the plates matched, which they did. She noted the make, and checked both side panels to make sure neither had any identifying marks, however faint, perhaps hastily painted over. She found nothing.

By then, the hood of her parka was soaked through. Chilled, her trousers clinging uncomfortably to her legs, she hurried back to the hotel. All she wanted was a hot bath, and a hot drink to sip while lounging in it.

Instead, she squelched her way to the telephones. Scumble answered on the first ring.

"Pencarrow, sir."

"What took you so long, Pencarrow?"

Her answer was an enormous sneeze. It took her by surprise, so she just had time to jerk the receiver aside.

"All right, all right, I heard that. Give me the number, quick, and go get yourself a hot toddy, on me."

Sometimes—occasionally—the guv'nor wasn't so bad. Thankfully she gave him the information, including the condition of the plates. "By the way, DS Faraday is reporting the two men to Sir Edward."

"But you agree they're not likely anything to do with him? Just remember, Pencarrow, you're only on loan to the pen-pusher. If your bad lads start any funny business on our turf, your first duty is to CaRaDoC."

"Yes, sir."

He grunted. She took that as a good-bye and hung up before he could come up with any further orders.

On her way to the stairs, Megan glanced round the lobby. No sign of the dubious pair, nor of Ken, though he must surely be back from the tower by now. She was in no condition to check thoroughly or poke her head into the bar. A few people gave her curious stares as she passed. She must look a complete disaster.

Plodding up the stairs, she relinquished the idea of a bath. Someone ought to be down below, keeping an eye on things. Ken was probably having a cosy man-to-man chat with Sir Edward over a glass of whisky. Strictly speaking, the men from London were not his problem as long as whatever mayhem they contemplated was planned to take place in Cornwall, as was almost certain. They couldn't be just passing through. Cornwall wasn't on the way to anywhere else.

Once again she changed into dry clothes and spread the wet ones on the radiator. They were so soggy now, there wasn't much hope that they'd dry by morning.

Downstairs again, Megan gave the lobby a quick scan. No Ken still, and no "bad lads." The latter she spotted as she entered the bar lounge, at the corner table where she and Ken had sat earlier. The room was about half-full now, the last diners having been chased from the restaurant, which was closed, as a sign on the door attested.

She went to the bar. The barman was not quite as spruce and alert as earlier, but he had a smile for her.

Smiling back, she said, "I bet three-quarters of the people in here have complained to you about the weather."

"You wouldn't be far off. What'll it be?"

"A hot toddy. I got rather wet."

"Rum or—"

"No, wait a minute. I'd better not." It had been a long day, and at least for the present she was the only pair of eyes on duty. What if she fell asleep? Where the hell was Ken?

As if reading her mind, the barman said, "Here he comes. I'll be back in half a mo, when you've decided." He went to serve another customer.

Megan leaned back against the bar and watched Ken cross the lounge. His face was laughingly guilty, but he had a jaunty spring in his step. "Sorry," he said as he reached her.

"Sir Edward must have had an awful lot to say. I hope you made notes, or you might forget all you have to tell me."

"It wasn't actually all that much. As a matter of fact, I stopped for a bit of a chat."

"With Aunt Nell?"

"Well, no. With the student I drove down here."

"The one who had you zigzagging all over southern England. Female, by any chance?"

"Yes, actually. Didn't I mention her?"

"You did not. It's nothing to do with me. We're only pretending to be a couple, remember. Which was entirely your idea. I could hardly deny it when you walked in and—"

"Have you decided what you want, madam?" asked the barman, altogether too close behind her.

"Yes, thanks. I'll have that rum toddy after all."

"Sir?"

"Seltzer with a dash of bitters." To Megan, Ken added, "*Some-one* has to stay awake."

"My guv'nor rang up and had me go out to get the van's number plate. I got soaked, again."

"Hard lines. Now why do I get the feeling that sooner or later we're going to have your chief and Sir Edward at odds?"

"I'd back the guv'nor against any pen-pusher—his description, not mine. What did Sir Edward say when you told him about our chummies?"

"He rather pooh-poohed them. They didn't sound at all the type he was expecting."

"What type is he expecting?"

"Probably a pretty straightforward colonial or ex-colonial who believes in the settlers' cause. He thinks it's unlikely Smith's government would resort to hiring a spy, but if they did, they're not so unsophisticated as to pick someone whose looks invite suspicion."

Megan frowned. "If he's right, then those two are my pigeon."

"I wish you the joy of them," said Ken. "Excuse me a moment. Nature calls."

The barman returned with their drinks. He leaned across the counter and said quietly to Megan, "You're rozzers, right? Busies?"

"Damn, is it that obvious?"

"My old man was a bobby. 'Sides, spend all my time watching people, don't I. That's what my profession's all about. To me, it's plain as the nose on your face, but I don't s'pose anyone else has noticed. I'd have to be thick as two planks not to see you and your 'boyfriend' don't give a sh—a hoot about each other, not in a romantic way, even if you did give him a key."

That was debatable, Megan thought. "Anyone else watching us?"

"Not so you'd notice. Nothing more'n a casual once-over in passing." He gave Megan the once-over and his eyes gleamed. "Here, if he's not—"

"You'd better stop right there, mate. I take it you've also been watching those two men sitting over in the corner?" She didn't look their way.

Nor did the barman. "Couldn't hardly miss them, could I."

"They haven't been watching us, Ken and me?"

"Don't think so. Should I be watching *them?*"

"We don't have any evidence. Just coppers' instinct. But if I was you I'd have a word with whoever handles your night security. If anyone?"

"Night porter. I'll warn him, no kipping tonight. Ta for the tip. They're ugly buggers."

"Dress up the tall one and take a few years off, and he might have been quite a ladies' man."

"On the con?"

"We have no evidence," Megan said again. "By the way, they both registered as Londoners. Have you heard them speak?"

"The con man talks BBC. Could be from anywhere. The brute, I've only heard a few words, but being a Londoner meself—"

"I couldn't have guessed," she teased.

He grinned. "Being a Londoner meself, I'd say the Borough is his home ground."

Ken returned in time to catch the barman's last words. He frowned at Megan. "You didn't tell—"

"I didn't need to. We're just not lovey-dovey enough to fool such a keen observer of human nature."

"That can be changed." He put his arms round her and kissed her mouth. Megan was pleased to discover that the Boy Wonder's kiss moved her not at all.

The barman laughed. "None of that stuff in my bar, if you please." He moved away.

She reported their conversation to Ken. "It can't hurt to have another pair of eyes on those two."

"I suppose not. Though their staying at the hotel doesn't necessarily mean their target is at the hotel. Could be something in the village."

"I doubt it. I'm pretty sure there are no big houses. It's mostly tourist traps like Arthur's Round Table, and those won't have much in the way of receipts at this time of year."

"All the same, one of us should go and poke about a bit tomorrow. It's your patch, so you're elected unanimously. I hope you have a good umbrella."

"Bastard," Megan said without heat. "As it happens, Scumble has already told me to scout the place, and he says the storm is forecast to blow over by morning. It'll be good to get out and get some fresh air."

Ken grinned. "Your trick. Was your guv'nor interested only in our shady acquaintances, or did he spare a thought for the matter that brought us here?"

"I hadn't told him yet about them when he gave the order. I might pick up a trace of an inquisitive stranger, but I can't see that I'm at all likely to find out anything about those two, unless I was lucky enough to happen to see them in commission of a felony."

ELEVEN

Waking on Saturday morning, Eleanor was instantly aware that something had changed. Eyes closed, still heavy with sleep, she listened. She had fallen asleep last night to the sound of rain beating against the windowpanes so violently, she hadn't been able to leave the window a few inches open, as was her custom. Now, through closed window and curtain, she heard faintly the cries of seagulls. Light sifting through tinted her eyelids rosy.

"*Wuff?*" A cold, wet nose poked her cheek.

"And *wuff* to you, too. Didn't I tell you not to get up on the bed, you cheeky beast?" The bright eyes peering into hers showed not a trace of guilt. "All right, I'll take you out, but I hope you're not in a hurry, because you'll have to wait till I'm dressed."

Slipping on her dressing gown and slippers, Eleanor went to the window and drew back the curtains. The sun shone down on Barras Nose, the headland's rough grass and granite outcrops ending abruptly at the drop to the sea, lapis blue streaked with whitecapped rollers. The storm had blown over; it was a glorious day.

There was no knowing how long it would last and it was too good to waste. Eleanor was determined to keep her appointment with Nick at the church on the cliffs on the far side of the village, no matter what Sir Edward's plans.

At breakfast, whether because of the weather or a good night's sleep, everyone seemed to be in a better temper than the previous evening. Nontando and Tariro were, if not cordial, at least scrupulously polite to each other. Gina's headache was gone. Sir Edward's mood was hopeful instead of discouraged. Only his secretary, Henry Payne, seemed unchanged. He was a reserved, distant man, with stiff manners and no personal warmth.

When Eleanor announced her intention of taking Teazle for a long walk, Sir Edward muttered but voiced no objection. He and Payne and the two young Africans were going to get down to serious talks right after breakfast.

"I'll go with you," said Gina. "I need to buy a couple of things in the village."

"Yes, do come." Eleanor was quite sure that her friend would not stir a step beyond the shops, so the semi-clandestine meeting with Nick would not reach Sir Edward's ears.

They walked down to the village at a strolling pace that allowed Teazle, though leashed, ample time to sniff every interesting smell she noticed. Eleanor found it far more wearisome than her usual brisk pace. They passed Castle Road, which led down steeply to the Haven and the island, and came to Vicarage Road.

"If you don't mind, Gina," she said, "I'll walk Teazle up here, so that I can let her off the leash. Don't bother to wait for me. I'll see you back at the hotel."

"I could tell you were itching to be off. I wasn't sure Edward wouldn't change his mind and try to stop you if you went alone. He has rather a bee in his bonnet about this meeting, I don't know why. He's not usually like this."

"Because of the many sympathisers Smith has in this country, including politicians, I should think. And young people being involved, perhaps."

"Young people are so unpredictable these days," said Gina vaguely. "I'll see you at lunch, if not before. Have a pleasant walk."

The air was still chilly, but the sun was warm on Eleanor's back as she and Teazle made their way up the hill towards the church. St. Materiana's was nearly half a mile beyond the village. It perched on its cliff-top, silhouetted against the pale blue sky, as if the world ended just beyond it. Low-profiled and solid, with a square, sturdy tower, it had withstood for eight hundred years everything the Atlantic gales flung at it.

The road jogged to the right. Teazle led the way straight ahead, up a couple of steps between stone benches, into the churchyard.

The burial ground boasted no sombre, symbolic yews, for the thin soil could not support trees. Bedrock was not far below the surface. Yet the path led between tombstones aplenty, standing and flat, a mausoleum or two, a half-dozen crosses. Noting that many of the flat memorial slabs were laid on top of stone walls a foot or two high, Eleanor wondered whether anyone had ever been buried a full six feet deep.

All the graves were surrounded by the typical wiry grass of the cliffs. A few clumps of pink thrift were already in bloom in spots sheltered by tombs. Rabbit droppings here and there explained Teazle's twisting nose-to-the-ground course. She ignored the sheep droppings, and the three sheep who raised their heads from grazing between the monuments to stare at her in alarm. Sheep were forbidden, as she well knew.

Nick came down the path to meet them. Teazle scampered ahead to give him a rapturous greeting.

"Morning, Eleanor! Delighted to see you haven't been carried off by spies."

"Isn't it a glorious morning? I was worried about you driving home in the storm last night."

"It was so hairy, I didn't." He stroked his unshaven chin. "Which is why I'm a trifle hairy. Just when I was wondering what on earth I was going to do, I saw a B and B sign without a 'Closed' addendum, so I stayed there. The landlady told me when I arrived that she actually was closed, but she took pity on me. Mrs. Mason, a very nice lady."

"I *am* glad you found shelter. In Tintagel?"

"No, over there." He gestured to the south. "In the middle of nowhere. Do you want to walk on the cliffs or sit down for a bit?"

"Let's walk."

They had reached the church porch. They turned in the direction Nick had waved, where a short path led to the continuation of the lane. A few yards farther on, the lane ended in a turnaround, and they joined a footpath along the cliffs. Rough ground tumbled steeply towards the cliff's edge and the sea beyond. From a patch of gorse in bloom wafted a fragrance like coconut.

"How kind of Mrs. Mason to let you stay."

"She's letting me stay a second night, too, so I'll be able to keep an eye on you."

"Nick, you didn't tell her about—"

"Of course not. I still haven't a clue what you and your friends are up to, and I didn't even breathe a word about you. I sort of gave her the impression I was going to paint, as I probably shall if the weather holds. She has one of mine in the house and she recognised my name."

"That was a lucky coincidence. Your fame spreads far and wide."

He grinned. "Or at least a dozen miles from home. Speaking of coincidence . . . Someone both you and I know is also staying with Mrs. Mason."

"Oh? Who? Teazle, come back here! I'm not climbing down the cliff to rescue you!"

"Alan Freeth."

"Mr. Freeth! That is a coincidence indeed. Especially as Megan is looking for him."

"Megan? He's wanted by the police? You don't think he's spying on your gathering, do you?"

"Good gracious, surely not! Such a pleasant man, and so generous with his time for LonStar. Do *you* suspect him?"

Nick frowned. "It doesn't seem at all likely. He's lived and worked in Port Mabyn for ages, since before I ended up there."

"You don't happen to know where he came from?"

"London."

"And before that? Hardly anyone really comes from London. Originally, they went to London from somewhere else. You've never heard anything suggesting Freeth started out in the colonies?"

"Not a whisper. So it's a spy from the colonies you're expecting? Not a Russian? You relieve my mind."

"Sir Edward doesn't seem to have considered . . . At least, he hasn't mentioned . . . Nick, I can't decide whether I ought to say something to him. I'd like to consult you, but I'm not supposed to talk about it."

"Silent as the grave." He glanced back towards the churchyard. "Cross my heart and hope to die."

"Be serious!"

"You know I won't tell anyone, unless a Russian pops out from behind a gorse bush and kidnaps you."

"Don't be silly, Nick. It's just that the Russians could be interested, and the Chinese, too. The Soviet Union and China are each supporting one of the factions Sir Edward is trying to bring together. Sort of."

"A Chinese spy would stick out like a sore thumb hereabouts. I suppose it's conceivable that Freeth could be a Russian 'sleeper,' but—"

"Sleeper?"

Nick grinned. "Clearly you don't read spy stories. A sleeper is a spy who lives in the enemy's country for many years, behaves like a native, lives a normal life, just waiting for the right moment to act."

"Not Alan Freeth," Eleanor said decidedly. "No one could have foreseen the present situation so long ago."

"That's just it; they're in place, waiting for a situation to arise. Which is not to suggest I suspect Freeth. The whole point is to lie low. He'd hardly have embarked on a gay way of life that at the time could have led to trouble with the police."

"Good. I'm glad he's in the clear."

"As far as being a spy is concerned. But why is Megan after him? What's he supposed to have done? Swiped some client's savings?"

"Nothing of the sort. She told me Mr. Bulwer reported him missing. He was upset because he left unexpectedly and didn't say where he was going."

"Let me get this straight: Bulwer was upset because Freeth left? I'm surprised the police are interested."

"They aren't terribly. It's one branch of the law keeping in with another, I gather. I wonder whether I should let Megan know you've seen him."

"And make me feel like a sneak!"

"I wouldn't say where. I don't actually know where. I'll tell you what, Nick, why don't I go back with you now and talk to him? Perhaps I can find out what the trouble is."

Nick groaned. "Eleanor, there's no earthly reason for you to involve yourself in their affairs."

"But if Roland Bulwer is unhappy and we might reconcile—"

"No!"

"Or at least persuade Alan to let Roland know where he is."

"It's much more complicated than you think, even the little bit I know."

"Complicated? What do you mean?"

"For a start, Freeth has known Mrs. Mason for yonks."

"How long," Eleanor enquired tartly, "is yonks?"

"Years and years. Since he was an articled clerk in London. He seems pretty . . . fond of her."

"But he's . . . He . . . You mean, he . . . ?"

"Swinging both ways, they call it these days. Could be, but I'm not going to jump to conclusions. It's quite possible that they're genuinely just old friends. He's been doing some legal business for her, drawing up a will, I think. She's not very well—heart trouble is my guess—so he's concerned for her. Only, why not tell Bulwer? And he could easily drive over from Port Mabyn to check on her, every day if necessary."

"It's odd. Complicated, you're right. Is that her house, by any chance?" Eleanor pointed down the slope at a solitary slate roof with a thread of smoke trickling upward from the chimney. They had been unconsciously following the dog, who was following some sort of smell along a barely visible path heading away from the cliff. "If so, Teazle's tracking your footsteps."

"All right." Nick sighed. "You may as well come down. He doesn't have to talk to you if he doesn't want to, and I suppose it's just as well if you tell him what Megan said. When did you see her, by the way? The police may have lost interest by now."

"Just last night. She's staying at the hotel as a watchdog for Sir Edward. Her friend from Scotland Yard is there, too."

"Faraday? What the hell does he keep coming down for? Poking his nose in where it's not wanted! She's told him time and again it's all over between them."

Hearing his tone, Teazle glanced back, ears cocked. Eleanor noted his annoyance with interest. "I doubt he had any choice, dear. Police officers go where they're sent."

"I suppose so."

"Besides, I rather think he has another interest at present."

"Who? Sir Edward's secretary?"

"Heavens no. Oh dear, I really shouldn't tell you."

"One of his party, then. Does Megan know?"

"I don't think so. But as you say, she's not interested."

With that, Nick had to be satisfied. They had reached the front door of Mrs. Mason's Bed and Breakfast Guest House. "Come in. If you'll wait in the hall, I'll see who's in."

"I'd better tie Teazle outside."

On either side, the slate path had white-painted posts connected by chains. Eleanor looped the lead round the nearest of these and hooked Teazle up, to her indignation.

"*Yip!*"

"Just for a few minutes, girl."

With a resigned "*Wuff*," she sat down.

TWELVE

Eleanor followed Nick through the green front door. In the hall, she immediately noticed his painting. It was of children playing in the sand at Kynance Cove, slightly impressionistic but basically straightforward. Remembering the abstract picture chosen by the two lawyers, Eleanor wondered what Alan Freeth had in common with Mrs. Mason.

"Hello?" Nick called out. "Anyone home?"

Freeth emerged from a room towards the back. "Rosie's popped out to the shops. Is there something I can—Mrs. Trewynn!"

"Good morning, Mr. Freeth. I was walking Teazle on the cliffs and I met Nick."

"Teazle? Oh, the dog." He looked distractedly round the hall. "Where is it?"

"I left her outside. I don't know how Mrs. Mason feels about dogs in the house."

"Neither do I. She'll be all right out there?"

"Oh yes, not pleased, but resigned." There was an awkward pause. Eleanor wished she had not come. Whyever Freeth was here, it was none of her business.

Nick had mentally absented himself in one of his brown studies. He moved towards the stairs.

"Nick! Where are you off to?"

"I need my sketchbook." He disappeared upward.

Eleanor and Freeth exchanged a glance and laughed.

"The artistic temperament," said Freeth. "Are you tired from walking? Would you like coffee? Or tea?"

So he was on such terms with Mrs. Mason that he felt free to offer an acquaintance refreshment in her absence. "Nothing to drink, thanks, but I'd be glad to sit down for a minute or two, while Nick's gathering his stuff."

"Of course." He turned towards the room he had just come from, but hesitated before pushing the door open. Eleanor saw that it had a PRIVATE sign. A bed-and-breakfast landlady had to have somewhere to retire to, she supposed. But Freeth decided to go ahead. "It's not very warm, I'm afraid, but the guest dining room and lounge aren't heated at all at present."

"I'm dressed for outdoors."

"Yes. Yes, of course." To all appearances, Freeth had been sitting at the desk, writing letters. A small fire flickered in the grate, its multicoloured flames dancing about the driftwood log. He invited Eleanor to take one of the armchairs beside it and, after a moment, sat in the other. Inevitably, remarks about the weather were exchanged.

"According to the wireless news," said Eleanor, "quite a number of people were stranded by the storm." She implied that she, like Nick, was among the stranded. "Some poor souls had to spend the night in their cars when they were caught by flooding in low-lying places."

"I take it you didn't suffer that fate?"

"No, I was quite comfortable, thank you." Deciding there was no circumspect way to inform a man the police were interested in his whereabouts, she went on, "As it happens, I ran into my niece. You and I being from the same village, she asked me whether I had any idea where you might be. You know she's a police officer?"

"What the deuce business is it of— Oh, hell! It's not Roland? Is he ill? Has he had an accident?"

"Nothing like that. It seems he has just the same concerns about you, only he reported you missing."

With a groan, Freeth sank his head into his hands. "I never thought of that."

"I don't want to meddle, but I have to say, couldn't you at least let him know you're all right?"

"I have. I wrote to him yesterday. He should have received it today if the floods haven't interfered with the post. And I'm going home tomorrow. Do you have to tell your niece where I am?"

"No. To tell the truth, she's not particularly interested. The police have too much on their hands to concern themselves with the wanderings of a grown man."

He summoned up a weak smile. "Well, that puts me firmly in my place, doesn't it?"

"If I see her, I'll tell her to call off the bloodhounds, always supposing your partner hasn't already done so. I hope I need not assure you I won't say a word to Mr. Bulwer about having seen you."

"Thank you."

"I wouldn't dream of it."

"I owe you some sort of explanation."

"Not at all," Eleanor demurred, dying of curiosity.

"It's . . . complicated. Rosie—Mrs. Mason—went through a lot for my sake. I owe her a huge debt of gratitude. Now, for her sake, I can't . . ." He hesitated.

"Nick mentioned that Mrs. Mason is unwell. Is there anything I can do to help?"

"That's very kind of you. She had a bad turn yesterday, but she's feeling much better today."

"Well enough to go to the shops, you said. It's quite a way to the village. I hope she drove." Eleanor spared a thought for the Incorruptible, doubtless sitting axle-deep—if not chassis-deep—in the flooded meadow.

"Yes, she took the car." He glanced at his watch. "She should be back any minute."

"Tell me honestly, Mr. Freeth—"

"Alan, please."

"Tell me honestly, Alan, would you rather I left before she gets home?"

He pondered a moment, then shook his head. "No. I appreciate the thought, but our web is more than sufficiently tangled already. Stay till you're ready to leave—or Gresham is. If she's not here by then, I'll tell her you dropped in—as a chance-met friend of Gresham."

"And one of your clients?"

"Yes. No. I don't know!"

"Sorry, it doesn't matter. I was just thinking, in case I ever met her again in a different context and the subject came up . . . But that's most unlikely, and there's no reason she should remember one way or the other."

"It sounds as if she's home."

A car drew up in the drive beside the house. In the silence after the engine cut off, Eleanor heard footsteps in the hall. Then Nick's cheerful voice called out, "Hold on, Mrs. Mason. Let me give you a hand with the shopping."

Freeth stood up.

"Would you like me to slip out by a different door?" Eleanor asked.

"N-no . . ." He made up his mind. "No, I'd like you to meet Rosie. Just a minute."

Left alone, Eleanor looked round the room. It was about twice the size of her own tiny combined sitting room and kitchen, but still small enough to be cosy. She would have hated to be so isolated, though. She liked living above the shop and right on the street. Solitude, when desired, could always be found on the cliffs or moors.

Perhaps Mrs. Mason had enough of people during the tourist season. She had plenty of books and records to keep her company in the winter, and being on higher ground, she probably had decent television reception, unlike residents of the lower reaches of Port Mabyn.

Eleanor was about to get up and look at the books, hoping she wouldn't appear nosy, when footsteps tick-tocked on the slates of the hall, approaching the open door. The woman who came in looked about twenty years younger than Eleanor. Unlike Eleanor, who carried a lipstick but rarely remembered to put it on, Rosie (Rosemary? Rosamund? Rosalind? Or just plain Rose?) Mason was fully and skilfully made-up. If her health was bad, her rouge hid it admirably.

"Mrs. Trewynn, how do you do? Mr. Gresham tells me he's your next-door neighbour. I expect you noticed I have one of his paintings in the hall."

"I did. I have one in my sitting room."

They shook hands, with the mutual smile of those who quickly find something pleasant in common with a new acquaintance.

"It's quite chilly in here," Mrs. Mason said with a shiver. "Alan should have built up the fire. He doesn't notice discomfort when he's busy." She gestured at the desk, where a neat pile of sealed envelopes testified to Freeth's diligence. "Would you like coffee? If you don't mind coming into the kitchen, where it's warm?"

"I'd love some."

In the kitchen, Nick was about to leave, slinging his satchel over his shoulder. "Eleanor, I want to get going while the sun is shining in the right direction. Are you coming?"

"Not yet. Mrs. Mason has invited me to stay for coffee."

"You'll find your way back all right."

"Of course, Nick. You go and catch your shadows before they vanish."

"Will you be back for lunch, Mr. Gresham?"

"I won't trespass on your kindness. I'll get a pasty in the village." With a wave, he was gone.

Freeth was making coffee. A shopping basket and three string bags lay on the table.

"I take my time putting things away," Mrs. Mason said apologetically. "Doctor's orders."

"I already put the frozen stuff in the fridge," said Freeth.

"In the freezer, Alan?"

"That little compartment at the top, yes. I'm reasonably domesticated. I'll deal with the rest, under your direction, but then, if you'll excuse me, Mrs. Trewynn, I'll go and finish my letters."

"Don't mind me," said Eleanor. "Mrs. Mason, I don't claim to be domesticated, but if you tell me where to put things, I can hardly go wrong."

"Heavens no, there's no need, honestly. There's no hurry, Alan. I'll do it in my own time later. You don't mind sitting at a table with shopping bags on it, Mrs. Trewynn?"

"Not at all."

"Here you are, ladies." Freeth set two cups of coffee on the table, and a jug of milk. "Sugar, Mrs. Trewynn?"

"Thanks. No sugar, thanks." She sat down.

While he poured his own coffee, Mrs. Mason produced a biscuit tin and joined Eleanor. "Do help yourself."

"Homemade shortbread—lovely!"

Freeth helped himself to a piece and ate it standing, obviously very much at home here. He picked up his cup of coffee. "Just a couple more letters, Rosie. I want to catch the afternoon post." A second piece of shortbread in his hand, he went out.

Mrs. Mason looked after him wistfully, then turned to Eleanor with a smile. "I've enjoyed having someone to bake for. It never seems worth the trouble just for myself."

"I know what you mean. Not that I've ever been a good baker. This is excellent. I gather Alan has to go home tomorrow. Will you be all right on your own? Nick said you're not well."

"Oh, that! As long as I don't overdo things, I don't need anyone hovering over me. That's not why I asked Alan to stay." She hesitated. Eleanor tried to look sympathetic but not inquisitive. "I was afraid of . . . of something else. But if it hasn't happened yet, I don't suppose it will. Alan has other commitments."

"It's not easy for a professional man to get away," Eleanor said tentatively.

Mrs. Mason gave her a surprised look, as if that wasn't at all what she'd been thinking of. "No. No, it isn't. Maybe I should get away for a while. Yes!" Her troubled face brightened. "That's a good idea. I don't know why I didn't think of it sooner."

"A few days in London, perhaps?"

"Oh no, not London! That's where— I mean, London wouldn't suit me at all."

"I expect you're right." *That's where what? Or who?* "Too much hustle and bustle. Bath? If you don't want to drive so far, it's quite easy to get to by train. No, too hilly."

"I'll have to think about it, and see what Alan thinks. Won't you have another piece of shortbread?"

"I'd better not, thank you. Would you happen to have an old dish or pan I could use to give my dog a drink? I left her tied in your front garden."

"I've got the very thing. Do bring her in. I'm sure she can't be happy tied up."

"Her whiskers drip when she drinks."

"Never mind. Fetch her in and I'll put the bowl on the backdoor mat. She can drip there."

Teazle was delighted to be rescued, fussed over, and fed a piece of shortbread.

"You'll have to go on a diet when we get home," Eleanor told her severely as they walked back towards the church half an hour later. "So will I. What a nice woman. I can't help wondering what she's so afraid of. If I knew what's frightening her, perhaps I could help. It's none of my business, though. Nor is her relationship, past, present, or future, with Alan Freeth. Even less so, in fact. Surely they can't be brother and sister. What reason could they have to conceal it?"

Teazle was not interested.

Talking to Freeth and Mrs. Mason had raised more questions than it had answered. Without revelations from one or both, they were unanswerable, though. The question that weighed on Eleanor, which her discussion with Nick had left open, was whether to remind Sir Edward—or perhaps Megan—of the Russian and Chinese connections.

"I don't think I will," she told Teazle. "They're watching for strangers already, and a foreigner would stick out like a sore thumb."

THIRTEEN

Eleanor saw no sign of Nick on her way back across the cliffs. She hoped he had found a secure eyrie with a good view of the castle ruins. The sun was warm and not a breath of breeze stirred as she and Teazle walked down through the churchyard. It was a pity Sir Edward was determined to keep the young people indoors on such a glorious day, with such glorious scenery close at hand.

Remembering Nontando's defiant look, Eleanor wasn't at all certain he'd succeed.

The track down to the Haven ran down a steep-sided cleft, making a shortcut to the hotel impossible, so they followed the lane. When Vicarage Hill met Fore Street, the main street, Eleanor turned right, heading into the village. She and Gina hadn't made any definite plans to meet—or any plans at all, actually—so Gina might be waiting for her somewhere. It wouldn't take long to stroll along, peering into shops and cafés, just in case.

It was midday. The shops were busy with housewives buying last-minute supplies for the weekend. Eleanor met three or four people she knew from her donation-collecting rounds. She had to stop to exchange a few words, so progress was slow.

Halfway back down the other side of the street, she ran into Megan, coming out of Boots chemist's carrying a shopping bag.

"Hello, dear. I'm glad you're able to get out on such a beautiful day. I rather thought you were confined to barracks, after a manner of speaking."

Megan drew her aside, out of the way of a large woman with a wheelie basket, into the deserted alley beside the shop. "Mr. Scumble told me to come down and chat with the locals, and Ken and I agreed one of us should amble round the village, asking about strangers. He said it should be me, because it's my district. He's right, of course, but he's up to something, I know it."

"What sort of something?"

"I'm not sure, but the signs are he's picked up another girl. How and where he found her, goodness knows. The maids all seem to be Greek, and he goes for blondes. Not good for our image as a holidaying couple. Still, I haven't heard anything to suggest we have a nosy-parker about the hotel, so I suppose it doesn't matter."

"You don't *mind*, do you, Megan?"

"Good lord no. Not the way you mean. But when it takes his mind off the job . . . I've been tramping round, buying tourist tat"—she hefted the shopping bag—"asking fatuous questions about the scarcity of visitors at this time of year, while I don't know whether he's even paying attention to those two fishy characters you didn't see last night, let alone anyone new who may turn up."

"Surely he wouldn't be so negligent."

"Probably not," Megan conceded reluctantly. "He's a good copper."

"Then trust him. Are you coming back to the hotel now? I'm going to be late for lunch if I don't hurry."

"No, I'm going to have a snack in a pub, and ask some more fatuous questions. I'll see you later."

Eleanor kissed her cheek and hurried off up the hill to the hotel, realising halfway there that she hadn't told Megan that Freeth was safe and had written to Bulwer. It would have to wait till later. She had barely time to brush her hair before shutting Teazle in her room and dashing down to the sitting room. Norton was hovering outside the door, clearly itching to announce that luncheon was served, so Eleanor refused Sir Edward's offer of sherry. The butler allowed thirty seconds for this exchange of courtesies before making his stately entrance.

They all trooped down to the dining room. By the time they reached it, Eleanor was certain the dissension she had sensed upstairs was no figment of her imagination.

As Sir Edward seated her, he leaned down to whisper, "Revolting students! Both want to parade about the countryside this afternoon. Perhaps you can dissuade them?"

"At least they agree on something," Eleanor responded. "Quite an achievement."

He shook his head, smiling. "Ever the optimist!"

When Aunt Nell left her, Megan strolled back along the street towards the pub where she'd decided to have lunch. As she approached the Old Post Office, a picturesquely ancient building with a sagging roof, she saw the so-called Adrian Arbuthnot coming out.

He looked annoyed. She guessed that like so many others, he had assumed it was still a working post office, whereas it was now yet another tourist trap.

Pretending to study a shop window—a collection of bits of driftwood topped with herring gulls in unlikely poses, made of some unidentifiable substance—she watched Arbuthnot from

CAROLA DUNN

the corner of her eye. He glanced left, in her direction, then turned right towards the Bossiney Road, where the current post office occupied a corner of a small grocer's.

It was almost closing time. He hurried, but managed nevertheless to appear surreptitious.

Megan dawdled along, keeping him just in sight. He went into the grocery. She crossed to the opposite side of the road and was almost level with the shop when he came out again after just a minute or two. In his hands was a small blue-covered booklet. Looking down at it with obvious satisfaction, he didn't notice Megan. He turned back in the direction of the King Arthur Hotel and went off almost jauntily.

"What the hell?" Megan murmured to herself.

She, too, turned back, but she was pretty certain he was going to the hotel, probably to report his success—whatever it was—to his confederate. She couldn't see much point in following him. When she reached the Trelawny Arms, she went in.

The first person she set eyes on was Nick Gresham. He stood up, grinning, as she marched over to his table.

"What are you doing here?"

"And hello to you, too." He held a chair for her—no one could say he wasn't a gentleman.

She sat down. "Sorry. Just a rather frustrating morning." She dumped the shopping bag on the floor, glancing at his beer mug. "Are you having a meal or just drinking?"

"You make me sound like a confirmed sot. I'm contemplating the alternatives: pasty or ploughman's. This, as the barman told me, is a ruddy pub, not a ruddy rest-oh-rong. What about you?"

"Ploughman's sounds all right." Megan glanced back at the barman. "Do you think you can persuade him to get me a cup of tea?"

"He's not a ruddy caff, but I'll try charm, and if that doesn't work, I'll speak to him severely."

"Fall-back position, bitter lemon."

He raised his eyebrows but didn't comment. Dropping a kiss on the top of her head in passing, he went to the bar. She couldn't hear what was said, but either the charm or the severity worked, because Nick returned a moment later to tell her "Tea coming up." He sat down and reached for her hand, meanwhile picking up his tankard with his other hand and taking a swallow. "I don't believe you followed me here, either for the sake of my beautiful eyes or in the course of your duties—"

"Hush!"

"Eleanor said you're mixed up in what's going on at the hotel."

"I am *not* 'mixed up' in it. I don't even know what they're doing."

"You're just watching out for strangers?"

"How the hell do you know so much about it? Aunt Nell told you? I met her in the street a few minutes ago and she didn't tell me you were in Tintagel."

"She didn't mention that I drove her here yesterday because the Incorruptible wouldn't start?"

"No."

"No credit for my good deed, alas," Nick said mournfully.

"Don't be an idiot. I hope that's all you learned from her, that something's going on and we're trying to keep track of strangers in the area?"

"Strangers who could be spies."

"She told you we're on the lookout for spies? You're not serious!" She stopped as Nick, looking beyond her, put his finger briefly to his lips.

"Here you go." The barman deposited a tray on the table: two ploughman's lunches, teapot, cup and saucer, milk jug, sugar basin.

"Thanks." Megan took out her purse.

"The gentleman already paid, miss." He withdrew.

"Oh, well, thanks, Nick. I'll put it on expenses and pay you back."

"That's all right, old girl."

"I'll add yours on, too. It's still cheaper than if I'd eaten at the hotel. What exactly did Aunt Nell say about spies?"

"Originally, she just said mysteriously that it was all very hush-hush. This morning she let slip that the spies would probably be colonialists. She didn't say which colony. We haven't many left, so I might be able to work it out if I put my mind to it, especially as the Russians and Chinese are involved."

"What? She said the Commies are involved?"

"Didn't you know?"

"No, I did not! Sir Edward never said anything about Russians."

"Eleanor was afraid he wasn't paying enough heed to that dimension. She couldn't decide whether she ought to remind him."

"This cheese is good, and the bread is fresh!"

"Davidstow Cheddar—I saw it on the counter. She didn't mention Russians to you?"

"No, not a word. She was in a hurry to get back for lunch," Megan excused her aunt. "Local butter, too, by the taste of it." She glanced round the dingy room. "Much better than the surroundings suggest."

"I was chatting to the barman before you arrived. Apparently there's a new owner who's going to tart the place up for the tourist trade. He's renaming it the Excalibur Inn."

Megan groaned. "Arthur, Arthur everywhere. You didn't happen to chat about the paucity of tourists at this time of year?"

"I was just coming to that. He said he wasn't complaining, because he was paid for it, but it was a waste of time opening in the middle of the day before the Easter hols. Locals come in only in the evening, and mine's the first strange—make that unknown— face he's seen in a week."

"Thanks, I won't have to ask."

"Neither of us mentioned Russians, however."

"A Russian would be just another stranger."

"A stranger stranger, you might say."

"*You* might. Chinese would be pretty obvious, though. Dammit, why did Aunt Nell talk to you about the conference at all?"

"I was giving her a lift, remember. I was mildly interested in where she was going and why."

"But why did you stay in Tintagel after dropping her at the hotel?"

"My dear girl, you aren't suspecting me of being a spy, are you?" he teased.

"Of course not. Don't be silly. Benighted by the storm?"

"Brilliant guess. And then I got an idea. . . ." His eyes took on a faraway look.

Megan reached over and shook his arm. "Don't you disappear into an artistic haze."

"Sorry. The storm was just descending in full force and I didn't fancy driving in it. I found a bed-and-breakfast willing to put me up for the night. When today turned out fine, I decided to stay on for a day or two. Did Eleanor tell you whom I found myself sharing digs with?"

"She did not," Megan said grimly. "Which seems to be becoming a refrain. What didn't she tell me this time?"

"If she didn't, I'm not sure I should."

"Why not? Does it involve something illegal?"

"Not to my knowledge. What a suspicious person you are!"

"Must be the company I keep. Come on, Nick, spill the beans."

"It's a matter of privacy. The person concerned was obviously dismayed that I was staying at the same bed-and-breakfast. Besides, he doesn't count as a coincidence for you. You've probably never met him. A chap from Port Mabyn."

"If he's a stranger to me, there can't be any harm in telling me." Megan had pretty much lost interest, but she was stubborn. "Wait a bit—a stranger to me *and* a stranger to Tintagel?"

"I've no idea. For all I know, he comes here every year for a hiking holiday. You're thinking he could be one of the spies you're watching for?"

"Well, couldn't he?"

"I doubt it. It would help if I knew what the conference is about, but I'd guess it was planned quite recently." Nick frowned, obviously pondering whether to give her the whole story. "This chap's lived in Port Mabyn for years, longer than I have."

"Port Mabyn? Then why would he come to Tintagel for a holiday?"

Nick shrugged. "Just for a change? I really can't see Freeth as a spy."

"Freeth! Not really? Alan Freeth, the solicitor?"

"Yes. Eleanor told me you're looking for him. But not that you suspected him of spying for the Chinese."

"For heaven's sake, Nick, that's not what I said. I shouldn't talk about it."

"But you're going to."

"If you swear to keep it under your hat."

"I solemnly swear to keep it under the hat I never wear."

Megan smiled, but said, "Seriously. I could get into deep trouble."

"Seriously, of course I won't breathe a word to a soul, idiot."

"And you won't let it slip accidentally, as you just did his name?"

"Ho, that was no accident. Carefully calculated to elicit a reaction if the name meant anything to you."

"You are impossible, Nick!"

"So my parents used to say."

"Oh, sorry." Megan was taken aback by the hint of bitterness in his tone. She didn't know much about his family, except that they had disapproved of his choice to become an artist. "I won't say it again."

"Never mind, old girl. I'm used to it. Now, what about Freeth?"

"His . . . partner reported him missing."

"Yes, that's what Eleanor said. So . . . ?"

"No suggestion of embezzlement or anything like that, and he's a competent adult. . . . At least, did he seem to you to have gone off the rails?"

"Not in the least. He seemed tense and wary, worried, and very pally with our landlady, but otherwise—"

"How pally?"

"Megan, you know he's gay?"

"That was obvious, and Mrs. Stearns confirmed it. As did Aunt Nell."

"Good lord, you don't mean to tell me you tackled our Jocelyn? You're a brave woman."

"She was very circumspect, if that's the word I want."

"Fits her to a T. I daresay Freeth may swing both ways, if that's what you're suggesting, though I doubt it. She's no dolly-bird, you know. A nice-looking middle-aged woman, not at all tarted up to look younger. More like brother and sister. Even if they are lovers, it's no business of the police."

"None whatsoever. But it would make it that much less likely that he's the sort of spy I'm supposed to keep an eye out for. Also, though it's equally none of my business, I feel I ought to—"

"Not to tell Bulwer where he is?"

"I wouldn't dream of it. No, to suggest to Freeth that it might be a good idea to let Bulwer know he's safe and sound, if not where he is or when and whether he's going home."

"I feel sure the estimable Scumble, for whom I begin to feel some sympathy, would strongly object. Besides, you're not supposed to know Freeth's here. Unless you're proposing to shatter my nice clean reputation as an innocuous member of the public?"

"Is that how you see yourself?" Megan teased. "I'd hate to tarnish that image."

"I'm beginning to wish I'd kept my mouth shut."

"I won't give you away, honestly. I'll fabricate a reason for looking for you, and hope to find him in. Where is the place?"

"I suppose it can't hurt." Nick gave her directions. "You're not expecting me to be there, are you? What sort of time, so I can be out?"

"I don't know. Depends when I can get away."

"I'm not so convinced it's a good idea. You said yourself, he's a competent adult."

"Old enough to run away from home if he wants to, for whatever reason."

"His reason remains obscure to me. '"And that," said John, "is that."' I'm off, before the light changes too much." He kissed her on the mouth, but a light, friendly kiss.

Noncommittal, Megan thought as she followed him out. That was all right. Though she was over thirty, she wasn't ready to settle down and wasn't sure she ever would be. Besides, an artist and a police officer just didn't belong together. She never knew when she'd be called out, and he might disappear in pursuit of his muse at any moment.

Better Nick than Ken, though. Almost worse than the girls was that he'd always hold a rank superior to hers in her own profession, by virtue of being male.

Not that either of them had ever breathed a word about marriage.

As for Freeth, why would a prosperous solicitor take a room at a bed-and-breakfast if his intention was to observe what was going on at the hotel? He wouldn't need to pinch pennies. And why should he spy for Ian Smith? Even less likely that he should be working for the African side, let alone the Russians or Chinese. Megan wished she paid more attention to the international news.

Whatever had caused him to walk out, he was surely a distraction, a red herring. All the same, if she could get away later, she would go and have a word with him.

FOURTEEN

Over lunch, Eleanor exerted her powers of persuasion to the utmost. Somewhat to her surprise, she succeeded in getting Nontando and Tariro to agree to a couple more hours of talks that afternoon, on condition that they be permitted to go outside later.

"Fresh air and exercise," Nontando said decidedly.

"And the view of the castle and the sea from the cliffs," Tariro added.

With more difficulty, Sir Edward was brought to admit that there was little danger in a walk on the cliffs, so long as they didn't show themselves in the village.

"And you must take a police escort," he insisted.

"Ken—Sergeant Faraday—will be happy to walk with me," Nontando said with confidence.

Forestalling Sir Edward's response, Eleanor quickly put in, "Mr. Faraday is not familiar with this district. It's just about impossible to walk from here without going through the village."

"Then I can't allow—"

"As I was about to suggest," Eleanor interrupted, "to avoid being seen, you'd have to go by car to a suitable spot."

"Your niece is local," Gina put in. "I expect she would know where to go."

"If not, I can easily explain to her."

"You could equally well give Ken directions, Mrs. Trewynn," Nontando pointed out. "He drove me all the way down from town without losing his way once."

"Of course."

"We'll sort that out later," Sir Edward said testily. "If you're determined to go out, we must get down to work at once."

Gina and Eleanor exchanged a glance and took themselves upstairs.

"You brought it off," said Gina, sinking into a chair. "I really thought poor Edward's talks were at a standstill, beyond even your wiles. I don't know how you managed it."

"I credit that divine pavlova, with Cornish cream and fresh strawberries. It was enough to melt the stubbornest resistance."

"One of Cook's masterpieces," Gina agreed complacently. "The persuasive effect of good food is not to be underestimated."

"Please pass on my appreciation to Cook. You don't mind if I fetch Teazle down? She does so dislike being shut up alone."

"Do bring her down. She's such a good little thing."

By the time Eleanor and Teazle reached the sitting room, another effect of good food was evident: somnolence. Gina's head lolled against the back of her chair and she was emitting gentle, ladylike snuffles that weren't quite snores.

With a sigh, Eleanor went over for a second look at the shelf of books. Previous guests apparently read nothing but thrillers and family sagas. Nothing appealed to her. She decided to go and see if Megan had returned. Their meeting this morning had been so rushed, she had forgotten to tell her that Alan Freeth was safe and sound.

In a drawer of a small writing table under one window, she found hotel notepaper and biros. She wrote a note to Gina to explain and excuse her absence; then she and Teazle went down to the ground floor and through to the main lobby.

DS Faraday was sitting alone in a corner of the lounge, reading a newspaper. Eleanor hesitated. She was never quite comfortable with the young man, unable to forget that he had let Megan down badly. To complicate matters, he and Nontando obviously had some sort of ill-defined understanding. Moreover, Eleanor was never sure whether to address him as Ken, Mr. Faraday, or Sergeant.

Nonsense, she told herself firmly. For one who had conferred with kings and cannibal chieftains, a mere detective, even one from Scotland Yard, was nothing.

She wound her way towards him between the groups of chairs and sofas and coffee tables, few occupied. Though he appeared completely absorbed in his paper, he laid it down and stood as she approached.

"Hello, Mrs. Trewynn. What can I do for you?" His voice was wary.

"I just wondered whether Megan's back yet."

"No. To be precise, not that I'm aware, and she's supposed to let me know."

"I hope she's all right."

"Do you have any reason to suppose she might not be?"

"No. I was just thinking about the suspicious pair you and Megan had your eyes on. . . ."

"You've seen them?"

"I wouldn't know. You two wouldn't let me take a look at them. Have you?"

"They had breakfast and lunch in the dining room. I didn't

see them in between, but they could have sneaked out unobserved. There are other doors, and anyway, I can't spend all my time in here watching the main door without drawing unwanted attention."

"Oh dear!"

"They're not really my pigeon, in any case. Megan and I agree that they're far more likely up to some local mischief than taking an interest in Commonwealth intrigues."

"So you won't help Megan foil them?" Eleanor asked indignantly.

"Of course I will, if it comes to that. At present, we have nothing against them except their looks."

"Describe them. How am I to help if I can't recognise them?"

"I'd much rather you didn't try to help. And I'm sure Megan would agree."

"All right, then, how am I to avoid being victim to their 'mischief' if I can't recognise them?"

Faraday blinked, and uttered something between a sigh and a groan. "You win. One is shortish, bulky in a muscular way, greying crew-cut hair, broad, unhealthily pale face, an expression that suggests he'd do over his granny for ten quid."

"He sounds most unattractive, the sort of person one would instinctively avoid."

"He goes by the name of Victor Jones, which is probably not his real name. The other currently calls himself Adrian Arbuthnot."

"I once knew an Adrian Arbuthnot," Eleanor said doubtfully. "He was a lieutenant in the Indian Army in the twenties, when I was sent out to find a husband. I don't know what became of him."

"This one isn't quite that old—I beg your pardon; that could have been better phrased. This one appears to be about fifty but desperately trying to look younger."

"A gigolo?"

"Gig— Oh, I hadn't thought of that."

Out-of-date, Eleanor thought. She wished the English language would just stand still for a while. "His companion doesn't fit a gigolo, though," she ventured. "He should be accompanied by an older woman with more money than sense, not a thug."

Ken Faraday looked surprised, amused, and approving. "Very true. The pairing is out of character. Nor do con men generally pal up with heavies. I wonder just what their game is."

"I suppose they might be taking a holiday from their nefarious activities?"

"Not together. Incompatible characters, unless we've completely misread them. Megan's been trying to get a snap of them for the CRO without alerting them, but they're leery customers."

"CRO?"

"Criminal Records Office. I know I've seen Victor's ugly mug somewhere before."

"One reads about criminal gangs in London. Could they both be working for the same gang?"

"You're full of ideas this afternoon, Mrs. Trewynn! It's possible. It would explain why they're working in cahoots, with different roles in a larger operation. The big gangs do carry out hits in the provinces. But they go for big cities, or at least the larger towns. I can't imagine what they would find in Tintagel's vicinity worth the trouble."

"Nor can I," Eleanor admitted. "And surely Ian Smith—or the Russians and Chinese—have too much nous to hire such obviously shady characters to do their dirty work."

"Russians? Chinese?"

"Bother, I wasn't going to mention them, as Sir Edward apparently didn't. I thought Nontando might have explained that they're each supporting one of the freedom-fighter groups. She seems to . . . repose great confidence in you on such brief acquaintance."

Ken Faraday blushed. Eleanor wouldn't have thought him capable of it.

"For pity's sake, we were together for hours! You wouldn't expect us to sit in silence? We got on well. She told me about her country, which was interesting, and she said she was a Marxist but not a Communist, whatever that means. Well, coppers are supposed to be above politics—outside politics. I switched off, stopped paying attention. If she talked about the Soviets or Chinese, I wasn't listening. Mostly, we talked about music and art, plays, that sort of thing. Dancing—she loves dancing, and I'm a bit of a dab at it myself . . . and why I'm telling you all this, I can't fathom."

"Nor can I," said Eleanor, "but thank you. The insight into her character may help with my job. By the way, perhaps I ought to warn you that *your* primary job here is about to get more complicated."

"What? What do you mean?"

"Nontando and Tariro found something they were able to agree on. They joined forces in revolt to persuade Sir Edward to let them go for a walk later on." Teazle, snoozing chin on paws, raised her head hopefully at the word *walk*.

"After dark," Ken said, equally hopeful.

"That wouldn't do at all. In the first place, they want to see the scenery, and in the second, the cliffs are far too hazardous. Nontando seems to be under the impression that you've already more or less offered to escort her."

"I may have said something like it on the drive down. I was thinking of when we get back to town, not here."

"Sir Edward says they're to have a police escort."

"How does he expect us to stop people seeing them? Has he given up on keeping their presence secret? The whole thing's turning into a bloody balls-up. Sorry, Mrs. Trewynn. A farce. A fiasco. I forgot you're not a colleague."

Eleanor gave him a kindly smile. "I'll take it as a compliment. To do poor Sir Edward justice, he didn't have much choice once Tariro and Nontando were at last in agreement, if only on a single subject. But it's not quite as bad as you may think." She explained about having to drive through the village and out the other side. "If they wear hats and keep their heads down, they shouldn't be noticed. The shops are shut, and you're not likely to meet hikers."

"'At this time of year,' a constant refrain. I don't know how Megan can stand it after London. When is this thrilling excursion to take place?"

"In a couple of hours. If you don't want to go, I'm sure Megan would be happy to take charge of both. She's used to *thrilling* walks on the cliffs. In fact, she's far better qualified to keep them to the safe paths and show them the best views."

"Touché, Mrs. Trewynn." Ken smiled, but it was with a degree of relief that he looked past her and announced, "Here she is now."

"Good. I need to talk to her."

"Am I to be a good boy and make myself scarce again?"

"I'm afraid so. But not right away."

"Okay. Just give me my marching orders when the moment comes."

"Marching orders?" Megan sat down, dropping her shopping bag at her feet. "Three Cornish piskies and a miniature plastic

Excalibur," she said bitterly. "At least I managed not to acquire a plaster seagull. I trust Sir Edward will reimburse me, because the guv'nor would explode if I put in a claim to CaRaDoC. Hello, Aunt Nell. I'm glad you're not back in seclusion. You rushed off in such a hurry, you didn't get round to telling me Nick's here."

"Oh, didn't I?"

"Nick Gresham?" Ken asked. "That artist bloke? What's he doing here? You don't suppose he's—"

"No," Eleanor and Megan both said vehemently.

"He drove me here and stayed to paint. How did you know, Megan?"

"I met him in the village and had lunch with him. And another thing you didn't tell me is that he's staying at the same place as—"

"We'll talk about that later, dear."

"Your aunt has just dropped a couple of bombshells. You and I are going to have to take Nontando and Tariro walkies." Teazle stood up and fixed him with a bright, expectant gaze.

"What!"

"We could go with you," Eleanor proposed. "Teazle's always ready for walkies." She explained Sir Edward's capitulation. "One or both may want to go over to King Arthur's castle."

"It's quite a climb. I hope Nontando's brought suitable footwear."

Ken looked gloomily at his feet, shod in glossy shoes suitable for London pavements. "I've got my boots in the car boot. I'd hoped not to have to wear them. I wonder if Nontando has anything other than those platform heels."

"Is that what she wore when you took her tramping round Stonehenge?" Megan asked.

"No, come to think of it. She changed into low heels, non-platform. Not what I'd call proper walking shoes."

"Well, if she wants to go, she'll have to manage. And if Sir Edward tells us to take 'em out, that's that. What was Aunt Nell's other bombshell?"

"Reds under the bed."

"Oh, that. The Russians and Chinese."

"You know already?" Ken was annoyed. "Sir Edward told you, and you didn't pass it on to me?"

"No. It was Nick." Megan avoided looking at her aunt, for which Eleanor was duly grateful. The less reason Ken had for suspecting her of spilling the beans to Nick, the better. Megan went on, "He said a Russian would be just another stranger. Of course I asked him what he meant. Apparently, he keeps up with international news. I don't know about you, Ken, but I certainly don't. Nothing but the headlines."

"Who has time? Gresham's right: A Russian who speaks good English would be just another stranger. A Chinese would stick out like a sore thumb, but not knowing the connection, we would have ignored him as irrelevant. Sir Edward ought to have warned us."

"When he briefed me, he was in shock at being faced with a woman detective. I'm surprised he managed to tell me anything useful at all."

"But he didn't mention them when I saw him later."

"He told me, earlier," said Eleanor, "before you arrived. I expect he got mixed up about who he'd told. I do, frequently."

"Oh well," Ken sighed, "now we know. I take it no one in the village reported a sinister Chinese character lurking in the vicinity, Meg?"

"No, but they wouldn't necessarily just because he was Chinese. Believe it or not, we do have a few Chinese restaurants out here in the wilds. People go to Bude or Camelford, or Launceston, come to that, for a Chinese meal. Though I can't think of anything in Tintagel that would bring the owners or staff here. They're very much a long shot. Don't let's waste time on them. I haven't told you yet who I saw in the village, besides Nick."

"Whom?" asked Ken.

She gave him a dirty look.

"Do tell us, dear," Eleanor intervened.

"Adrian Arbuthnot. The con man, Aunt Nell."

"Damn!" Ken exclaimed. "I missed him!"

"You didn't see him leave?"

"That's what I said, isn't it?"

"Which suggests he didn't want to be seen."

"Which just tells us they're up to no good, and we were already pretty sure of that."

"I think he must have walked down. I noticed as I crossed the car park that the van doesn't appear to have budged an inch."

"They were afraid it might draw attention."

"It's not exactly conspicuous, but I had worked that out for myself, thank you."

"Stop squabbling, children. What did he do in the village, Megan?"

"Went into the Old Post Office. For your information, Ken, it's no longer in use as a post office. It's a sort of museum. I think they charge for entrance. He came out right away, but he must have asked for directions to the actual post office, because that's where he headed for."

"Posting letters?"

"No, there's a postbox outside and he didn't stop beside it. He went in. It must have been just about closing—it was one o'clock. Again, he wasn't inside more than a minute. He came out with a sort of leaflet, more like a booklet." With her hands, she shaped a rectangle about half the size of a standard sheet of typing paper. "Lightish blue cover. I was on the other side of the road, so I couldn't read the printing on it."

"It sounds like a community directory," said Eleanor. "We have one for Port Mabyn. You probably don't in Launceston because it's bigger. It just lists names, addresses, and numbers for local people, with adverts for local businesses to pay for printing."

"He seemed pleased with himself, as if he'd found what he wanted."

"Your problem, Megan, as expected. A community directory can't have any bearing on Sir Edward's business."

Megan sighed. "I'd better ring the guv'nor. He may want me to concentrate on trying to find out what those two have in mind. In that case, you'll be taking Tariro and Nontando for their walk all on your own."

"He wouldn't pull you off—"

"Oh yes he would. He was very clear that CaRaDoC must take precedence if I'm needed. I'll see you later, Aunt Nell." She went off to telephone.

"Mrs. Trewynn," Ken said urgently, "you will go walking with us, won't you? I haven't a clue where to take them."

"We'll go along, won't we, Teazle?"

"*Wuff*," Teazle agreed.

"Not to climb over to the castle, though. We'll drive to the church; then you can walk north with Nontando, if you like, while I'll take Tariro and the dog south."

"I didn't say . . . I didn't mean—"

"Never mind, I was just teasing. We'll sort it out when we see if Megan's coming too."

"I count on you to persuade Nontando and Tariro to keep their heads down as we go through the village."

"I daresay Sir Edward will, too. I'd better get back to Gina—Lady Bellowe. I said I'd just be gone a few minutes."

Ken stood up. "Thank you for the information you've passed on to me, Mrs. Trewynn. I hope you're doing as well with keeping the talks running smoothly."

"As to that," said Eleanor, "it remains to be seen."

FIFTEEN

Megan dialled the Launceston nick. Keeping a watch out for eaves-droppers, she asked whether DCI Scumble was in. As she expected on a Saturday afternoon, he wasn't.

She rang his home. His wife answered.

"Hello, Mrs. Scumble. This is DS Pencarrow, I'm afraid. Sorry to disturb you. Is Mr. Scumble there?"

"I know you wouldn't if you didn't have to, dear." She had a very soft voice, as if she had decided years ago that she couldn't speak louder than her husband and would more easily catch his atten-tion if he had to shut up to hear her at all. "I'll call him to the phone. Just a minute."

"Thanks."

Megan had never met her guv'nor's wife, though she had waved to her several times while picking him up at his house. At first, she hadn't been able to reconcile the tough character she knew at work with the neat, colourful front garden and had presumed Mrs. Scumble was responsible for it. Once or twice, she had seen the short, thin, grey-haired woman dead-heading or on her knees weeding. By now she knew the garden was a joint enterprise and the chief inspector's pride and joy.

"Pencarrow. What's up? Better be something worth ringing me on a Saturday afternoon!"

"You wanted to be kept up-to-date, sir, on those London types."

"Caught them up to some funny business, have you?"

"Sort of. Well, nothing criminal. They've got hold of a community directory—at least I'm pretty sure that's what it is."

"*Pretty* sure, Pencarrow?"

"Sir, the shop and post office where he obtained it was just closing. I couldn't have gone in without a fuss, and I *am* supposed to be undercover. You told me not to contact Constable Yarrow directly, so—"

"All right, all right, describe the damn thing and I'll have someone get onto him." He listened without interruption while she described the booklet. "Got it. You're saying they're planning something in Tintagel."

"All I'm saying is that they seem to be looking for someone local. Could be a confederate who's lying low here, or someone they have a grudge against. Or one person who's both."

"Hmm. Did you get a snap of them yet?"

"No, sir. As I'm supposed to be trying to avoid attracting attention, I haven't had a chance." Attack being the best form of offence, Megan went on, "Have you heard back about the van's licence plates?"

"Not a chance till Monday earliest, and since the licensing people moved to Cardiff, they've been slower than ever. Could be a week, unless you can give me a solid reason for requesting priority."

"I can't."

"Then you'll just have to keep an eye on them as best you can."

"Which won't be very well, sir, unless you take me off this security job. I and . . . my colleague have to take the persons concerned for a walk on the cliffs this afternoon."

"What the hell? No, don't bother to explain. I'd rather not know. You know I can't take you off that job without orders from above, barring an emergency, much as I'd like to. All I can do is send over one of our plainclothes constables to give Yarrow a hand. Best of luck, Pencarrow. Just don't, for pity's sake, let any of them fall off a cliff."

With that cheerful word of advice, he hung up.

Which would irritate him more: if she rang back, or if she failed to let him know that Freeth had been found? Biting her lip, she redialled.

"Sir—"

"Not you again, Pencarrow!"

"Sorry, sir, but I didn't have a chance to tell you about the missing lawyer, and as the chief constable was interested . . ."

"All right, all right," Scumble grumbled. "So you've found him, have you?"

"I've found out where he is. Should I go to see him, sir?"

"Use your bloody initiative, Pencarrow! If you want your hand held, go and ask the Boy Wonder. I daresay he'll oblige." Again he hung up.

That was a low blow, Megan thought. She wanted to let off steam about his unreasonableness to someone who would understand, and at the moment, unfortunately, that meant Ken.

She turned away from the phone cubby and saw Aunt Nell waiting a few yards away, looking anxious.

"Megan, I left in such a rush down in the village, I forgot to tell you. . . . I didn't want to talk about it in front of Ken, though I'm sure, being a police officer, he's properly discreet."

"To give the devil his due, he is. What's wrong?"

"Nothing, really. I just felt you ought to know that Alan Freeth—"

"Oh, that's all right. Nick told me where he is."

"He did? I thought he'd decided not to. I wasn't going to tell you his whereabouts, just that you can stop searching for him. If you ever began. And he says he's written to Roland Bulwer."

"Good. Then I needn't bother him. I was wondering how to fit in a visit."

Aunt Nell frowned. "Only, the more I think about it, the more certain I am that he's in some sort of trouble. Or rather, his friend is."

"Bulwer?" Megan asked, startled. "Aren't his troubles over, now that his straying lamb has turned up safe?"

"Not him. Mrs. Mason, his friend here. The one he and Nick are staying with. Didn't Nick tell you about her?"

"He said she and Freeth are . . . 'very pally,' I think his words were. Just how 'pally' are they?"

"None of my business, nor yours. But I can tell you this: She's ill, the sort of thing that could carry her off any day, or she could live for years if she's careful. Alan's very concerned about her. The thing is, it seemed to me he has another reason to be worried about her, besides her health."

"What sort of reason?"

"I have no idea. That's what's so frustrating. I wish I knew whether there might be a way to help. As it is, what can I do?"

"You could call on her again, Aunt Nell, and try to find out what's wrong."

"Not today. It would look frightfully pushy. And I can't on Monday. I've got to get the Incorruptible repaired. Or at least find out if it's possible."

"I'd forgotten about the car."

"After the storm last night, it's probably sitting in several inches of water. Oh well, I'm sure Mrs. Mason has worse problems."

"Maybe I will drop in this afternoon after all. I may be able to get some indication for you. How long is it going to be before Tariro and the girl— The girl! It can't be her that Ken— But he's always fallen for blondes. I don't believe it."

"I wouldn't be surprised, dear. I've noticed several hints, in both directions. From him and from her, I mean. You aren't upset, are you? You've really got over him?"

"Oh yes," Megan said firmly. "I wish her luck, that's all. She'll need it. What time do you think they'll be ready to go?"

"Sir Edward said a couple of hours, and that was a bit after two. A couple of hours could mean anything, though, or Nontando and Tariro could decide to cut the session short."

"Damn, I'd better not risk it."

"How's this for a plan: You have to drive up to the cliff paths anyway, so instead of taking the nearest way—up Vicarage Hill to the church—you can go up the lane that leads to Mrs. Mason's."

"How do I get there?"

"I don't know what it's called, if it even has a name, but as Nick described it, it's the first right off the B3263 going south, just where the main road makes a sharp turn inland. Her house is right at the end, where it peters out into a farm track. It probably started as a shepherd's cottage. You pop in for a minute while the rest walk on; then you can catch up."

"Brilliant, Aunt Nell."

"I hope either you or Ken has a big-enough car for me and Teazle to squeeze in."

"I'm driving an 1100, so it's possible, but I've got a better idea. Ken can take the girl—"

"Nontando. She has a name!"

"Sorry. I've been thinking of her as just another of Ken's flock of totties. Obviously, Sir Edward wouldn't have chosen her if she was a dim-witted dolly-bird."

"He wouldn't have chosen her if he'd realised she was a woman, to tell the truth."

"Nor me, or that's the impression he gave me."

"He was quite put out. I'm not at all sure he even knew that there is such a thing as a woman detective. He's a bit behind the times."

"Telling me! Not that he hasn't got company. Yet he asks *you* for help. How does he reconcile it with his notion of the proper place of women?"

"My dear, men are just as capable as women of believing six impossible things before breakfast. If not more so."

Megan laughed. "Too true. How are the talks going, or am I not allowed to ask?"

"I don't know the details. Presumably Sir Edward sees progress, or he'd give up. My part has been reasonably successful. Nontando and Tariro are at least on civil terms, which they weren't at first. Some of the credit must go to Ken. If you ask me, a new man in Nontando's life has eased her grievance against Tariro."

"I hope she doesn't expect it to last. Maybe you should warn her."

"Not on your life. She's an adult. Also, I doubt she's looking for anything permanent. She's very serious about her studies and her country's politics."

"I wish her luck. He's not a bad bloke, on the whole. He'll give her a good time till he moves on. I'd better get back to him now and see what he thinks about splitting up for the walk."

"And I must get back to Gina before she thinks I've been kidnapped. Come on, Teazle."

Megan walked slowly back to where she had left Ken. As so often happened, she felt much better after talking to her aunt. In the face of her common sense and kindness, intractable problems melted away, or at least were reduced to a size that could be tackled.

If only Ken would just stay out of her life!

He wasn't where she had last seen him. For a moment she stared blankly at the neat pile of newspapers on the low table, then she sat down and shuffled through them, looking for a note, some cryptic indication of where he had gone.

She recognised instantly the sound of his approaching footsteps. "Oh, there you are!" she said in heartfelt relief.

He grinned. "Happy to see me?"

"Happy to see you haven't been carried off by Russian spies. It would have been such a bore to have to rush to the rescue."

"I thought it would be a good idea to check that your little white van is still in the car park. As it is, large as life and twice as natural. Didn't you say the number plate was filthy?"

"Yes, I could barely read it, even close to, with my torch."

"The rain last night must have come down so hard, it bounced off the asphalt and washed them down. The front one, at least, is fairly clean and clear. I didn't go round the back. Did you have a nice chat with your guv'nor?"

"Not how I'd describe it. He just wants the impossible, as usual."

"I've always considered that to be the essential function of chief inspectors. Keeps you on your toes."

"Maybe I could manage if I had three feet."

"Our friends from London; Sir Edward; what's the third?"

"Not something you need to know about."

"Okay-ay. Allow me to commiserate anyway from the depths of my ignorance. How about a cuppa, as it looks as if we'll be out merrily hiking at teatime?"

"Good thinking. Let's see if we can have it in the bar, where we can watch the van. And I have to talk to you about the hike."

The obliging barman agreed to arrange for tea. "I've been keeping an eye on your suspects," he informed them in a low voice. "The tough always drinks Guinness, so I reckon he must be Irish, though he don't sound it. Borough-born and -bred, if you ask me, me being a Londoner meself. And t'other one drinks vodka, usually neat. D'you reckon he's a Russki?"

Megan and Ken raised eyebrows at each other. "Does he sound Russian?" Megan asked.

"Not that I can tell," the barman said regretfully. "More posh, if you get me. Another thing, the con-man type started to call the tough something beginning with S and got an elbow in the ribs that made him wince. He changed it to 'Vic,' pretty quick."

"The plot thickens," said Ken. "That's the lot?"

"Yeah, they're not the sort to chat at the bar."

"Thanks." The pound note he slid across the counter was swiftly pocketed.

"My pleasure. Tea for two coming up."

They took a table by the window. Megan had a view across the car park, though she couldn't actually see the van because of the protruding portico. She could see the exit drive, however. Adrian Arbuthnot and Victor Jones couldn't leave without her spotting them.

"Irish? Russian?" she queried.

"I can't see what finger the IRA can have in this pie. Our Russian?"

Megan shook her head. "There is no art to find a man's nationality in his favourite tipple."

"Oh, very clever, ha ha. Though I agree with you. No Russian spy worth his salt would touch the stuff."

"I wish I could guess—"

"Wait a minute! I've remembered his ugly mug. The S gave it to me. Victor Stone, sent down for manslaughter. Strong-arm robbery, a specialist—in fact, an expert—with a sandbag. He was very fast, and very clever at hitting just hard enough in just the right spot to knock out his opponent for just long enough, but he didn't reckon on someone's thin skull, and the victim died. His brief persuaded a soft-minded jury he hadn't intended to kill the poor chap."

"I have a vague memory. . . . Long time ago?"

"Yes, he got quite a stretch. Must have been back when I was on the beat."

"Me too."

"Are we growing old?" Ken misquoted.

"Oh no, not us. He had a nickname—S again! Wasn't he called the 'Sandman'? That's why I remember him at all. Banks, jewellers, goldsmiths, wasn't he? Not corner shops."

"I think so."

"What on earth is there in Tintagel that he'd consider worth knocking over? I've walked round the whole place, and there's nothing." Megan gazed out over the car park and the drive to the village spread out at the bottom of the hill. She could also see the sky to the southwest. "Oh no, more clouds on the horizon!"

"Not another storm! I'm not mucking about on the cliffs in a gale."

"I don't live on the coast, so I'm no expert, but it looks to me like the kind of low cloud layer that drifts in and hangs there.

Could be a bit of drizzle but probably just overcast or mist, depending how high it is. Stratus, is it?"

"Don't ask me. Not a beautiful sunny day with a boundless view of the sea followed by a glorious sunset?"

" 'Fraid not."

"Perhaps Non—they will decide not to go."

"I doubt it. When Tariro first saw this building last night—as much as he could see through the storm—he said it looked like a prison. I think they'll be raring to get outside. As Aunt Nell wants to go too, with Teazle—"

"As a matter of fact, I asked her to come with us."

"You did?"

"Don't sound so startled. I like your aunt. Besides, she's supposed to be persuasive, isn't she? We're going to have to persuade our charges to keep their heads down as we drive through the village."

"And they're going to want to see the sights. It's a point. I was going to suggest we take both cars, as there will be five, plus dog."

"Sir Edward and/or Payne may decide to join us."

"Heaven forbid! In that case we'd have no choice but to split up, but we might as well anyway. Besides not being crammed in, the two of them wouldn't have each other's support in going against Sir Edward's wishes. You take Nontando and I'll take Tariro and Aunt Nell."

Ken grinned. "You've tumbled to it, eh? I must say, I never thought I was the sort to fall for a coloured girl, but I've never met any girl like her, black, white, brown, yellow, or blue. She's—"

"That's quite as much as I want to hear," Megan said firmly. "Here comes our tea."

SIXTEEN

Returning to the sitting room, Eleanor found Gina playing a game of patience on the writing table by the window.

"I *am* sorry to have deserted you for so long. I didn't expect to be gone more than a couple of minutes."

"It's quite all right. I've had two out of three games come out already, which hardly ever happens. This one is looking quite promising. . . ."

"Don't let me interrupt."

Gina turned a couple more cards, sighed, and collected the pack together. "You'd think I'd know by now that 'promising' doesn't promise anything. You told your niece and her colleague about the proposed outing? I hope they weren't too upset."

"Not noticeably. Well, Megan was surprised but not upset. Ken—DS Faraday—wasn't very happy, but I talked him round."

"Just what you're so good at, Eleanor," Gina said warmly. "You seem to know him quite well."

"He turns up every now and then. I gather his superiors prefer to send an officer who's familiar with the local police, on the rare occasions when they have to send someone. He and Megan used to work together when she was in London."

"Ah, I see. I have the impression he and Nontando were making eyes at each other, as we used to say. I was a little concerned that Megan might be upset."

"She has no reason to be upset," Eleanor prevaricated. Her opinion was that Megan was well rid of Ken.

"I'm so glad. Sergeant Faraday has known Nontando only since yesterday—but really, young people nowadays are in such a hurry!"

"*Plus ça change . . .*"

"*Autre temps, autre moeurs,*" Gina retorted. "Well, they're old enough to sort things out for themselves."

She put the cards away in the desk drawer and they moved over to the comfortable chairs by the fire. Eleanor asked her friend, a keen theatre-goer, about the latest plays in London. Gina gave her an exhaustive—and exhausting—analysis, including a fair share of theatrical gossip, and assured her she would always be welcome to stay if she came up to town to see a few shows.

Eleanor put in an occasional "Good heavens!" or "Not really?" or "That sounds interesting," as appropriate, while half her mind pondered the puzzle of Alan Freeth and Rosie Mason.

Was it possible she, and a good many others, had misinterpreted a close friendship between Bulwer and Freeth as a closer, more intimate relationship? Eleanor didn't think so. Jocelyn, for one, was convinced they were homosexual though she would have preferred not to believe it. While inclined to be judgemental, Joce was always fair.

Yet Freeth had gone off without explanation to assist Mrs. Mason. They must have been *very* good friends in childhood.

Whether or not brother and sister, could they have been brought up together? Now she had time to ponder, it seemed unlikely. Alan

Freeth was so clearly professional middle-class, and something about Rosie Mason spoke of lower-middle or upper-lower, that in-between group whose watchword was *respectability*.

The English class system be damned! thought Eleanor. Perhaps she was completely wrong about the whole thing, having spent so much of her life overseas.

"Yes, American musicals can be amusing," she said to Gina. "The local cinemas show the films, but I have to confess, mostly they come and go before I get round to going to see them."

Gina laughed. Giving up on theatrical chitchat, she switched to reminiscing about the distant parts of the world where their paths had crossed. Eleanor's attention was engaged and she stopped worrying about Alan Freeth.

At about quarter to four, the negotiators appeared, Norton close behind with tea for all. Eleanor couldn't tell from Sir Edward's expression how the meeting had gone, but she reckoned that if he were meeting with notable success, he'd be visibly cheerful, which he wasn't.

On the other hand, Nontando, spectacular today in bright purple and electric blue, was definitely cheerful. "I can't wait to get outside into the fresh air," she said. "If you'll excuse me, Lady Bellowe, I'll go and get my coat."

"I really don't believe it's wise," grumbled Sir Edward, fighting a rearguard action, "but if you insist. . . . Norton, send for the police officers, please."

The butler ushered out Nontando and followed her. Gina poured tea. Tariro collected two cups and came over to give one to Eleanor. Teazle greeted him with a soft *wuff* and a wagging stump of a tail.

"May I join you, Mrs. Trewynn?"

"Of course. How did it go?"

He pulled a wry face. "Could be better. Could be worse. Sir Edward is probably correct. Sanctions will work in time and the settlers will have to accept majority rule. Bishop Muzorewa, as head of the only legal African party, will be well placed to take advantage. But Sir Edward doesn't understand our impatience and frustration. We are tired of waiting. And naturally, he strongly disapproves of our guerrillas accepting support from the Commies. What can they do when the West won't supply arms?"

"Which they use to fight each other," Eleanor pointed out with a sigh.

"That's why I can't bring myself to support either group. I'm going to keep my head down and get my degree. Maybe by then it will be clearer who is worthy of support."

"Or sanctions may have worked. I'd say that's a wise decision. What about Nontando?"

"Oh, she's a fire-breather. Her problem is that she prefers the Maoists to the Soviets, but they are supporting ZAPU and she doesn't like Nkomo, even though he's Ndebele, whereas ZANU's leader, Mugabe, is Shona."

"And she's Ndebele. What a dilemma!"

"Also, she—"

"Here she is now," Eleanor said with relief. She was never going to be able to keep ZANU and ZAPU straight. "And she's sensibly dressed for a country walk on a chilly spring day. I'd better go and fetch my coat."

On the landing, Eleanor met Megan and Ken.

"Ready to go, Aunt Nell?"

"Just about. Give me five minutes."

"I expect Sir Edward will lecture us on our duties for at least that long."

"Nontando's not wearing high heels, is she?" Ken asked.

"No, jeans and proper walking shoes."

He blenched. "I hope it doesn't mean she's expecting to climb over to the ruins."

Megan grinned, slightly maliciously. "Probably. The tide should be right. I checked. Just make sure you get back before it starts to get dark, or you'll find yourselves stranded for the night. Sir Edward would not be pleased. See you shortly, Aunt Nell." She went into the sitting room, with Ken following.

When Eleanor returned downstairs, she found she need not have hurried. Sir Edward was minutely questioning Megan about exactly where they were going.

"*Not* along the main street of the village," Megan was saying, as if not for the first time. She turned to Eleanor with relief. "Aunt Nell, could you please explain to Sir Edward where we're taking Miss Nontando and Mr. Tariro?"

"We'll be turning off the main road before we reach the main shopping area. The shops will be closed anyway on a Saturday afternoon. The tourist places stay open over the weekend in the summer, but not now. No one will be out and about."

"If you say so. . . . I suppose it will be all right. But be careful!"

The five, plus Teazle, trooped down to the ground floor. As Sir Edward had insisted, Nontando and Tariro waited at the tower door for Megan and Ken to bring the cars right to the spot.

"I'll go with you to fetch the car, Megan," said Eleanor, to whom Sir Edward had not issued orders. "Seeing a little old lady and a dog get into your car should make you look innocuous."

Megan laughed. "Little do they know you! All right, it's in front. We'll go out through the main door."

They went through to the hotel lobby. Megan held the main door open for Eleanor and followed her out.

"Damn and blast, the van's gone!"

"Van? Oh, your crooks' van?"

"Yes. They must have driven off while Sir Edward was haranguing us. I'd better call it in."

Eleanor scurried after her niece to the car, Teazle scampering alongside. Megan unlocked the driver's door, got in, leaned over to unlock the passenger door, then reached for the radio set. As soon as Eleanor opened the door, Teazle hopped in and sprang over the gear lever to the backseat.

Megan spoke urgently into the radio transmitter. Eleanor paused to look at the sky before getting into the car. A pall of low cloud hung over sea and land. She hoped Tariro and Nontando wouldn't be disappointed not to see waves sparkling in sunlight.

The radio squawked. Megan replied and it squawked again.

"Oh hell! Okay, thanks, Launceston. CaRaDoC L6 over and out."

"What's wrong?" asked Eleanor, settling in her seat.

"They've sent Dawson."

"Dawson?"

"PC Dawson, the Speed Demon, Terror of the Highways and Byways. The only thing he does well is drive. His idea of fun would be careering at eighty miles an hour round the lanes, pretending to hunt for the van."

"Oh dear!"

"And if he finds it by crashing into it, guess who the guv'nor's going to blame?"

"Freddy!"

"Hello, Sis."

"What are you— Vic!"

"Hello, Rosie. Happy to see dear hubby? C'mon, give us a kiss."

"No! Vic, don't!"

"Have it your own way. Aren't you going to invite us in? What a way to welcome your lawful wedded husband that's been away for years."

"You're not—"

"Now hold on, Vic!"

"You trying to tell me how to treat my own wife?"

"No, Vic, of course not. But can't you give her time to get used—"

"Ah, that's better. Nice place you got here. Comfy, like. Doing well, are you, duckie? Bit too far from the Smoke, though."

"How did you find me?"

"Now, that'd be telling. Maybe you forgot I have my ways. What's this 'ere? 'Private'? Looks like a good spot for a little *private* chat. You and me've got things to discuss. Anyone else in the house, Rosie? Bed-and-breakfasters, like?"

"They'll be back soon. Any minute."

"We better get a move on then, hadn't we. That desk, it was your pa's, wasn't it? Always knew quality when he saw it, your pa. I don't know what prices are these days, but I bet it'd fetch a pretty penny. Sit down, Rosie. Make yourself at home. Oh, ha ha, you are at home, aren't you? Good old home sweet home. Don't want to sit down? All right, stand, then; just don't try any funny business."

"I won't, Vic. Please—"

"Now, I seem to remember you always kept the stuff you thought was important in the bottom drawer. Freddy, see what you can find."

"No! I'll give you money, everything Dad owed you. I've got cash in the top drawer. I'll write you a cheque—"

"Get out of the way. Forgot your lessons, have you? This'll teach you!"

"No, Vic, don't!"

"Vic, there was no call for that."

"That's for me to decide. I won't have my wife cheeking me. Go look in that drawer."

Nick was in a foul mood as he trudged down the hill towards Mrs. Mason's house. His vision of a ghostly host emerging through the remaining arch from the ruins on the island had deserted him. Replacing them in his mind's eye were a Pre-Raphaelite knight with inevitable drooping damsel, most definitely not his thing. He couldn't get rid of them.

From the hillside, he saw a van in the drive, backed in, in front of Mrs. Mason's car. She had a visitor, or perhaps a shop delivery, though that seemed unlikely on a Saturday afternoon. As he approached the back door, he heard voices in her private room.

Good. He was in no mood to be introduced to strangers. Slipping in through the kitchen, he could avoid them.

It was a measure of her hospitable nature that he didn't hesitate to enter her house unannounced. He wanted a cup of tea but was not quite enough at home to set about making himself one. Going through into the hall, he made for the stairs.

A thought struck him. Could her visitors be people wanting a bed for the night? Perhaps he should tell her that he'd be quite happy to go home right away. With inspiration fled, he had plenty of work to do in his studio. It would be easy enough to come back on Sunday night or Monday morning to pick up Eleanor.

He dumped his equipment at the foot of the stairs and turned towards the front of the house.

From the front room came Mrs. Mason's voice, raised in protest: "Vic, no!" followed by a heavy thump.

Two strides took Nick to the door. As he moved, he heard a different voice, high but recognisably male: "Vic, you shouldn't have!"

"She asked for it."

Nick turned the handle. It was locked.

"How long d'you put her out for?"

"Dunno, do I. Haven't got the old skill back yet. Didn't hit that hard. Coupla minutes, I reckon."

"Rosie? Rosie! Oh my God, Vic, what have you done?"

Nick took a step back and ran at the door shoulder-first. It shook, but the lock held. He was about to try again, when Freeth came hurrying along the hall towards him.

"What's going on? Who's in there?"

"I don't know, but it doesn't sound good. Help me break in."

"A good kick just below the lock—or so I've been told. By a felonious client."

Not waiting for the explanation, Nick kicked. The door burst open. Facing them was a burly man, arm raised. Beyond him, Nick caught a glimpse of Mrs. Mason sprawled on her back, her head resting on the edge of the raised slate hearth.

Behind Nick, Freeth uttered an inarticulate cry. Nick had just time enough to take in that much before the man's arm, oddly lengthened, swung down with a sideways flick and the world went black.

SEVENTEEN

"Are you going to see Mr. Freeth?" Eleanor asked as the police car rolled down the hotel drive, Megan at the wheel, Tariro in the back with Teazle on his knee.

"Yes, I think so, just for the sake of my report. It shouldn't take more than a minute or two."

"And after that? Tariro and I can walk back to the hotel if you have to go chasing off after your two malefactors, can't we, Tariro?"

"If you say so, Mrs. Trewynn. I'll be glad to stretch my legs."

"No," Megan said decidedly. "They're only prospective malefactors. As far as I know, they haven't actually done anything illegal, and for all I know, they're heading straight back to London. If not, Dawson and Yarrow can manage without me for the present. Besides, Sir Edward would have a fit."

"Which reminds me," said Eleanor, looking back, "you're supposed to keep your head down, Tariro."

"Okay." He grinned at her and leaned forward over the dog, who kissed his nose.

"Teazle, really! I'm so sorry. Here, hand her over; she can sit on my lap."

"That's all right. She was just being friendly." Still bent double, he took out a handkerchief and wiped the dog slobber off his face. "How long do I have to stay bent double?"

"I've got to stop for petrol," said Megan after a glance at the gauge. "I'm afraid you really ought to get down on the floor. Sorry!"

Tariro groaned. "This is all such rubbish!" But he slithered off the seat and managed an awkward crouch, knees on one side of the bump and hands on the other side.

Teazle regarded this manoeuvre with interest, then hopped up on his back, eliciting another groan.

Megan made the petrol stop as brief as possible by asking for four quids' worth instead of a fill-up, and having four pound coins ready.

Pulling out of the petrol station, she said, "You can get up on the seat now, if you can do it without bobbing up in the process."

Tariro clambered up. With a few contortions—Teazle scrambling to adjust—he ended up on his back, knees in the air and the dog on his stomach. She turned three times and settled to sleep.

By that time, with next to no traffic in the streets, they had almost passed the built-up area.

"You can get up now," said Megan cheerfully.

Tariro groaned. Teazle strongly objected to another upheaval. She took a leap and landed on Eleanor just as the car made an abrupt turn off the main road into a narrow lane. The dog slithered to the floor with an indignant yip.

Eleanor leaned down to help her. When she straightened up, they were turning off the narrow lane into a narrower lane with slate walls on either side. A short way ahead, an isolated house stood at the point where the lane turned into an unpaved farm track. The sign in front now announced NO VACANCIES.

"Bloody hell! That's the van, in the drive!"

"The one you're looking for?" Eleanor asked. "Are you sure? There must be thousands like that on the roads."

"I'm sure. I'm going to drive on a bit up the track and walk down to see what's going on. That's where Freeth and Nick are staying?"

"Yes, Mrs. Mason's."

Luckily, there was no rattling cattle grid. A five-barred gate stood open. On their left, an enclosure surrounded by dry-stone walls held a flock of ewes and lambs. Beyond, the stony track, unwalled, sloped up towards the crest of the cliffs. Megan stopped after fifty yards or so and turned the car to face downhill.

"May I come with you?" Tariro asked.

"No, better wait here. Aunt Nell, explain to him, would you?" She retrieved her binoculars, got out, and closed the door with a faint click.

Eleanor held on to the dog, who wanted to follow. While she told Tariro what little she knew about the two men, she and Tariro watched Megan circle round behind the house. She ran half-crouched, ducking behind gorse bushes bright yellow with bloom, then took up a position concealed by an outcrop of granite. The house hid the van from them, but Megan must have a good view, Eleanor assumed.

From Megan's vantage point, looking down at the house, she saw a small car parked in the drive behind the van. Fortunately, the vehicles were far enough apart for the van's licence plate to be visible to her. She focussed the binoculars on it. She could imagine the ructions if she spent Sir Edward's time watching a perfectly innocent anonymous white van.

The number was her quarry's. She widened the focus to take in the van, the side of the house, and the space between.

Settling down into a reasonably comfortable position, she wondered what on earth the two men could want with Mrs. Mason. Had Adrian Arbuthnot gone so far to seed that he could no longer prey on wealthy women and had to make do with the proprietress of a guest house? Had he come alone, or brought his thuggish crony along?

Megan wished she knew whether Victor "Jones"—Stone, if Ken was right—was in the house. If he was, she'd be inclined to go down and prospect more closely, perhaps knock on the door and ask for Freeth. Maybe she should anyway. She might wait for hours here without being any the wiser as to what he, or they, were up to.

In the meantime, what were Aunt Nell and Tariro up to? It was only a matter of time before they got fed up with waiting and either went off for a walk or came down to see what she was doing.

She glanced over towards her car, partly concealed by the intervening gorse. No sign of movement. So far, so good.

A pair of jackdaws landed on the grass a few feet from her. Inveterate beggars, they doubtless hoped she was having a solitary picnic. Attracted by their insistent *chuck-chuck,* a gull wheeled overhead, screaming. A pair of Londoners probably wouldn't notice, or if they did, wouldn't draw the conclusion that the birds were interested in an intruder. Anyway, they were still inside the—

Click.

At the sound of a latch, Megan swung the binoculars back to the house. The con man came out of the side door. His appearance was more furtive than ever. He slunk down the drive to the lane and peered down towards the village, then turned and came back. Megan zoomed in on his face. It was ghastly, a mix of horror and terror.

Whatever he had looked for in the lane, he didn't raise his eyes to the hillside. The London mind-set: A barren hillside could present no danger.

He went back into the house.

His expression had shocked Megan. Something appalling had happened in the house. Now she had to decide whether duty required her to dash down to investigate or to hurry back to the car and radio for assistance.

If she called for help, she'd face teasing from her male colleagues. If she went to the house and ran into trouble she couldn't handle, teasing would be the least of it. Against Arbuthnot alone, she would expect to prevail. But she remembered Victor Stone's burly form and couldn't help quailing.

She could call Ken on the two-way. He was probably within range. He didn't know the area, though. He'd have trouble finding the isolated house. And he had the girl with him. . . .

A sudden stray breeze wafted the scent of gorse to her nostrils. The gull took advantage of the gust to sail away with a mournful cry. The jackdaws had given up and flapped off a minute or two earlier.

The breeze dropped as suddenly as it had started, leaving an ominous stillness in the air. Overhead, the low pall of grey cloud crept slowly inland, extinguishing the last vestiges of blue sky to the east. Calling it the "pathetic fallacy" didn't prevent brooding nature's increasing Megan's uneasiness. What should she do?

The squawk of the radio made Eleanor jump. "CaRaDoC L6, come in, please."

Tariro pointed to a small metal plate on the radio console: "L6, that's us!"

"Hello, L6, are you receiving me? Come in, please."

They exchanged a look. Gingerly, Eleanor picked up the thing that looked like a telephone receiver. "Hello?" She listened. "Hello, this is L6." No response.

"I think you have to push something, one of those buttons."

"L6, Pencarrow, are you receiving me?"

"On the dashboard? Which one?"

She pressed a button. The Launceston operator was cut off in mid-word. Hastily Tariro climbed over into the driver's seat and took a closer look at the radio panel. "This one—"

"—lo, L6, come in, please."

"Hello?" said Eleanor.

"CaRaDoC L6, are you receiving me?"

"I bet it's the one on the transmitter. The thing you're holding. Here." He pressed a button on the gadget Eleanor held out to him.

"Hello?" she said into it yet again. "This is L6. CaRaDoC L6, I mean."

"Hello? Hello?"

"Hello, this is L6, can you hear me now?"

"I am receiving you, L6. Who is speaking?"

"This is Eleanor Trewynn. Megan—DS Pencarrow—went to investigate a van."

"The van she reported as having left the hotel?"

"Yes."

"Can you give me your location, Mrs. Trewynn, and the location of the van?"

Eleanor described how to get to Mrs. Mason's guest house and the position of the police car. "Megan's behind the house, concealed behind a rock, watching to see what's going on. Should I go and fetch her?"

"On no account! The men involved may be dangerous. We

have a probable identification for one of them. Stand by a moment, L6."

"I'll go and warn Megan," Tariro whispered.

"No! You'd be more likely to draw their attention to her than to help. And I need you here. I'm bound to get in a muddle with the—"

"L6, are you there?"

"Yes, I'm here. Hello?" She reached for the console.

Grinning, Tariro intercepted her hand and hit the correct button, not the one she'd aimed at.

"Yes, L6 here."

"I'm authorised to give you the information, Mrs. Trewynn. Please listen carefully so that you can pass it on to Megan. I shall ask you to repeat it to me to make certain you've got it correctly. Understood?"

"Yes. I mean, understood."

"Here goes, then. The man using the name Victor Jones is almost certainly Victor Stone, alias the Sandman because of his expertise with a sandbag. Recently released from Dartmoor after a long stretch—that is, after a prison term—for manslaughter in the course of a robbery. Repeat, please."

Eleanor repeated, with a little prompting from Tariro. "I'll tell Megan. She said you're sending—I can't remember his name—the Speed Demon, she called him?"

"DC Dawson." The radio operator's dry tone came through in spite of the crackling. "Yes, he's on his way, but even he can't arrive for twenty minutes at least, more likely half an hour."

Barring tractors, flocks of sheep, and herds of cattle, Eleanor thought. "Oh dear!"

Luckily, Tariro did not transmit this unconstabulary exclamation.

"I'll alert PC Yarrow," the voice continued. "Please continue to listen for further news or instructions. Over."

Eleanor hesitated for a moment, then replaced the receiver— or transmitter, or whatever it was she'd been speaking into—in its place on the console. "Is that right, d'you think, or should I keep holding it?"

"We heard their original call before you picked it up. I suspect you should have acknowledged what was said before hanging up, but I'm no expert. They know you're an amateur. No doubt they'll make allowances."

"I hope so! I hope they won't tease Megan about her incompetent aunt."

"You managed very well, if you ask me. I still think I ought to go and warn Megan. Suppose she tries to tackle this Sandman bloke on her own, not realising how dangerous he is?"

"She wouldn't do anything so foolhardy." Eleanor sounded doubtful to her own ears. She knew the pressure Megan felt to keep up with her male colleagues. "No, I'm sure she won't. The other man is bound to be there too, and she knows it."

"Oh yes, the operator said 'men.' Who are these men? I've got only one little piece of the puzzle."

"I haven't got much more." She told him what Megan and Ken had said about them.

"So they haven't actually done anything illegal here? That we know about, at least. They could be just visiting Mrs. Mason?"

"It's possible, certainly. From what little I've seen of her, she wouldn't be worth going to all that trouble to rob. *Mason*," she reflected, frowning, "*Stone*. A coincidence. But not much of one. Neither name is particularly uncommon. It does make me wonder, though. . . ."

"Perhaps they are related, and Mrs. Mason changed her name to prevent discovery of the relationship."

"It's a nice theory, isn't it? I'm sure Megan would say Stone is too common a name for anyone to imagine such a connection. Besides, why choose a name that's . . . not similar, exactly, but linked, if you see what I mean?"

"The name suggested itself to her because of the link, and she didn't realise until after she had established herself as Mrs. Mason? It would not be easy to start again somewhere new."

"True." Could it all be true, their tissue of speculation? Was it worth presenting the theory to Megan?

At least it had served to distract Tariro from his intention of joining her niece. Eleanor rather doubted Megan would be pleased had he appeared at her side.

On the other hand, perhaps Megan ought to know the alarming news about Stone. What exactly was a sandbag? It didn't sound dangerous, but evidently it became a lethal weapon in the hands of an expert. Should Eleanor let Tariro go and warn Megan, at the risk of alerting the villains to her presence?

The question changed suddenly: Could she stop him?

Tariro opened the door and got out, saying, "I'm going to tell her one of them is a killer. For all we know, the second man might be another. She can't face those odds alone."

EIGHTEEN

Megan decided it would be just plain stupid to act without further information. She scanned the hillside between her and the house. There was little cover between her sheltering rock and the low wall that kept sheep out of Mrs. Mason's back garden. A dark line slanting down the slope, brought into focus, turned out to be sedge defining a rill, too low-growing to be useful unless she lay flat behind it.

The streamlet was almost certainly too shallow for her to hide herself by slithering into it. In fact, she'd easily be able to jump over it, if it weren't that she wanted to remain as invisible as humanly possible.

Off to her left was a small hawthorn tree, leaning away from the onshore winds. The trunk wasn't anywhere near wide enough to conceal her, but anyone just glancing round could possibly overlook her in her dark green parka.

And the Londoner hadn't even glanced that way.

Halfway down, the thorn tree would provide a meagre shelter from which she might be able to see more. It seemed the best bet.

Before making a dash for it, Megan focussed the glasses again on the house and van. For a moment, the scene was just as when she had first seen it. She could almost believe that the terror on Arbuthnot's face must have been a figment of her imagination, that he was paying a perfectly ordinary visit to Mrs. Mason and had had some innocuous, if obscure, reason for looking down the road.

And then he came out again. For a moment, Megan couldn't make out what she was seeing, or perhaps refused to believe it. Arbuthnot, stooped and staggering a little, carried a man draped over his shoulders. The slumped body wore hiking boots; legs in dark grey corduroy trousers dangled limply. His ankles were bound together over the trousers with multiple loops of household string, the straw-coloured, hairy kind. A blue pullover and, as Arbuthnot turned towards the van, a sandy head, lolling, came into view. The dangling arms were also tied, a pink stretch bandage binding his wrists.

Arbuthnot momentarily let go of the legs to make an ineffectual grab at the handle of the van's back doors.

"Moron!" The snarled word came clearly to Megan's ears. "Why the hell didn't you open it up before?"

Victor Stone had come out of the house while Megan was concentrating on his mate. His expression was vicious, without a sign of shock or fear. Like the other crook, he had a limp body over his burly shoulders. Megan instantly recognised Nick.

Her heart skipped a beat; her breath caught in her throat; her vision blurred.

The scene came back into focus. Nick, too, was trussed up, which surely must mean he was alive! He appeared to be tied with white gauze at both wrists and ankles.

Megan's brain began to work again. The two villains had not come with the intention of tying anyone up. When the need arose, they had used whatever came to hand. What had happened to make such an expedient necessary in their eyes? Was Mrs. Mason complicit? Or were they going to carry out her unconscious body next?

Stone let Nick slide to the ground, feet first. Megan winced as he landed, crumpled to his knees, and fell forward. Stone opened the rear of the van, swinging the doors wide. The sole contents seemed to be two suitcases, but it was dark inside, apparently lacking a window to the cab. He shoved the cases to the front.

Arbuthnot turned his back and made a clumsy attempt to unload his burden into the van. With contemptuous ease, Stone took the unconscious man from his shoulders and slung him casually to the corrugated metal floor. Picking up Nick, he dropped him on top of the other and slammed the doors on them.

Megan expected them to go back into the house. They had left the door open. But Stone tramped round the van to the passenger door. Arbuthnot locked the back doors and went round the driver's side.

It was too late to think of trying to intervene. Megan headed for her car as fast as she could run.

As Tariro closed the car door, so carefully it made not a sound, Eleanor saw Megan coming up the hill.

"Wait," she said sharply. "Here she comes."

Tariro looked over the roof of the car, then hastily opened the driver's door again. "She's in a terrific hurry. I wonder what's happened? Look, the van's leaving." He jumped into the backseat. Teazle deserted Eleanor and joined him.

Megan arrived, slightly out of breath, swung in behind the wheel, and turned the key. "Don't ask," she snapped. "You'll hear soon enough. Aunt Nell," she went on as the car rolled down the track, gathering speed, "you see that van? Keep your eyes on it and watch where it goes, in case I'm distracted. Tariro, I've got to use the radio and I need both hands for driving. Can you lean over and get the transmitter, and hold it where I can speak into it?"

"Of course." He slid over to the middle of the backseat, reached between the front seats, and unhooked the gadget. "Mrs. Trewynn's been in communication with your HQ."

"What!"

"They rang up," said Eleanor, "or whatever you call it. Do you want to hear what they said?"

"In a minute. I must get things moving fast." She took her left hand from the steering wheel to press the transmit button, but Tariro was there before her. "CaRaDoC L6 calling Launceston. Urgent. Emergency."

Tariro hit the receive button.

"I am receiving you, L6. Emergency, understood. Details, please."

Eleanor listened with mounting horror as Megan described what she had observed. "I am following the van, Jenny. Just turned south on B3263. Request assistance with tailing and interception. Dawson knows the lanes. And someone needs to check on Mrs. Mason."

"Roger, L6," said the operator. "I'll notify Dawson and the Tintagel bobby—PC Yarrow, right?—immediately, then clear it with DI Eliot. He's in charge here. D'you want Mr. Scumble informed, Megan?"

"Yes. Even if he's— Hold on. The road's wiggling. And here's a village."

"Trewarmett," said Eleanor, glad to see no one and no traffic in the street.

Megan reported the name.

As the car skidded round a bend and Megan expertly corrected, Tariro exclaimed, "Oh, well done!"

Beyond the hamlet the road straightened, going uphill with quarries on the left. Megan stepped on the accelerator. Nonetheless, the white van was pulling away. "It's moving fast."

"Souped-up engine," Tariro said.

"Jen, he knows we're after him."

"L6, I'm switching you to Channel 3. It will remain open for you to keep us informed of your location. Please confirm when you have switched."

Tariro leaned over farther to peer at the console and Megan told him how to change channels. Eleanor, her gaze on the van, didn't see what he did, but he said, "I think that's it."

"Penbethy," said Eleanor as they whizzed past a few buildings, followed by stone-walled fields on either side.

"L6 reporting on Channel 3. Are you receiving me, Launceston?"

"Roger, Pencarrow." It was a male voice. "Wharton here. Jen roped me in temporary-like. Eliot's sent for Tina."

"Sarge, we're coming up to a T-junction. He's turned right—and right again, and left."

"Railway bridge ahead," said Eleanor, "and Camelford Station. There's a crossroads."

"Railway bridge, station, and crossroads coming up. He's charging straight across." Megan slowed just enough to glance both ways before following. "Shortcut to the A39, Aunt Nell?"

"Yes, via Slaughter Bridge. It's a narrow, winding lane." Her wanderings in search of donations were proving useful once again.

"Heading for Slaughter Bridge, Sarge."

"I heard that. You've got your auntie along for the ride, Sarge?"

Megan flushed. Eleanor didn't listen to her response. The van had disappeared round a bend and she had lost sight of it. "They can't turn off before Slaughter Bridge," she said, reassuring herself as well as Megan.

They were passing through yet another tiny hamlet. The police car swept round the curve and there was the van, rocketing down a straight stretch into a wooded valley.

"The River Camel, but it's just a stream here."

"Dangerous bend sign," Tariro commented as the van vanished again, swinging wide round the sharp curve.

"Thank goodness it's not August!" Eleanor exclaimed. In summer, even these back roads got a fair amount of tourist traffic.

They rounded the corner in time to see the van dash over an ancient humpbacked bridge. It might have taken off if the hump had been a little more pronounced. Immediately on the other side, the lane made an acute-angle turn to the right.

The van slowed, and Megan caught up bumper-to-bumper. "I wish I had a gong and roof light," she moaned. "I don't dare try to overtake."

"I doubt flashing lights would stop them," said Tariro. "The girl said it's a convict called Stone."

"Ken was right, then."

"The next bend is even sharper," Eleanor warned. "Left. Or if they go straight ahead, straight but much too narrow to pass."

Round the tight curve crawled the van, with the police car on its heels. A farm lorry coming the other way, far too close to the centre line, veered back to its own side. A lane leading off to the left had a FARMS ONLY sign. Eleanor usually took that way in her quest for donations for the shop. Now they swept past, the van speeding up into the next curve.

Once past that, the van began to get away from them. High hedge-banks hid even its roof from Eleanor. "No turnoffs except for farm tracks," she said worriedly, "but the A39 isn't far, just a mile or so."

"On the main road they'll beat us hollow," Tariro said.

"That doesn't matter so much," said Megan, "as long as we manage to see whether they turn south or north. Sarge, I'm approaching the A39."

"So's Dawson, in L13, on the A395 a mile east of Davidstow."

"Tell him to turn south. If they go north, we'll trap them between us."

"Hold on. Mr. Scumble's arrived."

"Already? He must have driven like a bat out of hell."

"I heard that, Pencarrow. Do not—repeat—do *not* tackle these men."

"I doubt I can catch them, sir. The van looks grotty, but the engine's better than mine. If Dawson and I together manage to stop them . . . and I have an able-bodied assistant—"

"Sure thing!" Tariro said with an American accent.

Eleanor started planning how to use Aikido to disarm a large man wielding a sandbag. She wasn't sure what a sandbag looked like, what length, thickness, weight, flexibility, or how it was swung. At the same time, she kept her eyes on the van.

The road bent slightly to the right before debouching onto the A39. As the van reached the junction, for a moment only its roof was visible. It didn't pause before swinging left onto the main road.

"North," said Eleanor.

"They've turned north," Megan reported. "Damn!" She had to stop at the intersection as a lorry thundered by, closely followed by a sports car unable to pass because of traffic coming the other way. "Turning north on the A39, two vehicles between us."

"Roger, L6," responded the radio in the sergeant's voice.

"I can't see them," Eleanor said anxiously.

"Better get out the map book, Aunt Nell. In there."

The lorry gradually slowed on the uphill slope. The sports car zipped round it; then more vehicles came down the opposite lane.

"Damn, I wish I had a gong and a light! All right, here goes."

As Megan pulled out to overtake, Eleanor saw the van rocket across the southbound lane to take a narrow road leading east.

"They've turned right, Sarge. May think it's the 395? Will follow."

"It goes to the old Davidstow aerodrome," said Eleanor. "After that, it gets confusing, even with a map. I usually end up at Altarnun but I'm never quite sure where I am."

Megan's language deteriorated. "Bloody hell!"

"Sorry, I don't come this way very often."

"Turning right, Sarge, towards Altarnun."

"Got it. Hold on half a mo, Sarge."

The road ran fairly straight for a mile or so. To the south, the tors of Brown Willy and Rough Tor were hidden in mist. Or low cloud cover, depending on how one looked at it. Wisps of mist drifted across their path, but the van was in sight ahead most of the time, steadily increasing the distance between them.

"L6, Dawson has turned south on a road that meets yours on the aerodrome."

After a moment's thought, Eleanor said, "I know it. I don't think even your Speed Demon will get there in time to cut off the van. Besides, there's plenty of room on the runways for them to dodge."

"Old aerodrome?" asked Tariro. "How old can an aerodrome be?"

"*Abandoned* would be a better word. It was used to train Allied airmen in the war. It's a good place to walk the dog in wet weather because of the tarmac. Look!"

The plateau of the airfield was before them, crisscrossed with roads and runways, mysterious paved circles where Eleanor had always assumed aircraft had been parked, and a cluster of buildings to the north. To one side of the buildings, the road Dawson was on—

And here he came, gong blaring, blue light flashing. Eleanor held her breath as the police car and the van raced towards the vee where the two roads merged.

The van got there first by inches. All three in L6 gasped as the Speed Demon's brakes screeched and he veered a moment before he would have rammed the side of the van.

Eleanor let out her breath. "Thank heaven he remembered the men in the back!" Eleanor breathed.

"And the hot water he landed in last time he wrecked a car," Megan said sardonically. "L6 calling Launceston. L13 and I are both chasing the van across the airport."

"Roger, Megan. Tina here."

"The van's holding the centre of the road."

"I hope Dawson doesn't try to pass it on the grass," said Eleanor. "It'll be very boggy in places after the storm."

"Hear that, Tina?"

"I'll tell L13." Tina's voice became muffled, then returned. "Thank you, Mrs. Trewynn."

"The next crossroads just leads to farms in both directions."

"If they take either, we'll have them cornered," Tariro crowed.

The van sped straight across, with Dawson close behind. Megan kept up as well as she could. Thus when the van took the next right, the Speed Demon overshot the turn but Megan had time to follow.

"Straight on's a dead end. But if they turn left . . ."

They did.

"Where does this go, Aunt Nell?"

"All over the place," Eleanor said gloomily. "A network of lanes. They could go on to Altarnun and the A30, or double back, or cut across to the A395. It's mostly farms, not villages, so there aren't many signs. It's anyone's guess where they'll end up."

The van turned left. In the narrow lane—one and a half cars

wide, with cutouts and farm gates for passing—it could no longer take advantage of its superior speed, so for a while Megan kept up with it. She glanced in her rearview mirror. "And here's Dawson to join the party. Speed won't help him now."

They were descending off the moor into lower terrain, hedged and wooded country, trees and bushes putting out their spring green. The lane began to wind. Eleanor lost sight of the van in Bowithick, though at least she knew the name of the place. But with the tiny village behind them, their quarry had disappeared. The lane split, and split again.

They had no way of knowing which way the van had gone.

"We've lost them," Megan reported reluctantly.

"Mr. Scumble says to split up," Tina told her. "We're sending out spotters, but we can't cover everywhere."

Megan took the right fork. Dawson peeled off to the left.

"We're on our own again," Tariro observed, sounding pleased.

Eleanor hoped he wasn't nursing expectations of heroic deeds. "I have no idea where we are," she said as they crossed Penpont Water for the second time, "and I'd be surprised if they do, but I'm pretty sure we, at least, will end up at Altarnun. Dawson may get back to the aerodrome road. He could join us in Altarnun or reach the A30 farther north. Or not."

"Pencarrow." It was Scumble's gruff voice. "Yarrow just reported from Mrs. Mason's house. She's dead. I've sent Eliot, and Dr. Prthnavi is on his way."

Eleanor blinked back tears. She had only just met Mrs. Mason, but she had liked her and hoped to get to know her better. Then a still more horrible thought struck her. "Oh, Megan, what about Nick?"

"He's alive," Megan said fiercely. "If he was dead, why tie him up?" But her tone lacked conviction.

NINETEEN

Nick had a horrendous headache, the worst he could remember, worse than anything he had suffered on the rugger field. It was even worse than the migraines that had afflicted him when he was battling his family over his determination to become an artist.

He couldn't remember what had happened to make his head hurt. That was alarming. Still more alarming was that when he opened his eyes, he couldn't see.

The surface beneath him shifted. *Ambulance,* he thought fuzzily. Listening, he heard the roar of the motor and the whir of wheels on asphalt. A damned uncomfortable ambulance. He seemed to be lying on cold, ridged metal.

The vehicle swerved. Nick rolled helplessly, unable to brace himself, until he hit an obstacle. That was when he realised he hurt all over, and that his wrists and ankles were tied. Another swerve and again he tumbled across the floor. This time he fetched up against something soft.

Memory slunk back.

"Freeth!"

No response.

Not Freeth? Freeth unconscious? Not Freeth dead! Taking advantage of a smooth, straight stretch of road, Nick manoevred until he could put his ear to the man's chest. He was breathing, his heartbeat strong.

The van—the white van Nick had seen in Mrs. Mason's drive, of course—went over a bump. Both he and the inert Freeth jolted sickeningly. He had to find a way to immobilise them both. The first step was to explore their prison. Surely there must be some way to tie down the van's usual cargo, some sort of hooks or rails attached to the sides, if he could only find them.

Freeth was lying against a side wall, where the last lurch had tossed him. Nick managed a sort of crawl-cum-scramble that was hard on the elbows but carried him past his companion's head.

He found the wall with his own sore head. Kneeling, he felt with numbing hands from the floor upward. Just as he straightened to reach higher, they zipped round another corner and he went flying. Somehow, with his arms, he shielded his head from the collision.

A sudden slowing sent him slithering to the front of the van. He and Freeth and two heavy rectangular objects came together against the front wall. And he heard voices in the cab.

". . . roads you've been taking aren't even on the lousy map! I don't know where the hell we are."

"I told you, we have to go east." The second voice was equally angry but with an unpleasant whine to it. "I showed you on the map which direction is east."

"A fat lot of good that is when I don't know where we are, you bloody moron! Damn these clouds."

The whiner's response was muted. Nick was glad that their captors had troubles of their own, but it wasn't a lot of help.

His groping fingers found a handhold. For as long as he could

{ 184 }

hang on, there would be no more battering. For him, at least. What about Freeth? Was there any way to help him?

Stretching out his legs, Nick fished for his fellow victim. One of the objects sharing their all too spacious accommodations was between them. He kicked it away. They were going uphill, so it slid all the way to the back doors and thudded against them. The sound seemed very loud to Nick and he held his breath for a moment, but their captors apparently didn't hear.

Or they didn't realise that, unlike previous thumps, the road provided no reason for this one.

His questing feet found Freeth. Lying on his back, he managed to hook his legs over the man's body. His position was uncomfortable and tiring, but as long as the road was straight and smooth, he didn't have to exert himself much. If they started veering all over the place again, it would be a different story.

Freeth's body—Nick wished his mind had not provided that phrase. Freeth was alive, and would doubtless have an even worse headache than Nick's when he came round.

Mrs. Mason, though . . . He had been trying not to think about her lying on the floor. Was she dead? It seemed all too likely when he recalled what he had heard through the door.

Besides, what else could explain the kidnapping of himself and Freeth but that they were witnesses to her murder? They were being taken to some suitably remote spot to be disposed of.

Yet this scenario didn't make sense. Mrs. Mason's house was well off the main road, with the nearest neighbours some distance away. Why not finish them off on the spot and make a clean getaway? Why go to the trouble and delay of knocking them out, trussing them up like chickens, and carrying them off, if they were to be permanently disposed of?

Nick would have shrugged had it been physically possible.

Maybe Megan would be able to guess their reasons. He sincerely hoped he'd be present—and alive—to hear her explanation.

A stretch of smooth, straight road had lulled him into relaxing his grip. When the next, inevitable, sudden swerve came, centrifugal force nearly tore him loose, and Freeth with him. He barely hung on, his arms a fiery agony. Tyres squealed. The strain went on and on, as if the van was doing a 180-degree turn. His fingers were slipping when it straightened out.

Another one like that and he and Freeth would be bouncing back and forth again, helpless to protect themselves against further battering.

"If you don't mind my asking," said Tariro, "who is Nick?"

"My next-door neighbour, and a dear friend." Eleanor waited hopefully for Megan to add "And my boyfriend," but she didn't.

Megan had to concentrate on driving, Eleanor consoled herself. If Nick came out of this affair in one piece, perhaps the two of them would make up their minds at last.

As Eleanor had predicted, the winding, branching lanes took them to Altarnun. They also slowed the van and no doubt confused its driver with a multiplicity of choices. After crossing Penpont Water yet again, the road straightened as it entered the village and continued straight for a few hundred feet, and Eleanor caught the first glimpse of the van in several miles.

"I knew it," she said triumphantly. "We're almost at the A30. We absolutely must see which way they turn. Step on it, Megan."

"Not at the risk of running down a pedestrian." Megan veered round a stout woman coming out of her garden gate, which opened directly on to the street. She was holding a lead. "Or a dog."

"*Wuff?*" Teazle rushed to peer out of the window.

"Too late, pup." Tariro ruffled the dog's head as Megan accelerated. He had long since given up trying to hide. He had also taken over most of the radio reports and was thoroughly enjoying the job. "Tina, L6 passing through Altarnun. We have a sighting, repeat, we have a sighting."

"Good job, L6." The Launceston operator hadn't been told his name, still—to his amusement—an official secret. "L13 has just reached the A30 at Holywell Cross. He got stuck behind a herd of cows."

"Almost back in Launceston," said Eleanor. "That's the way the van will turn, don't you think? I can't believe they'd want to go farther south. Unless they've completely lost their bearings trying to dodge us."

"If you ask me, they have," said Megan. "One is definitely a Londoner and the other probably never walked a country mile in his life. He's the sort that bounces between resort hotels, cruise ships, and cheap digs in London. And the odd spell in clink, I shouldn't be surprised."

The lane was winding again. The van was intermittently visible. Eleanor couldn't see it when it stopped—if it stopped—at the stop sign. But they were close enough behind that when they, in turn, reached the junction, the van was in plain sight, speeding southwest.

There was little other traffic. Megan raced after them while Tariro reported the right turn onto the main road.

"They're going to Bodmin?" Tina asked incredulously. "Are you sure?"

"Mrs. Trewynn says we are going towards Bodmin. The only signpost I had time to see said Jamaica Inn. And Lewannick the other way, which I gather is the way to Launceston."

"Oh, I know those signs. A big new one to Jamaica Inn, and

CAROLA DUNN

just an old fingerpost to Bodmin and Launceston. Very mislead-
ing."

"Megan thinks the men in the van are lost."

"Megan's usually— Hold on, L6."

They were dropping behind the van again. The road was mostly
uphill, from the valley back up onto the moors. The low, unbro-
ken clouds had brought an early twilight. Soon it would be difficult to distinguish the van's rear lights from any other vehicle's.

"Pencarrow!" Scumble's voice. Tariro hurriedly held the mike
close to Megan's mouth.

"Sir."

"I'm sending L13 after you. If the target stays on the A30,
Dawson will pass you. I'll have a car come up from Bodmin—they
have one on stand-by already. Between them, they should be able
to stop the van. In that case, when you catch up, you will observe
and not intervene unless absolutely necessary. And for chrissake,
keep those bloody civilians out of it. Beg pardon, Mrs. Trewynn, but
please just stay in the car."

Luckily, he continued to give instructions to Megan without requiring Eleanor's word. She was quite willing to leave the capture
to three or four policemen, but her thoughts were on the captives
in the back of the van. Her first concern would be to free them.

The van came into sight again as they approached the turnoff
to Jamaica Inn. It was caught in a slanting shaft of light from the
sun, which broke through the clouds for a moment as it sank
towards the horizon.

The brief gleam must have been a revelation to the villains in
the van. If that was west, they were hastening farther and farther
from London. Coming to the next side road, they swung round
the sharp left turn at high speed, leaving black tyre marks on the
road, as Eleanor saw when they came to the spot.

As Megan followed, not much slower, Eleanor hung on and glanced back and saw with relief that Tariro was holding Teazle.

"Aunt Nell, where . . . ?"

Tariro moved the mike over towards Eleanor. She wasn't as familiar with this district, so she checked the map, holding it up to her face in the fading light.

"It starts out going northeast, Mr. Scumble, then bends to the southeast and follows the River Fowey, wiggling like mad. It ends up near Liskeard, but if they realise they're going south again, they'll take the road to Alton."

"Roger," said Tina's voice. "Hold on, L6."

"If it's wiggly," said Tariro, "we should catch up a bit. Megan's a better driver."

"Thank you!" said Megan.

"I hope so," said Eleanor, "because we'll lose sight of them again, what with wiggles and the trees along the river."

"Are there any side roads they could take?" Megan asked.

Eleanor peered. "I can't really see. Not enough light for map reading."

"There's a torch in the map pocket."

"All right. Here we are. No, there's only very minor lanes and they all seem to go to farms or to high points on the moors. Or hut circles. Prehistoric, I presume. It doesn't seem likely they'll choose to wander off into the wilderness with night coming on."

"It's getting foggy up in the hills, too," said Tariro, twisting his neck to look up the slope of the moors to their right. "Or the clouds coming lower, maybe."

"Just what we need," Megan grumbled.

"It's going to get worse if they turn east at Redgate," said Eleanor, her finger following the line on the map. "It's higher land. And it's the logical way for them to take."

"*If* they realise they're heading south. I wouldn't count on any logic coming into their movements. I wish I had the faintest idea what's in their minds."

"L6 . . . you receiv . . . me?"

"Reception is bad," Tariro said, the clipped clarity of his accent noticeable. "L6 is in a valley."

"Un . . . stood. Sending L . . . to Upton, repeat, . . . ing L13, that . . . Dawson . . . Upton. Do you . . ."

"Roger, Launceston. L13, the Speed Demon, to Upton."

Half a laugh came over the radio. "L6, send . . . B . . . Red . . . peat, sending B16 to Redgate."

"B, that's Bodmin? B16 to Redgate. That came in clear."

"L6, can you give me your exact position?"

"The middle of nowhere," said Tariro.

TWENTY

Once again, Eleanor's prophesy came true. When they reached the junction at the tiny village of Redgate, they were just in time to see that the van had turned left and was heading northeast towards Upton.

"Perhaps they worked out how to read the map," said Megan as Tariro reported to Launceston.

The road was wider and straighter than the lane along the Fowey. Inevitably the van pulled away again. They left hedges behind, though. As they ascended gradually towards the moors, Eleanor caught glimpses of the roof of the van over the banked stone walls.

Better still, she had a clear view when it reached a Y-junction and branched off to the left.

"Towards Upton," she said with satisfaction. "If only Dawson gets there in time to head them off!"

Rough moorland spread on either side now. Weirdly shaped gorse bushes and hawthorn rose from the rough, tussocky grass and heather, and sheep grazed freely right beside the road. Tariro was thrilled by the sight of a herd of wild ponies. Here and there, the incongruous ruins of mine engine houses remained as tumbledown witnesses to the industrial history of this desolate place.

Eleanor loved the moor—on a sunny day. With low clouds hiding the crest of the hills and wisps of mist drifting across their way, it was dank and unwelcoming.

"Perfect for the Hound of the Baskervilles," Tariro commented.

The windscreen started fogging up. Megan wound down her window a few inches. The chilly air battled the car heater for supremacy. Overall, the heater won, but cold currents circulated. Eleanor was glad to be wearing a warm jacket.

The road narrowed. Contending with sheep, ponies, and mist, Megan slowed down.

"L6, Dawson is at Upton. How far away are you?"

Frowning at the map, Eleanor said, "About three miles? We haven't gone through Minions yet."

Tariro relayed their position. "Bad driving conditions," he added. "Patchy fog, getting worse."

"Can you see the target vehicle?"

"No. Not for several minutes."

"Could it have turned off the road without you seeing it?"

"Yes," said Eleanor, "but none of the turnings appear to go anywhere. At least till we get to Minions, they're just farm tracks. And even the streets in Minions all seem to peter out at farms or quarries."

"They could have gone off the road and doubled back," Megan said gloomily.

"Roger, L6. L13 is coming to meet you."

"I hope he isn't going to run into us!"

Scumble's voice took over from Tina. "Pencarrow, if you meet Dawson without seeing the van, you'll have to turn back and see if you can find it. All roads east are covered, so they can't leave

Cornwall, but if they go to ground—I'm worried about the witnesses—hostages—or whatever they are."

"Believe me, sir, so am I."

"So find 'em," he growled. "Launceston, over."

Eleanor, busy with the map and with looking out for the van, had managed to put Nick's plight to the back of her mind. Now the full force of the horror flooded back. Was he still alive? And if so, what was Victor Stone's purpose in kidnapping him and poor Alan Freeth?

Freeth was going to be upset by Mrs. Mason's death. Upset, or devastated? Eleanor couldn't guess. Their relationship was still a complete mystery.

Realising her attention was wandering, she dragged it back to focus on the road ahead. The white mist, perfect camouflage for a white vehicle, eddied and swirled past as the car set it in motion. Ahead, apart from the slow, steady drift from west to east, it was still. Which must mean it hadn't been recently disturbed, which meant the van was not just ahead. But whether it had passed long enough before for the air currents to disperse or had turned off somewhere behind them, there was no way to know.

Eleanor dismissed her fruitless speculation as the Minions sign appeared. Before she spoke, Tariro had reported it.

The village might as well have been deserted for all they saw of its inhabitants, though curtained windows glowed dimly. A couple of side streets led off their road, "But they don't seem to go anywhere," said Eleanor again as they passed the Cheesewring pub, a welcoming lamp illuminating its sign. "That looks very inviting," she added wistfully.

"Doesn't it!" Tariro exclaimed.

Megan braked. "There's no reason on earth why I shouldn't drop you off here. My guv'nor would be delighted."

"Not likely!"

"No thank you, dear. I won't be able to relax until I see Nick safe and sound, and as long as I might be able to help—"

A police car with a flashing blue light pulled up next to them on the opposite side of the street, blocking it.

"Dawson," said Megan, opening her window all the way.

The detective constable had already opened his. In the passenger seat beside him, a uniformed officer was reporting their meeting. Another stepped out from the backseat, closing the door behind him.

"The guv'nor sent an extra man for you, Sarge. No sign of the van?"

"It's vanished. Must have driven off up a farm track."

The bobby in the street walked round the back of Megan's car.

Dawson tut-tutted. "If they watched you drive past and then went back the other way, we're f—fried," he amended as he noticed Eleanor's face beyond Megan.

"There's a Bodmin car on the way."

The bobby came to the front passenger door, saw Eleanor, turned towards the back door, and opened it.

Megan asked, "They couldn't have passed you in the mist?"

"Not a chance. It's pretty clear back to Launceston."

"It's coming in from the west."

The bobby slid into the backseat and yelped as Teazle greeted him with her usual enthusiasm.

"It's all right," said Tariro, "she doesn't bite."

Looking back, Eleanor saw the constable do a double-take. "U-u-uh . . ." he stuttered, fending off Teazle's licks. "Uh, I'm glad to hear it. Thank you . . . , sir."

Meanwhile, Scumble's voice came over the radio. "So between you, you've lost them? Let's hope they're just lying low. Each of you continue in the direction you're facing and investigate every possible turning."

"Yes, sir," said Megan, and Eleanor heard Dawson echo the words from the other car.

"All right, get going." As the cars began to move, he added grimly, "And in case you were wondering, Mrs. Mason's death was homicide."

In silence, Megan drove on a few hundred feet, then turned left off the road. A track, little more than wide enough for a single car, led straight ahead, and another went off to the right. Between them was a car park. She stopped.

"Homicide," said Tariro, his voice hushed. "That means it was murder?"

"Murder or manslaughter," Megan said curtly. "That's for a jury to decide. No one in the car park. We'll keep left." She continued along the track, which disappeared into the mist ahead.

A moment later, Dawson's flashing blue light appeared on their left.

"Aunt Nell?"

"The map doesn't show these tracks. The scale's too small. Or do I mean big? He must have turned back to check the side street."

Tariro pointed: "Look, there's a bit joining our track to his."

As he spoke, Dawson saw it too and turned towards them. His car and Megan's met nose-to-nose at right angles. Eleanor rolled down her window.

"Hello, Mrs. Trewynn," Dawson said cheerfully. "Sarge, d'you want us to check this one or will you?"

Megan leaned across in front of Eleanor. "You might as well, as you're on it already. For pity's sake, turn off your roof light. You can use it when you're sure you want them to know who and where you are."

"Right y'are, Sarge." The blue light went off.

"And no headlamps."

"Headlamps just reflect off the fog anyway. Good job we've got fog lamps."

They all gazed up the slope to where the low clouds met the higher ground as a solid-looking bank of dense fog, lying like a barrier across the hillside. The patches of mist they had encountered so far were mere tatters from its edge. More abandoned mine engine houses stood like watchtowers guarding the moor.

Eleanor glanced at the dashboard clock. The sun was just setting somewhere beyond the fog. Increasing darkness wasn't going to make it any easier to save Nick and Alan Freeth.

Dawson backed away at an alarming speed. At a more moderate pace, Megan continued up the track. It had grass growing up the centre. On both sides was the tough moorland grass, relieved by twisted hawthorns, patches of gorse and heather, and randomly scattered boulders.

"Your name, Constable?"

"Barnicot, Sergeant."

"Well, Barnicot, for reasons I won't go into, I have with me my aunt, Mrs. Trewynn, and . . . If we're to work together, we need names. And Mr. Tariro, whose name is not to be bandied about, Barnicot, if you value your badge."

"Mum's the word, Sarge." Not unnaturally, the constable sounded baffled. He was a comfortingly large, solid individual.

"All the windows open, please, and everyone, keep your eyes open."

As they approached the mass of fog, the track became narrower and rougher, its edges ill-defined. The car jolted over stones and into potholes. The shaking would have reduced the Incorruptible to its component parts, Eleanor thought, with a sigh, about her car, doubtless irremediably rusted by now.

The fringed edge of the fog, which had looked so solid, was as ill-defined as the track. At first, mist billowed around them, yellow in the fog lamps' glare, barely impeding visibility. It thickened as Megan drove on, until she stopped and said, "Barnicot, you're going to have to hop out and walk in front with a torch. Do you have one? Good. Otherwise, we'd end up in a bog or take out the transmission on one of those rocks."

The constable hopped. He walked on at a fast pace, keeping the torch beam playing on the driver's side of the track and casting an occasional nervous glance behind him. Megan kept the car a steady couple of yards from his boot heels.

"If they came up here and drove off the road," said Tariro, "we'll never see them."

"We have to check anyway."

"If they have any sense at all," said Eleanor, "they'll have stayed on the track. You don't know the moors, Tariro. They're full of hazards, from bogs to old mine shafts."

"Poisonous snakes? Man-eating beasts?"

Megan laughed. "You don't have to worry about any but the human beasts. And if we find them, you're to leave them to me and PC Barnicot." She paused, but if she was waiting for his consent, she didn't get it. She didn't press him. "Aunt Nell, I haven't any reason to think they're any more familiar with the perils of moorland than Tariro. They're townees."

"Victor Stone was in the prison on Dartmoor. He's sure to have heard stories about escapees lost on the moors."

"I wish I knew more about him. That type often believes mistakes are something only other people make. Too clever by half. That's why they land behind bars."

The fog thinned for a few yards. On one side, a stretch of sedge and marsh grass was a timely example of the dangers of wandering on the moor, as Eleanor pointed out to Tariro.

"Got it. Green means *don't* go."

The grey veil closed in again. PC Barnicot trudged on for a hundred feet or so, then stopped and waved the torch at the car. Megan stopped and he called out, "Looks like something went off the track here, Sarge. Can't tell how long ago."

"I'll take a look."

Tariro followed her. "Need a native tracker?"

Barnicot stared at him.

"Are you one?" Megan asked.

"No, actually. Sorry, I was being facetious."

"Pity. Take a look anyway."

The three of them bent over the side of the track, shining three torch beams on whatever Barnicot had seen. What was it? Eleanor had to know. She and Teazle went to join them.

The track veered slightly to the right at that point. Splitting off leftward was a much fainter track, a stretch a few feet wide where the grass grew thinly.

"It's where one of them old mine railways used to run," said Barnicot. "The grass still don't grow proper 'cause the rails were fixed to slabs of stone from the Cheesewring quarry. They took 'em up—the rails—for salvage in the first war."

"Thanks for the history lesson, Constable," Megan said tartly.

" 'S true. My granfer was a miner."

"I daresay. More to the point, it's obviously now more for hikers than vehicles."

"But look here, Sarge." Barnicot crouched and pointed. "If you slant your torch from the side, you can see the grass along that way is flattened-like about a wheel width apart."

"Constable Barnicot is your native tracker!" crowed Tariro.

"Well spotted, Barnicot," Megan said. "The grass would spring back quite quickly, I imagine. It does look as if they went that way."

Eleanor didn't fancy driving along the old mine railway, with barely a few inches clearance on either side. "Both tracks are going towards the Cheesewring," she pointed out. "And the one we're on is much wider. It'd be awfully easy to drive off the side of this one."

"You're right, Aunt Nell. There's a fair chance they've come to grief not too far away. Let's go and see."

Not the response Eleanor had hoped for. Suppressing a sigh, she climbed back into the car with Teazle, who gave a yip of protest.

"For pity's sake, keep her quiet, Aunt Nell. We don't want her broadcasting our approach."

Eleanor put her hand round the little dog's muzzle and said softly, "Hush!" It usually worked, at least for a while. Teazle curled up in her lap, a warm spot in the cold twilight.

Megan turned down the loudspeaker.

They jolted over the ridge. Bumping over the stone sleepers, they followed Barnicot. He walked on ahead up the middle of the path, his torch held behind him now, so that Megan could aim the car at the centre. She had little room for error.

Eleanor kept watch out to the side, staring into the fluctuating fog, straining to see into its depths, sometimes an intangible wall, sometimes pale, filmy veils. If only the murderous pair had chosen a bright-coloured van to make their getaway! The grassy ground on her side was not very different-looking from the surface of the path. If they had driven off course, they could have gone quite some way before encountering trouble.

A little farther on, the path was edged with sizeable boulders that must have been cleared out of the way to put the rails in. For a few hundred feet, Megan had no fear of going astray, but the fog closed in denser than ever, so they moved no faster. Eleanor blinked and rubbed her tired eyes.

The constable, still in the vanguard, turned and waved his torch. Megan stopped the car and he came back to speak to her.

"The rail bed's cut through solid rock just ahead, Sarge. There's stuff tumbled down from the sides that you don't want to hit."

"All right, Barnicot."

"There's a bit of a stream wandering down the slope, but it's not deep. I reckon rainfall off the hill gets funnelled down the zawn and scours it out, 'cause there's no grass growing. Plenty of mud for tyre tracks, though. For sartin sure, someone came this way since the rain last night."

"Good! You go on ahead and see how it looks farther on. "

The constable strode off. He disappeared after a couple of yards into dense fog that some quirk of nature had collected in the cutting. It was darker in its depths than on the open moor, too, the rugged walls on either side shutting out what little light remained. They were barely visible, though not much more than an arm's length from the car. How high they reached was impossible to tell.

Megan drove up the chasm at a slow but steady pace. The car jerked over unavoidable rubble, but after a short distance they were back on the grass-grown stone sleepers. The mist had once more thinned, but night was almost upon them.

Teazle raised her head. Conscious of the movement and afraid she might bark, Eleanor glanced down. "Hush, girl."

Teazle's nostrils quivered, then flared. She stood up on her back feet, front paws against the bottom of the window frame. Head high, she sniffed the air. Looking up at Eleanor, she whined.

"Megan, the dog smells something."

"A rabbit. A sheep, a horse, a fox—"

"Or a person, a person she knows." Tariro's eyes gleamed as he shifted across the seat to Eleanor's side of the car. Their gazes strove to pierce the grey veils in the near dark.

"Rubbish!"

"You never know, Megan. Do stop for just a moment."

"Look!" Tariro managed to shout in a near whisper. He pointed. "Over there. No, it's gone. No! Look!"

At that moment, Barnicot swung round and waved his torch wildly. Megan stopped the car and he came back at a run.

"They went off, Sarge! Somewhere near here. Just ahead, one of the blocks of the rail bed has sunk a bit, crooked-like. The dip's full of mud, but there's no tyre marks."

Tariro jumped out of the car.

"Stop!" Megan hissed at him. "I'm not having you disappear next." She got out and went round the front of the car to meet him. "As it is, I dread to think what Sir Edward's going to say. What did you see?"

"A light."

"Headlights?"

"No, a rectangle. Like a window, but tilted." He pointed again, and Megan stared. "It's gone again. The mist keeps moving."

"There's a bit of a breeze coming up. With luck, it'll clear out the lot."

Eleanor felt on the floor for Teazle's lead, hooked her up, and got out to join them. Teazle tugged on the lead. When Eleanor didn't follow, the little dog squatted and peed, then returned resignedly to Eleanor's side. All four humans gazed in the direction Tariro was pointing, and suddenly there it was, just as he'd described it, a tilted rectangle of pale yellowish light.

"The back doors of the van," said Megan.

"Looks like it came to grief," Barnicot suggested. "Quarter of a mile or so, I reckon. Want me to take a look, Sarge?"

"No. Let's not rush blindly into a situation we don't understand." In Megan's voice, Eleanor heard an echo of her own fear that in the back of the van they would find the bodies of Nick and Freeth.

TWENTY-ONE

Megan forced herself not to imagine Nick lying dead. She had to believe he was alive and that she could rescue him. Call for help first or find out what had happened, what was going on? She wasn't even sure the square of light was the van they sought, though the odds were very much in favour. She shuffled the pieces in her mind.

"I could reconnoitre," Tariro volunteered. "They wouldn't see me." He took off his yellow hat. In the dark, he would all but vanish.

"I'm supposed to be keeping you safe." Megan hesitated, looking at him. "Besides, you don't know the moors."

"I do," said Aunt Nell. "And I'm small. I can hide behind a gorse bush."

"Not likely! You'll stay here, Aunt Nell, and keep Teazle quiet. Barnicot, call in and report the situation. Close the windows and keep your voice down. Launceston will be listening on three. And don't mention Mr. Tariro."

"Right, Sarge."

"Okay, Tariro, I'm trusting you to do this right. Follow me and don't take a step without my say-so. Let's go."

The breath of air had died as quickly as it came up. The fog had closed down again, hiding the van, but also hiding their approach. They knew the direction roughly, and Barnicot was sure it had gone off the main track, so Megan set off, followed by Tariro, keeping to the left side, with her torch directed at the ground to her left. She shielded it with her hand to make it less visible from a distance, though Stone and his partner were not necessarily near the van. They could be anywhere within ten to fifteen minutes' walking distance.

The track was edged with boulders of all sizes and shapes, some in heaps, some scattered at irregular intervals. Walking was an irritating process, as the sleepers were just too far apart for Megan's natural stride. In between, the ground was a little bit lower and softer, and she kept almost stumbling. It wasn't far, though, before she came to a gap wide enough for a vehicle to drive through.

She stooped to look for signs. Tariro crouched beside her.

The extra pair of eyes was not needed: The muddy morass was pocked with sheep hoof marks, with nary a trace of tyre ruts. They walked on. A twisted hawthorn bush, bent and contorted by winds sweeping over the moor, loomed out of the mist, a black silhouette against the all-pervading grey. Beyond it was flat, grassy ground in all directions as far as Megan could see.

"This looks a likely place to go astray," she said in a low voice. "Seems to me, with no obvious route they'd probably have driven straight ahead. Let's have you explore straight ahead while I stay here to keep our bearings. Look back every few steps to make sure you can still see me. When another step would take you out of sight, come back."

"Whatever you say, baas."

Tariro walked away. After four strides, he glanced back. She pointed. Correcting his course slightly, he went on. After four more steps, his figure was hazy. Megan must have looked hazy to him, too. He paused, as if calculating, before taking another pace, and another.

A dark shadow, he stopped. As far as Megan could make out, he was examining his surroundings. He turned and waved to her, then took several steps to his right and bent down. He waved again and backtracked, going off to her left, westwards, in the direction of the van. If it was the van. They had no evidence but a fleeting glimpse of an unidentified light in the fog. She refused to believe they were wasting precious time following a will-o'-the-wisp.

Tariro obviously shared her sense of urgency. He came running back towards her. "They went thataway!" He pointed to the north-west.

"Did you actually see tyre marks, or are you guessing?"

"I'm theorising, based on Constable Barnicot's report that they didn't stay on the railway. It curves the other way, over there. You can tell by the sleepers, of course, even in the fog. The path I found is wide and forks off to the left. If they weren't paying attention to the bumps, they'd have had no reason to choose one branch over the other."

"Or perhaps they thought they'd be safer leaving the main track."

"Yes! Then either the path they took curves back towards the village or they drove off it."

"On purpose or by accident," Megan agreed, "or it petered out. A lot of paths on the moors just sort of fade away. But no tyre marks."

"Not that I saw. It's very short grass—grazed by sheep and ponies, judging by the—uh—droppings. I didn't see hoofprints, though, so the ground must be pretty hard."

"I expect there's bedrock under a thin layer of soil just here.

Good enough." Megan set off at a swift walk in the direction Tariro had come from.

He lagged behind. "So what next?"

"We find the van. It should be quite easy now, unless they turn off the light."

"Yes. But . . . I don't want to be a wet blanket, but how will we return to your car? It'll be pitch-dark in quarter of an hour, not to mention the fog."

"We'll find it, or they'll find us, sooner or later," Megan said impatiently. Anxiety and the need for haste drove her on. "You needn't come."

"Of course I'll come, but just wait half a tick while I tie my handkerchief on that bush." He darted back to the hawthorn.

"Good idea. I'm sorry I snapped."

"You're worried about your friends. I understand. It can't be far now."

They soon found proof of Tariro's theory in a muddy patch: tyre marks overlying the prints of sheep and ponies and what might have been a fox. The path veered more and more to the north, away from the village, rising steadily.

"It's not going towards where we saw the van," Megan said in dismay.

"Shall we turn back?"

"Yes. But not all the way to the hawthorn. That'd be pointless. Turn off your torch for a moment. It's so dark now, we might be able to spot the light even through the mist."

After a few seconds, their eyes adjusted. The fog seemed less impenetrably dark. Megan checked her luminous watch dial. Though the sun had set, the faint afterglow filtered down, directionless, the particles of moisture scattering the light. They stared down the slope.

"There!" Again, Tariro was the first to spot the van. They were facing its side, not the rear, but the light inside cast a pool of illumination on the ground and reflected dimly from the nearby mist. "It doesn't look as if the headlamps are on. I wonder why they left the doors open and the light on. The battery must be running down."

Megan started off in a straight line towards the van. "Let's go and find out. Come on."

"No torches?"

"No torches. We don't need them to follow a track now. There's still just enough light to see obstacles." She promptly tripped over a stone.

Tariro caught her arm. "Careful!"

"I was talking instead of looking. Thanks."

He switched on his torch and shaded it with his hand. Beyond the stone was a dark pool bordered by mire pocked with pony-hoof prints. Megan would have landed flat on her face in it if he hadn't saved her. She didn't comment when he kept his torch on.

They circled the muck, widdershins because on its left were a bank of reeds and a massive boulder. By the time they cleared it, the fog had thickened between them and the van and it was once more invisible.

"That way," said Tariro.

"I think it's more that way. We'll split the difference and we should end up close enough to see the damn thing."

The downward slope was steeper than Megan recalled having walked up. It took them into a narrow valley they had certainly not crossed before. Along the bottom, a belt of sedges marked the presence of a bog or a small brook. A rift in the fog gave them a view of a drystone wall marching across the farther slope. From beyond came the sleepy bleats of sheep settling down for the night.

CAROLA DUNN

"Oh hell," Megan said wearily. "They couldn't have driven through that lot."

"Unless there's a bridge and a gate. Which way now?"

"Damned if I know. One thing's certain: We won't spot the van from down there, fog or no fog. We'll cut diagonally back up the hill and hope to get high enough to see something recognisable. If we happen to come across the railway, we'll follow it back to the car and start again. Sorry. I seem to have made an almighty mess of this."

"Not to worry," said Tariro, infuriatingly cheerful. "It's a side of England I haven't seen before. Though perhaps *seen* is the wrong word, as I haven't seen anything much but fog. *Experienced* would be more accurate."

Megan nearly snapped at him, but after all, he didn't have a friend in deadly peril. He had never even met Nick. Aware that he might be marching into danger, he had volunteered to help. Why shouldn't he regard it as no more than an interesting expedition?

"I just hope we find your friends safe and sound," he added, heaping coals of fire, especially as, in her fear for Nick, she had almost forgotten Freeth. "We should have brought Teazle with us. I bet she could have led us straight to the van."

"She may have caught a trace of Nick's scent. She knows him very well. Or it might have been just a rabbit."

"What we need is the hound of the Baskervilles. Don't the police have search dogs? . . . Ouch!" He had heedlessly brushed against a gorse bush. "Dammit, what's that?"

"Gorse. 'Furze,' some people call it. A hazard Aunt Nell didn't warn you about. No leaves, only prickles. It looks like a big patch. We'll have to go round it."

By the time they had circled the thicket, Megan was more dis-

{ 208 }

orientated than ever. If the guv'nor sent for the canine team—which sounded like an excellent idea—they would have to search for her and Tariro as well as the villains and their victims. She could just imagine the flak she'd take for that, from both Scumble and her colleagues.

The brow of the hill was visible ahead, a dark curve against the fog. The contrast was greater than Megan would have expected. A pallid luminescence suffused the veils of mist. On the far side of the ridge, a light was shining, a light brighter than the van's interior.

"Headlamps? Theirs or ours? I said to keep them off, but at this point I wouldn't quibble."

They reached the top.

"The moon!" Tariro exclaimed.

"So that's east. I wouldn't have guessed. Which way is the van from here, would you say?"

He shrugged, then turned slowly through a full circle, as if estimating the route they had walked. "Southwest? But it's pure guesswork."

"We don't seem to have any choice." Megan stretched out her arm in front of him. "We're on the edge of a quarry. Don't take a step forward. Look."

The ground in front of them levelled off for a few feet, then came to an abrupt end.

"Whew! Lucky we stopped to take our bearings. And lucky the moon has risen! Is this the Cheesewring that Mrs. Trewynn and the constable were talking about?"

"Could be, but I rather think not. There are several quarries in the area. The Cheesewring is cut into quite a high hill and I don't think we've climbed that high. Also, it has two or three tors at the top. I would have thought we'd be able to see at least one.

There seems to be a sort of path here, parallel to the edge. We'd better follow it, but for goodness' sake, walk carefully."

"Don't worry, I will. What's a tor? And, come to that, does Cheesewring mean something?"

"A tor is a stack of enormous, flattish boulders balanced in a pile at the crest of a hill. The legends say they were heaped up by giants. They sort of look like an old cheese press, or at least the biggest local one does. That's *wring* with a *w*, as in squeeze out the whey. That's *whey* with an *he*."

"Little Miss Muffet . . . I learned that at school and always wondered what curds and whey are, but never wondered hard enough to look it up."

"Now you know as much as I do. Careful, there's some loose stones here. It's a bit slippery."

They safely negotiated the bad patch. The path became steeper. The sheer edge came to an end, but the slope on that side was too steep and rocky to walk down.

Ahead, the ground flattened. The footpath widened slightly and continued in more or less the same direction. It wound about a good deal, skirting outcrops, narrowing between banks of dead bracken, sometimes hard to distinguish from the grass it crossed. When in doubt, Megan kept to her right. Sooner or later, whether they came across the van or not, they would reach the road and at least would know where they were.

A shadow moved. Startled, Megan gasped, then realised they had come upon a small herd of ponies. In the diffuse moonlight, they stood with drooping heads, seemingly drowsing on their feet. One was alert, a large piebald that stopped cropping the grass, stamped a hoof, and whickered. The dozers raised their heads; a couple lying down awoke and scrambled to their feet.

"They're bigger than I expected," Tariro whispered. "Do they bite? Will they stampede?"

"They're used to people," Megan said hopefully. "They usually just move aside if you get closer than they like."

The two of them must have looked singularly unthreatening, because the ponies just stared at them, scarcely twitching the odd ear. Megan took a step forward. They shifted uneasily. She walked slowly and steadily forward, Tariro close at her heels, and they parted before her, ambling to one side or the other.

The last two moved apart to let them through.

"The van!" they exclaimed in unison, Tariro's voice as hushed as Megan's, to her relief. She had instinctively ducked behind a gorse bush, and he followed suit.

The white van was no more than twenty yards away, facing them. Megan saw it plainly through the straggly gorse. The headlamps were off, so she couldn't see whether one was yellow glass, but there was little doubt in her mind.

Nothing stirred except the ever-shifting mist. The only sound came from the ponies cropping grass.

"You're not a copper," Megan whispered. "I can't tell you what to do. But I would very much appreciate it if you would go and see if anyone's in the cab of the van."

"Of course. I offered, didn't I?" He dropped to his knees and started to crawl round the bush. "I'll circle round and approach on driver's side."

"Go carefully!"

And then a piercing shriek sliced through the quiet night.

"Ye gods!" Tariro stopped in his tracks. "What was that? Not . . ."

"I *hope* it was a rabbit caught by a fox or stoat."

"Are you sure?"

"No." Urgency gripped her. "Go on. Count off fifteen seconds, then stop and watch the van while I catch up. If anything moves, give a *pssst*. Got it?"

"Got it."

He slithered away. Counting, she kept her eyes on the van. Nothing moved. The only sound was the *tu-whit* of an owl. She hoped it wouldn't catch a rabbit within earshot. Another scream like that would shred her taut nerves to tatters.

Fifteen. On hands and knees, she set off after Tariro, glad she was wearing gloves.

Once past the gorse, she looked for him. Hatless, in jeans and a dark pullover, he was invisible. Guessing, she crawled onward. She managed not to put her hands in any pony droppings, but sheep and rabbit pellets were unavoidable.

How far could he go in fifteen seconds? Either farther than she'd expected or she had missed him. Should she change course?

So still was he sitting, cross-legged, that she almost bumped her nose on his knee.

She straightened up and gauged the van's position. From here she couldn't see the offside headlamp. "Nothing?"

"Nothing."

"All right, make it ten seconds this time."

He pointed the way he intended to go and then was gone, melding into the darkness.

. . . *Eight. Nine. Ten.* This time the hazard wasn't animal droppings, it was random rocks strewn in Megan's path. The larger ones were easy to avoid but she put her knee down painfully on a small one. If one could be said to limp while crawling, she limped the rest of the way.

Tariro crouched at right angles to the side of the van, about halfway along. "I'll approach the window from behind. Okay?"

"Perfect. Remember Stone's an expert with a sandbag."

"I'll remember, but I'm not exactly sure what it is."

"A long bag filled with sand. It may not sound like much, but he can kill with it. He won't have much room to use it, though, and as far as I can see, the window's closed, which will limit him still more. But watch out."

"Yes, baas."

"If you see someone, come straight back to me. Unless they see you, in which case get out of here as fast as you can."

He grinned. "Yes, baas."

The next she saw of him was a silhouette against the white door of the van, rising from the ground. She held her breath as the top of his head reached and passed the bottom of the window.

He stayed there, looking into the cab rather than racing for safety. Megan breathed again.

Half a minute later, he was back at her side, shaking his head. "Empty. That is, I can't swear there's no one hiding on the floor on the other side, but I'm pretty sure. The back now!"

"Yes. Will you go to the far side? Not that I ought to let you—"

"Try to stop me."

"—but you crawl faster."

"Boy Scouts. What are we going to do?"

"We'll go up under cover of the open doors. Try not to touch the van."

"Fingerprints?"

"Fingerprints. After that, it depends whether we can hear anything. If they're in there and talking, we'll listen. My 'baas' told me to find out the situation, not to rush in and grab them."

"Pity!"

"If you hear nothing, wait for two minutes just in case. Then we'll back away and move off. How far would you say we can go and still see who—or what—is in the back?"

"Standing?"

"Probably, though there's an upward slope, so maybe not."

"Thirty feet? Twenty-five? Unless the fog closes down."

"Make it thirty. It'll be guesswork anyway. We can always move closer. Let's go."

Megan's knee hurt. She hoped she wouldn't have to do much more crawling. It was a relief to stand up behind the cover of the van's back door. She listened.

The silence was so profound, she ought to be able to hear field mice scampering through the bracken. She shivered, only partly from cold.

Cold and silent as death . . .

One hundred and twenty, said the automatic counter in her head. She managed not to groan as she sank to her knees again. Crawling away from the van, she felt her back exposed as a target. The Sandman was unlikely to carry a gun—villains tended to stick to their own tried-and-true methods. But his pal was an unknown quantity. That he was just a con man was a guess based unreliably on his looks.

Megan found Tariro, already seated cross-legged facing the van. His expression was unreadable. Reluctantly she sat beside him.

"Empty. I'm sorry we haven't found your friends."

Panic threatened. She must not panic. *Police officers do not panic.* "At least we haven't found them dead. I must get back to my car to report." Turning her back on the van, picturing how it had looked from the car, she set off in what she hoped was the right direction.

Tariro didn't question her choice. "What I don't understand," he said, "is why they abandoned it. Leaving the light on, which will run down the battery."

"I hadn't thought of that, but I've got plenty of other questions. For a start, why bring Nick and Freeth with them? No, to go back further, what was their connection with Mrs. Mason that led to her death? Because it's obvious it wasn't just a burglary gone wrong. But the only important question now is where are Nick and Freeth?"

"And," Tariro said soberly, "wherever they are, are they still alive?"

TWENTY-TWO

Eleanor and PC Barnicot had watched Megan and Tariro disappear into the fog, Eleanor seething with impatience. She was sure she and Teazle knew this bit of Bodmin Moor better than Megan, let alone Tariro. Even though they didn't come this way very often, she was familiar with the relative positions of the main landmarks: the village; the Hurlers stone circles; Stowe's Hill, with the Cheesewring quarry and other, lesser diggings; and the engine houses.

In spite of the fog, now hiding, now revealing, her knowledge might help.

At least Megan realised that on the moors a straight line was rarely the shortest way between two points. If they managed to follow the van's trail, they ought to be all right.

"I don't like it." Barnicot sounded both affronted and uneasy. "I don't like the sergeant going off alone with that coloured laddie."

"Tariro."

"She oughter've taken me along. It's my job. This Truro fellow's not a copper. Leastways, he's not from Scotland Yard, is he? I heard tell there's a CID man came down to these parts."

CAROLA DUNN

"That's a rumour you should not pass on. *If it's true, you should assume he doesn't want it generally known.*" *Rather neatly phrased,* Eleanor congratulated herself. "Shouldn't you report to Mr. Scumble? That's what Megan left you here to do."

A bit chilled from standing still, she got into the car, and Teazle hopped up on her lap. She closed the door carefully, with the tiniest click, wound up the window, then displaced the dog to reach back and close the rear window.

Barnicot didn't immediately get in. He stood staring after Megan and Tariro, then turned to gaze in the direction of the van's brief appearance. It was none of Eleanor's business to tell him what to do, but she was on the point of doing just that when at last he tired of looking at fog and got in.

He turned down the volume on the radio and reluctantly picked up the thingamajig—microphone, was it? Transmitter?

"Launceston, this is L6. PC Barnicot reporting."

In spite of the lowered volume, Eleanor could hear the voice at the other end. "Hold on, L6. DCI Scumble wants to talk to you."

Half a minute later: "Barnicot? Where the hell is Pencarrow?"

"That's what I called to tell you, sir."

"Well, get on with it, Constable! Where is she?"

"Umm, I don't know exactly, sir."

The response was an inarticulate explosion at the other end.

Eleanor took the microphone from his hand. "Mr. Scumble," she said severely, hoping she'd pressed the right button, "this is Eleanor Trewynn. Will you please let Mr. Barnicot explain? It's not simple."

"All right, all right. Why don't *you* tell me, Mrs. Trewynn. Do you know where your niece is?"

"No, and I very much doubt whether she does. It's easy enough to lose one's bearings on the moor without fog. We saw what ap-

BURIED IN THE COUNTRY

peared to be the van we've been following, just momentarily before the fog hid it again. They—she went to investigate. She disappeared from our sight almost immediately. So we know roughly where she's aiming at, but not, as Constable Barnicot said, exactly where she is."

"They? Who's 'they'?"

Oh botheration, Eleanor thought. That had been a nasty slip of the tongue. Cravenly, she gave the mike back to Barnicot.

"The black bloke, sir, with the funny name. He went with Sergeant Pencarrow."

During the ensuing silence, Eleanor was pretty sure she couldn't actually hear heavy breathing over the radio, not with the volume turned down, but she was also pretty sure that was what was going on.

In a carefully controlled voice, the DCI said, "I'd appreciate it if you'd keep that information to yourself, Constable. Not to be mentioned to a soul. Can you tell me what DS Pencarrow's plans are when and if she finds and identifies the van?"

"To come back here, sir, and report."

"She's not thinking of attempting to collar the suspects, she and the . . . person you mentioned?"

"Oh no, sir. You told her not to."

"And I would have told her to keep the young man out of it, had I thought for a moment that— But it's no use crying over spilt milk. I suppose it's no use asking how long she'll be gone."

"The van wasn't too far away, sir. But the fog—some places it's really thick."

"Bugger the fog. Beg pardon, Mrs. Trewynn—you're listening in, I presume? Last time we had trouble on the moor, I put in a request for compasses, but have we got 'em? We have not. Tell the sergeant to call in immediately when she gets back. I can't pull any men off the road watch till I know what's what. You'd better report every five minutes. Over."

The constable hung up the transmitter and sat staring glumly out at the fog. There was nothing else to see.

Eleanor endured the silence as long as she could, then asked, "Do you live in Launceston, Mr. Barnicot?"

He gave her a suspicious frown. "Why?"

"I'm just trying to make conversation."

"Oh. No, madam, in Egloskerry."

"Are you their village policeman?"

"No, I'm stationed at Launceston HQ. I've got a motorbike."

"Oh." Eleanor didn't know enough about motorbikes to ask any sensible questions. "How convenient."

Unlike many young men with motorbikes, Barnicot did not elaborate on the glories of his machine. Eleanor decided that any more questions would begin to sound like interrogation or nosy-parkerism.

She gave up on conversation but ventured to say, "Don't you think it might be a little warmer with all the windows up?"

"They'll all fog up."

Which wouldn't make much difference to overall visibility. "I suppose so. I'm getting cold. I'm going to walk the dog a bit."

"I don't think that's a good idea."

"Why not?"

"You might get lost."

"I won't. The dog would always be able to find our way back here. But if you want, I'll stick to the tracks. I'll even stay within sight of the car and just go round and round it."

"I still don't think that's a good idea. It's my job to keep you safe."

"No, it isn't. Megan never said anything of the sort. I'm quite capable of taking care of myself, thank you. Besides, if she'd taken you with her, Tariro and I would have been alone here and could have done whatever we wanted." She got out quickly before he realised that argument was a two-edged sword, since Megan had, in fact, left him behind.

She was about to let Teazle off the lead, knowing she would come when called, but realised just in time that shouting the dog's name might well bring unwanted attention.

Had Megan taken into account that if the van was stranded, the villains would be looking for alternative transportation? A police car might not be their first choice, even an unmarked one, but needs must when the devil drives, and the devil was certainly driving those two. Megan hadn't warned Barnicot of the possibility. Perhaps she had thought it too obvious to mention. Eleanor wasn't sure the constable was capable of working it out for himself. His acuity with regard to tyre tracks didn't mean he wasn't as thick as two planks in other respects.

Should she draw it to his attention? He'd be justifiably annoyed if he was already aware of the danger. On the other hand, even if he wasn't, he'd be annoyed to have a little old lady teaching him his business.

There must be a tactful way . . . Eleanor's working life had been based on the premise that there was always a tactful way to present information the listener would prefer not to hear.

She returned to the car, approaching the driver's side, where Barnicot was sitting. He had rolled down the windows she had closed, she noted.

He saw her in the side mirror and said gloomily, "Don't blame me if you get sandbagged."

"How likely is it, would you say, that Stone and Co. will try to steal this car?"

"Not very, but you'd be surprised at the stupid things crooks try on. That's why I'm sitting here with an open radio channel to Launceston. Even if they was to try, see, they wouldn't get far before they was picked up. Unless they bash you on the head and use you as a hostage."

"They already have two hostages. Besides, they couldn't get near me unnoticed. Teazle would bark at the first sign of anyone she doesn't recognise. She can smell someone coming long before I can hear them, far less see them in these conditions."

"That's as may be. I still wish you'd come and sit in the car. Tell you what, I'll check if there's a rug in the boot. Patrol cars mostly keep one for accident victims. For shock and that. Dunno about unmarked cars, but I'll take a look-see."

He produced a hideous red-and-green tartan blanket. Eleanor gave in. Well wrapped, she sat beside him and of course found herself, like him, staring fruitlessly into the mist. She noticed that he regularly checked the rearview mirror and both wing mirrors. No one was going to creep up on him unseen.

After a few minutes, Barnicot radioed to report no change in the situation.

"The boss is getting impatient," the operator told him.

"Nothing I can do about it. I'll check back in five minutes, unless they turn up sooner."

"Okay. I'm not going anywhere. Over."

"How long since Megan and Tariro left?" Eleanor asked.

"Twenty minutes."

"How long before Mr. Scumble decides they're lost and sends reinforcements?"

The constable shrugged. "How much longer would you give them?"

"In normal circumstances, I'd probably wait to see if they turned up in the morning before I kicked up a fuss. Given a couple of murderers wandering out there with them, I'd have as many searchers as I could get hold of out there right now."

"If my guv'nor knew for certain the murderers are here . . . But he doesn't want to call off the road patrols when there's still a chance the van we spotted may be the wrong 'un and the right one is still trying to escape with a couple of kidnap victims aboard. I'm glad it's not up to me to choose."

Eleanor admitted to herself that she had misjudged him based on his inability or unwillingness to indulge in small talk. "Any idea how long he's going to wait?" she asked meekly.

"You heard Tina say he's getting impatient."

"So am I," said Eleanor, wondering whether Teazle could be persuaded to hunt for Megan. She was very good at tracking rabbits, but what they really needed was a bloodhound. Or a police dog, as Tariro had suggested. "Jay!"

"Whassat?"

"Sergeant Ajay Nayak. The Indian policeman from Kenya who joined CaRaDoC. He took up dog handling."

"Oh, him. Based in Bodmin, he is, being in the middle of the moor and most likely to be useful. I dessay they'll send for him. I've heard the dog's a proper wonder. Kelly, it's called."

"Kali."

"Prob'ly a Carly Simon fan." He flashed his shielded torch at the dashboard clock. "Time to call in. L6 reporting."

"Still no sign of them, I take it."

"Not a whisker."

"Half a mo. Here's Mr. Scumble."

"Constable, I'm directing L13 to join you immediately. Describe exactly how to reach your position."

"I . . . er . . . I'm not exactly sure, sir. I was in the backseat. I didn't see which turning the sergeant took."

DCI Scumble adopted his infuriating long-suffering tone: "Give me Mrs. Trewynn."

"Yes, sir."

"Hello, Mr. Scumble. I can explain the first part, but about half-way here, Constable Barnicot started walking ahead to lead the way. Because of the fog. So he can best tell you that bit."

"Whatever you say, Mrs. Trewynn." His ultra-patient voice was even more infuriating. "Tina's ready to take it all down. Or half of it, as the case may be. Go ahead. Please."

Eleanor complied. When she reached the point where Megan had sent the constable to walk ahead, she said, "Mr. Barnicot can take over from here, but you know, it's difficult to describe the way. It might be best if he walks down to meet them." And while he was gone, she might as well take Teazle for a little walk, just in case Megan and Tariro were in the vicinity.

"No!" Scumble quashed her scheme instantly. She should have guessed he'd still be listening in. "I'm not letting any more people loose to wander about in the fog on Bodmin's patch! Put Barnicot on."

On Bodmin's patch—Eleanor remembered Megan mentioning more than once that Scumble was at daggers drawn with the Bodmin superintendent. He'd hate having to ask for help, as protocol dictated, in hunting for not only a pair of villains and a pair of hostages but one or two of his own subordinates. And an Official Secret. How long would he wait?

If Megan and Tariro didn't turn up soon—

Teazle yipped and stood up on her back feet, her paws on the window edge. Was it Eleanor's imagination, or had the fog thinned a bit? Two dark figures came down the slope towards the car.

"Here they are!"

"Who?" demanded Barnicot, who appeared to have been unable to concentrate on keeping watch while recalling and describing their route. "Could be the—"

"Teazle would be barking her head off if they were strangers."

"DS Pencarrow is back, Tina."

"You heard that, sir? . . . Yes, sir. Finish the directions, please, Constable."

"That's about it. We're just past the end of the ravine. For chrissake, tell the Speed Demon to take it carefully! Here's the sergeant." He scrambled out of the car and Megan sank into the driver's seat.

"Tina?"

"Glad you're safe, Megan. Here's Mr. Scumble."

"What took you so long, Pencarrow? Never mind, rhetorical question. What's up?"

Eleanor listened with dismay to Megan's brief report. She and Tariro had found the right van. That was hardly surprising; who else would be out here on a foggy night? The van was empty, apparently abandoned, no sign of Stone or his partner, no sign of Nick or Freeth.

Nick was more than a mere neighbour to Eleanor, more like a favourite nephew. She was far fonder of him than of Megan's brother, who had enthusiastically joined the rat race and was some kind of broker in the City of London, with a glossy wife whose picture often appeared in _Tatler_. Eleanor rarely bothered to notify them when she spent a few days in town.

She cherished a secret hope that someday Nick and Megan would realise how ideally suited to each other they were, despite the unlikely mix of an artist and a police officer. Recently the odds had seemed to be improving. . . .

And now Nick was somewhere out on the moor, injured or dead. Megan was holding up well so far, speaking in a clear, steady voice, but the search was going to test her stiff upper lip.

"All right, Pencarrow, Bodmin's sending searchers from Liskeard. They're on their way and should be with you in fifteen to twenty minutes. It'll take nearly half an hour for the people from Bodmin to reach you. Our people will trickle in, depending on where they're patrolling. I'll be there soon as I can make it, but don't wait for me. Till then, you're in charge, and don't let any jumped-up inspector from Bodmin tell you otherwise, so get busy planning your search. Questions?"

"No, sir."

They signed off.

"I hear DC Dawson's car, Sarge," said Barnicot.

"Go and wave your torch at him so he doesn't run into our bumper."

One of many questions had risen to the top of Eleanor's mind. "Megan, why Alan Freeth?"

"For the same reason as Nick," Megan said impatiently. "They saw Mrs. Mason killed."

"Not that. Why was he there? Why did she send for him and why did he stay so long?"

"Aunt Nell, I've got a search to organise. You know the terrain hereabouts. Can you describe the lie of the land?"

"In broad terms, it goes uphill from the village to the north and northwest, getting steeper and steeper. The top's called Stowe's Hill. The biggest quarry, the Cheesewring, is at the nearer end of the hill. From the west end of the village, it's a more gradual slope. That's where the Hurlers are, the three ancient standing-stone circles. To the east, it slopes down to a river valley. The Linney, I think, but I wouldn't swear to it. Is that what you want?"

"Perfect."

"There are the mine engine houses all over the place, not to mention bogs—"

"Tariro and I encountered a couple. People will just have to avoid them and keep the line as much as they can. Thanks, Aunt Nell." She leaned over to kiss Eleanor's cheek, then got out and walked back to join Barnicot and Dawson.

Eleanor turned to Tariro, who had settled in the back of the car. "I can't just sit here. I'm going to go and take a look for myself. Before Mr. Scumble arrives."

"I'll go with you," Tariro said eagerly.

"Better not. He'll be angry that I've gone, but if you went missing, he'd burst a blood vessel. You can tell him I'm searching, not kidnapped. And as Megan already let you go with her, I daresay she will again. She's going to need everyone she can get."

He sighed. "If you say so. Don't get lost."

"The fog seems to be lifting a bit." In fact, it appeared to be crawling up the slope. The blanket of cloud was rising to higher elevations for some obscure but doubtless explicable meteorological reason.

"What will you do, out there alone, if you find one of them?"

"I've got the torch I used for reading the map. A police torch. It's really bright. I'll wave it until someone sees it. Also—" She felt in her pocket. "Yes, I've got a little whistle. A friend gave it to me. She's a vicar's wife and rather old-fashioned in some ways. She doesn't think it's quite dignified for an old lady like me to be shouting in public for my dog. I promised to try to remember to take it when I walk Teazle, though I'm afraid I've never taught her to come to it, so I never use it. Between the torch and the whistle, some-one will notice."

"That's all very well, but you're forgetting you may find the crooks, not your friends."

"Don't you worry about that," Eleanor said with confidence. "I can handle them."

TWENTY-THREE

"The guv'nor's on his way," Megan told Dawson as he handed her a two-way personal radio. The one already weighing down her pocket was a twin to the one she had lent Ken, on a different frequency and useless to her now. She must remember to dump it in the car. "So let's get this show on the road."

"Sooner the better."

"We're going to have a lot more cars arriving." Dawson's car was close behind hers, its boot not quite clear of the narrow ravine. "They'll have trouble getting out of their vehicles back there, even though the fog seems to be just about gone. Barnicot, take the car up the track to where the van turned off."

"Can I use the headlights, Sarge?"

"Umm . . . yes. They'll know very soon we're here, if they haven't worked it out already."

Dawson told the constable who had stayed with him to drive on, following Barnicot. Before Megan's car started to move, Tariro jumped out and came back to join Megan and the DC.

"Who the—"

"Mr. Anonymous," Megan said quickly. "Don't ask. He's part of

an unrelated job I was on when this business came up. T—
Mr. Anon, this is Detective Constable Dawson."

"Alias the Speed Demon?" Tariro's grin flashed.

"That's me. I'll take you for a spin sometime and—"

"Come on, fellas, enough gossip. We've got a job of work to do."
Megan hurried them along after the cars.

Both motors shut off. Their footsteps, even Dawson's heavy
tread, made very little sound. In the hush, a distant hum made
itself heard.

Dawson cocked his head. "A car."

"Coming this way." Tariro swung round, his hand cupping his
ear. "Fast. From the way we came, I'm pretty sure, Megan."

"Reinforcements from Liskeard. I hope they've had the sense
to bring a six-inch map. I didn't think to suggest it to the guv'nor."

"Six inches to the mile?" Tariro asked. "Wouldn't they keep
them in their cars? For when they have to rescue hikers lost on
the moors?"

"That's mostly volunteer search-and-rescue people," Dawson explained. "They must have at least one at the Liskeard nick, though."

"Nick?"

"Cop shop. Police station."

"I hope so," said Megan, "and that they think to bring it, because
any sketch map I produced from what my aunt's told me wouldn't
be detailed nor, probably, very accurate."

Tariro was a step or two ahead when they reached the cars. He
stopped and looked back. Megan and Dawson also turned to watch
for the Liskeard car. Some trick of the atmosphere had dissipated
the ground mist. The cloud cover had thickened, though, and
hung low overhead. It now hid the moon, and the night was ap-
preciably darker.

Barnicot and the other uniform joined them. Megan expected

Aunt Nell, too, but she didn't come. She must be tired. She usually had so much energy, one forgot her age, but she had had a very active day accompanied by exhausting emotions.

"I hope my aunt isn't getting cold, sitting in the car."

"Mr. Barnicot gave her a rug," said Tariro.

"She must've got into the backseat and gone to sleep—the little dog, too, 'cause I didn't hear a peep out of either of 'em just now."

"That's funny. Teazle—"

"Look!" Tariro interrupted. "Isn't that headlights turning off the road?"

They were high enough on the hillside to see over the eastern slope of the mound through which the route had been blasted for the railway. The five watchers saw the car come up the track, hesitate at the Y-junction, take the left branch, and disappear into the cutting, the sound of its engine muffled.

The Liskeard driver was a cautious man, taking the rock-strewn path at a snail's pace. It seemed a long time before the twin beams appeared at the mouth of the ravine and approached up the slope, bumping over the sleepers.

"Dang it!" he said when he got out of the panda. "That's not done my bleddy suspension any good." He caught sight of Megan. "Begging your pardon, ma'am."

The uniformed sergeant who emerged from the front passenger seat said crisply, "DS Pencarrow? Sergeant Roberts, from Liskeard. We're at your orders."

Megan had already decided not to wait for her entire force to arrive. Her sense of urgency was far too great. "Thank you, Sergeant. This is DC Dawson."

"We've met. Wotcher, mate."

"Have you got a large-scale OS map?"

Roberts dived headfirst back into the car and produced a map.

Megan unfolded it on the warm bonnet of his car. She, Roberts, and Dawson pored over it, with Tariro peering over their shoulders.

The lie of the land was just as Aunt Nell had described it, here shown in detail, footpaths, bogs, and all. Seeing it didn't alter Megan's plan, which was as devoid of specifics as her sketch map. She would make sure all searchers had a good look at the section of the OS map for the area they were responsible for covering. After that, it was up to them to avoid the hazards they were bound to come across.

"Megan, the van just disappeared."

She swung round to stare at Tariro. "What the hell . . ." She followed his pointing finger. "Disappeared? What do you mean?"

"I've been keeping half an eye on it."

"It drove away?"

"No, no. The light started flickering a couple of minutes ago, and it just went out. Sorry to alarm you."

"It wasn't the doors closing? You're sure?"

"Ninety-nine percent."

"Battery ran down, I shouldn't wonder," said the Liskeard bobby, "or the lightbulb's kaput."

"Could be. Ta—Mr. Anon, can you pinpoint its position on the map?" Megan was already pretty sure she could, but she wanted to know if he agreed.

He bent over the map, studied it for a minute, then pointed. "Just about there?" he said uncertainly.

"That's more or less where I'd put it. You"—she turned to Roberts's driver—"what's your name?"

"Johnson, Sergeant."

"Johnson, you were bemoaning possible damage to your transmission. Does that mean you know about cars?"

"Spends all his spare time tinkering with 'em," said Sergeant Roberts. "He's got ambitions to be another Speed Demon, too."

"Does he, now!" Dawson exclaimed.

"Johnson, can you read maps?"

"Er . . . road maps, Sergeant."

"So you can't read this map? Mr. Anon, take a good look at it, please, and then escort this would-be demon to the van, preferably by a shorter route than you and I took."

Tariro studied the map, consulted the key to the symbols, traced out a route with his finger, and announced confidently, "I foresee no insuperable difficulty, if we may use torches. It's much darker now."

Megan wondered what Scumble would do. If the killers were on the lookout, they must know by now that there was a significant police presence. "Yes, use torches. And look about you on the way. As we have no idea why they took hostages, or why they removed them from the van, they could have left them absolutely anywhere. When you get there, I want to know whether it is in fact disabled, and what's wrong with it. And if either of you smudges any prints or destroys other evidence . . ." She left the threat hanging. "Oh, and if the keys are in it, I want them. Pick them up carefully with a handkerchief and bring them here. Come back here to report anyway, unless someone urgently needs your help."

"Right, baas. Let's go, Officer."

While she gave them her orders—or in Tariro's case, instructions—Roberts was talking on the radio in his car. He came back and told her, "Two cars from Bodmin just reached Minions. They weren't sure where to turn off the road, but I've set 'em straight. Should be here in a couple of minutes."

"Did they bring Sergeant Nayak and the dog?"

"Yes, and there's an ambulance following them."

"Good." But it was an unpleasant reminder that at best Nick and Freeth would be found suffering from concussion; at worst . . . She wasn't going to think about at worst. She had a job to do.

Her own car's radio called for attention.

"I'll get it, Sarge." Dawson hurried to the front of the queue of cars. A moment later he called, "The chief inspector wants a word, Sarge. Launceston's patched his car through." He handed over the mike.

"Pencarrow, sir."

"Give me an update, Pencarrow."

She told him about the Bodmin contingents, those present and those about to arrive. "Including the dog and his handler, sir."

"Your Indian pal, eh? Good, good. How's the African gentleman doing?"

"Cheerful, sir." Enjoying himself no end.

"I've heard through channels that Sir Edward Bellowe is not happy. Too bad. I told him we can't spare a driver to take his chap back to Tintagel. You've got my backing if he kicks up a fuss. But that's by the way. Two of our patrol cars are nearly with you. I'm inclined to tell 'em to block the road a mile or so outside Minions, in both directions. It strikes me that your villains, if they're not completely clueless, will make for the village, hoping to pinch another vehicle. Assuming theirs really is disabled."

"I sent one of the Liskeard officers, a car nut, to check the van, sir. I hate to lose any searchers, but roadblocks sound like a good idea."

"Right. Carry on. I'll be with you in about ten minutes."

Megan remembered to drop off the superfluous two-way in the car. That was when she realised her aunt wasn't there.

"Aunt Nell?" No answer. She'd probably "gone behind a bush" not too far off, but a discreet distance from the swarms of coppers. No doubt she'd be back any minute, begging to be allowed to join the search. Megan hadn't time to worry about her. She hurried back to greet the newcomers.

One of the Bodmin vehicles was a minibus with a dozen or so officers aboard, including a uniformed sergeant in charge, the other a car into which they had crammed five large men. They had brought three more six-inch maps of the area.

A moment later, a van drove up behind them: Sergeant Nayak with his black-and-tan Alsatian.

Megan reminded them all that two murderous crooks were out there, as well as the two victims. She quickly sorted them into pairs and sent them off in different directions to start combing the moor, all but DC Dawson and Jay and his dog. Kali sat at attention and watched, her eyes alert.

"Jay, it's my understanding that Kali needs a scent to follow, right?"

"It is more efficient, certainly. Otherwise, she is not a great deal better than a man."

Dawson snorted.

"You'll have to let her sniff around inside the van, then. It's more important to find these people than to preserve trace evidence. Anyway, I'm an eyewitness."

"I myself need not enter the vehicle, Megan. Kali's paw prints will not confuse the SOCO team. They are not here yet?"

"No. I assume they're in Tintagel, where the murder took place. If you haven't heard the whole story, DC Dawson can tell you, as he's about to show you the way to the van. Dawson, I hope you were watching when Ta—Mr. Anon pointed out the way."

"Uh . . ."

"Come and look now." Megan heard herself using Scumble's too-patient tone.

"Stay," Jay told Kali, who sat still while Megan showed the two men the path Tariro had traced.

"Jay, you've done searches on the moor before? You're aware of the dangers?"

"Yes, to be sure. Kali will not let me step into a bog."

"I hope not. Dawson, call me on the two-way when you meet the two who went to the van. They should be on their way back by now, if Johnson is half as clever as he claims. And when Sergeant Nayak—or rather, Kali—is finished with the van, stick with them."

"Sure you won't need me back here, Sarge?" Dawson asked hopefully.

"I need you to assist Sergeant Nayak with whatever Kali finds."

They left. Megan weighted down the map with several stones and returned to her own car.

"Aunt Nell?" Where the hell had she got to?

She heard a car approaching, and a moment later saw the headlight beams emerge from the ravine. The detective chief inspector had arrived. Shielding her eyes against the glare, Megan hurried down the row of cars to meet him.

As Scumble heaved his bulk out of the passenger seat, the driver also got out, as well as three large constables who had somehow squeezed into the backseat. The car's suspension groaned in relief. So did Scumble, who disliked being driven.

He gestured at the cars ahead, still illuminated by the headlights. "You sent 'em all out already?"

"Yes, sir."

"Fast work. Denton, turn the damn lights off, will you, so our eyes can get accustomed to the dark. Pencarrow, tell this lot what you want them to do; then we can talk."

She led them to the map and directed them to two gaps in her

line of searchers. "You've all got torches? . . . Good." As the constables trudged off, she said to Scumble, "I wish we had a personal
radio for each pair."

"Tell that to the ratepayers. I wish we had one for every man—
and woman—on the force. Didn't you take a pair of two-ways to
Tintagel?"

"Yes, sir, and mine's in my car, but it's no use here because DS
Faraday has the other. Dawson brought two with him. He kept one
and I have the second. He's gone with Sergeant Nayak and the
dog to the van. I'm expecting him to call any minute."

"Lucky the fog's dissipated. The Met says a southeasterly breeze
will begin to break up the cloud layer, too." Scumble and Megan
both looked up. The moon was faintly visible now, as if the thick
blanket had worn as thin as a sheet.

"It'll make the search easier," said Megan, "but if—when—
someone wants to attract our attention with a torch, it won't be
as visible in full moonlight."

"Every cloud has a silver lining, and every rose has its thorn.
Explain to me how you've set up this—"

"Sergeant!" the radio in Megan's pocket bleated tinnily.

"Excuse me, sir. Yes, Dawson?"

"We met Johnson—the bloke that wants to be a second Me—
and . . . the bloke you sent with him."

Megan appreciated his caution. The longer she could put off
Scumble's discovery of the use she had made of Tariro, the better.
"Yes?"

"He says the van won't be going anywhere without a new transmission and a new oil pan. They drove it over a rock that was
bigger than they reckoned. Or, likely, they didn't even see it in the
fog."

"Tell him thanks."

"Too late, Sarge. They've gone off to join the hunt. Made a bet with Sergeant Nayak they'd find someone before the dog does. Me, I wouldn't bet against her. She's already tracking something, and they're moving fast. I better get going or I'll lose them."

"All right, Dawson. Keep in touch." As she returned the radio to her pocket, she exclaimed, "Damn! You heard that, sir?"

"The van's out of action and the dog is in action."

"And that twit Johnson has 'joined the hunt' off his own bat, without waiting to be told where to go." Though she guessed that the initiative had been Tariro's, regarding both the wager and the unauthorised departure. He was afraid if he returned, he too would be out of action. She sighed. "Still, given the terrain, the pattern's probably all fouled up by now anyway."

"Bad, is it?"

"It's Bodmin Moor, sir. Here comes another car. Good. Whoever it is can be my partner. It's time I got going."

"Searching, you mean? No, Pencarrow, I need you here, for liaison."

"Sir, you can't be serious! Nick's out there somewhere, and Freeth. You sent me to find Freeth. I've got to do my bit!"

"Your 'bit' is organising. You're doing a good job. Stick with it. I'm going to join your auntie in the car—the first car, I take it?— to find out what she knows about Freeth and Mrs. Mason. This isn't the primary crime scene, remember?"

Before she could argue, the car she had spotted arrived. Both front doors opened. Two men: One could go with her and the other stay with the guv'nor to man the radio. Scumble was quite capable of both organising and talking to Aunt Nell at the same time.

If Aunt Nell had returned to the car by now—

"Sarge!" the two-way squawked. "Sarge, someone over to the north of us is flashing a torch and blowing a whistle fit to bust!"

TWENTY-FOUR

Eleanor ran out of breath. Her ears ringing, she wondered whether anyone within a mile or two could have failed to hear the whistle.

The moon sailed out from behind the clouds and illuminated what lay at her feet, which she had much rather not have seen so clearly. Teazle had alerted her to the body sprawling face-down in the bog, first whining and then, when she didn't respond in the desired fashion at once, uttering shrill, anxious yelps.

At first Eleanor had had no room for anything but relief that the man was neither Nick nor Alan Freeth. The lifting of the burden of fear made her feel positively giddy.

That it should be a person unconnected with the murder and kidnapping, who just happened to be rambling on the moor this foggy evening, would be altogether too much of a coincidence. If not one of her friends, then who? Nick was tall and lanky, Freeth slight and slim. The man who had died so gruesomely in the mud was burly, with a thick neck and bristly hair. He must surely be one of the villains who had abducted them after killing poor Mrs. Mason: probably Stone, alias the Sandman.

It was difficult to feel any real sorrow for his death. But was he dead? His face was buried in mud up to his ears. He certainly wasn't breathing now. How long had he lain there? Could she save his life if she managed to get him out and somehow clear his airway?

Though fit, and strong for her age and size, she very much doubted she was capable of hauling a hefty, inert body from the glutinous muck. That was when she had remembered her whistle.

Now, recovering her breath, she flashed the torch in what she hoped was the Morse SOS signal. Dot dot dot, dash dash dash, dot dot dot—or was it the other way round? Never mind, one or more of the searchers was bound to realise what she meant. She gazed down the slope and saw several of the powerful police torch beams turning her way.

Her forefinger was tired of pressing the button on and off, so she left it on and swung it in an arc to indicate her position. While she waited, having got over the first shock and revulsion, she studied the body and its surroundings by the light of the moon, now shining bright.

For a start, how had he ended up in the bog? Did he fall, or was he pushed? A quarrel between the crooks, leading to blows, would probably have landed him on his back, or perhaps his side. Besides, from what Megan had said, Eleanor had gathered that the second man didn't look like a violent thug who could overcome Stone. A sneak shove from behind might have done the trick.

More likely, she thought, he had tripped over the rock that lay on the brim close to his feet. How ironic that rocks invisible in the fog had brought both him and his vehicle to grief.

The position of his arms, raised and bent at the elbows, showed that he had put out his hands to break his fall. But why had he not scrambled out of the bog? Few were more than thigh-deep, most much shallower. The surface was too liquid to retain the marks if he'd struggled and failed to rescue himself.

Teazle barked.

"Ma'am? What are you doing— What have you found?" A constable unknown to Eleanor was the first to arrive. He gasped as he caught sight of the body. "Omigawd, that's a nasty way to go!"

"He may not be dead yet. You'd better get him out of there and find out."

"Move him? Before they take photos?"

"What if he dies because you won't?"

The Speed Demon came up, panting. "What you got here, Mrs. Trewynn? Oh, lor! DC Dawson, Constable. You better get in there and try for a pulse in his neck."

"Me?"

"You, mate. I didn't study to be a detective so I could go playing in the mud. Hurry up about it. What d'you reckon, Mrs. Trewynn? Who is it? Not one of your friends, I take it."

"No, thank heaven. No, I'd guess it's Stone, the one they call the Sandman. But that's just a guess, based on what I've heard."

"Course. Well, man, what about it?" Dawson asked the unhappy constable, now over the top of his wellies in the smelly bog. "Is he alive or is he dead?"

"I can't feel a pulse."

"Then he's dead."

"But I might just be missing it. . . ."

"I s'pose we'd better get him out." He looked down at his suit and shoes with a sigh. "Not what I passed Driver Grade One for, neither. Oh well."

He was saved by the arrival of two more common-or-garden bobbies, whom he happily sent to join the first. While they were busy, he took out a pocket radio and called Megan.

"Sarge, your auntie found Stone's body."

"Couldn't happen to a more deserving fellow."

"Leastways, we think that's who it is, and we think he's dead."

"*Think* he's dead?"

"Drowned in a bog. Or suffocated, same difference. I've got some lads hauling him out in case there's anything we can do."

"Did you . . . I hope I misheard you. You didn't say my aunt found him?"

" 'Fraid so, Sarge."

"Oh hell! Luckily the guv'nor is talking to Launceston, but that's only postponing the thunderbolt. Did she notice any sign of life when she found him?"

"You want to talk to her?"

"No, I might say something I'd regret. Ask her."

"You hear, Mrs. Trewynn?"

"I could hardly help it," said Eleanor drily. "No, there was no sign of life that I could see."

Dawson told Megan, who said, "Seven minutes since she blew the whistle. Even if he'd just fallen in, he'd likely be dead now, but try anyway. Dr. Prthnavi will be grateful not to have to wade in to examine him. He's on his way. An ambulance has arrived. It's stayed down in the car park so as not to get stuck up here with cars behind it. A couple of men are bringing up a stretcher."

"Strikes me they're going to need more than one."

"I hope not," said Megan. Eleanor silently echoed her words. "Was it an accident, do you think? Or is the guv'nor going to have to beg for Bodmin's SOCO team?"

"Dunno, Sarge. There's a muddy mark on his back that could be significant."

"Make sure it's not messed up. I've got a Minicam on me, but I don't suppose you do. "

"Nah. Do me a favour: Come up and take over."

"Be careful what you wish for. Mr. Scumble's making 'see for myself' noises."

"Oh lor'! Hold on a mo. They've got him out. Gotta go."

Jay and Kali had come up and now stood nearby, watching the struggles of the men in the bog. When the body was at last heaved out onto solid ground, Jay said, "You are DC Dawson? I'd like to let my dog get the scent of this man."

"Go ahead, Sergeant, but we're not looking for him any longer."

"Kali will discover which way he came and we'll backtrack him, which may lead to others."

"Oh, right."

As Kali sniffed at the inert body, one of the constables asked, "We don't have to do kiss of life, do we?"

"Nah," said Dawson, "Just hold him up by the heels and whack him on the back. That'll bring the stuff out and get his heart and breathing going if anything will. Mind out for that blotch on the back of his coat there, see?"

Eleanor couldn't watch. She considered following Jay as Kali, nose to the ground, led him away at a trot. That was what Teazle obviously wanted, but Eleanor was afraid the little dog's presence might distract the big dog from whatever trail she had found.

She decided to climb right to the top of the Cheesewring quarry. There was a footpath up there on what was left of the flattish top of the hill where the tors still stood. It ran a few feet back from the edge of the sheer face where granite had been blasted out of the hillside. From there, now that the fog was gone and the moon shone, she would have a view of the whole stretch of moor down to the village. With luck, she'd be able to spot the searchers. If she saw any large gaps between them, she would try to make her way there to concentrate her efforts in an area no one else was covering.

After a few false starts among a jumble of rocks, she found the path she wanted. Teazle, still full of energy, led the way up the steep slope, Eleanor trudging after her.

As they got higher, she met wisps of mist. Higher still, she could see that the clouds had cleared only to the south and east. The hill blocked the breeze and the leeward side was still draped in fog. The crest of the hill rose above it though. Reaching the top, she looked out to the northwest across a silver plain, as if the valley were filled to the brim with snow. In the far distance, Rough Tor and Brown Willy stood like islands in the sea of clouds.

Eleanor and Teazle came to the first tor, a huge pile of rock slabs, like an uneven stack of Scotch pancakes, all different sizes. The biggest was near the top. It was hard to believe Mother Nature had piled them up or eroded their surroundings so thoroughly and strangely. No wonder legends of giants abounded.

Standing in the moon-shadow of the tor, Eleanor gazed out over the wide expanse to the south. The line of cars was easy to see. The nearest had its interior light on. She couldn't really tell from this distance, but she guessed the two silhouettes behind the windscreen were those of Scumble and Megan. She hoped Megan wasn't getting an earful about letting her aunt and Tariro become involved.

Here and there on the slopes, torches were visible, bobbing up and down, disappearing momentarily behind bushes or rocks, flickering through gorse bushes. A lot more men had arrived since she had slipped away from Megan's car.

In finding Stone, she could be said to have done her part, but that was not what she wanted. Until Nick and Freeth were safe, or beyond help—

Teazle whined. It was a soft, anxious sound, not insistent like when she had drawn attention to the body in the bog. She was staring at the tor as if she could see right through it.

"Hush," Eleanor whispered. "Good girl. Stay."

Inch by inch, she crept round the north side of the tor, setting each foot down with care. A loose pebble rolled against another with a *chink*. She stopped and held her breath.

From beyond the tor, she could now hear a low, intermittent mutter. Nothing about it suggested that her approach had been noticed. The impression it gave was of someone arguing with his own silent inner voice. She strained her ears to catch a second voice. Nothing.

Cautiously, she took two more steps and peeped round the tor, through the sideways vee between two of its rocks.

Between her tor and the next stretched a space of grass and tumbled boulders. On one of the smaller stones, much too close to the edge for comfort, a man sat with his head in his hands.

As she watched, he stood, stiffly, and took a step towards the edge, then hesitated. His silhouette against the moon-bright sky suggested he was taller than Freeth, shorter than Nick, thicker at the waist of his belted raincoat than either, or so it seemed to Eleanor. Nor could she imagine any reason why Nick or Freeth might contemplate suicide.

For that was undoubtedly what was going through the man's mind, she realised. Two more steps and he would plummet down the vertical face of the quarry.

What was she to do?

On the one hand, she was virtually certain he was a crook, a murderer, the partner of the man in the bog. Many would say good riddance; he was no loss to the world. It was his life and his choice. It wasn't even as if suicide was still considered a crime, and in

Eleanor's philosophy, the only "sin" was any action that deliberately harmed another.

On the other hand, every life was precious, and killing oneself in a moment of despair ended the possibility of making amends, of becoming a better person and making a contribution to the world. She knew nothing of his history, circumstances, or background. Who was she to judge?

Another factor, one she ought not to allow to influence her, was curiosity. He might be the only person who could explain the events leading to the present situation.

As all this flashed through her head, she was simultaneously working out how to stop him jumping. If she spoke, tried to dissuade him, she could precipitate immediate action.

Teazle whined at her feet. *Stay* was a flexible, short-term concept to the Westie.

The man swung round. "Who's there?" He sounded terrified, not at all aggressive.

"It's just me." Meaningless, but perhaps her equally unaggressive tone would reassure him. "And my little dog." She stepped forward, still in the shadow of the second tor.

"*Wuff?*" Teazle barked uncertainly. She couldn't possibly have sounded less threatening.

"What do you want? Come out where I can see you!"

"Teazle, stay!" Eleanor used her most commanding tone. She didn't want to find herself tripping over the dog. Taking a long pace into the moonlight, she was just a few feet from him now.

He stepped back. "That's close enough!"

"Be careful. You're awfully close to the edge."

"What does it matter? I'm going to jump. In a minute."

"Why?" Eleanor's skills and experience had not prepared her to argue someone out of committing suicide. Was she saying the wrong thing, in the wrong way? She had no idea.

"None of your business. You can't stop me. What are you doing here?"

"Looking at the view. It's beautiful from up here, in the moonlight. There are so many beautiful things in the world."

"Not in a prison cell."

"Prison isn't forever these days. They don't lock you up and throw away the key."

"What do you know about it! Kill the soul but not the body, that's what they do these days." He spoke in a monotone now, more chilling than any histrionics. "I killed him. I murdered him." He thumped with his fist on the nearest boulder. "Too many rocks here. One tripped the van and killed it. One tripped Vic, but it was I who killed him. He fell over it and landed in the muck. It wasn't that deep. He was pushing himself up and I put my foot on his back and held him down till he stopped moving. He deserved it, the dirty rotten bastard. He killed my sister."

With that, he turned and moved without hesitation towards the brink.

For a moment, Eleanor was frozen in disbelief. Then she launched herself at him. By the time she grabbed one shoulder, one of his feet was already over the abyss. Quickly she seized the other shoulder, dropping her weight backwards, stepping out of the way as he fell on his back.

He landed with a thud and lay still. Either he was stunned by the fall or he'd had the breath knocked out of him. He had fallen on grass, thank goodness, not against a stone. Eleanor was quick to take advantage to grip his arm, pull it across his body, and flip him onto his stomach.

Breathing heavily now, he lay there, showing no sign of trying to get up.

Eleanor sat down cross-legged beside him, holding one wrist lightly, alert to the slightest motion. In a second or two she could move into position to be ready to put him in an armlock if necessary. She'd have immobilised him already had he shown the slightest sign of fight, but he seemed to have had the stuffing knocked out of him physically and, she suspected, emotionally.

She had dropped the torch when she'd leaped at him and she couldn't see it anywhere. It must have broken. She took her whistle from her pocket and blew a blast.

The man shuddered. Teazle came trotting up. She sniffed him with interest, then jumped onto his back and curled up for a nap after all the excitement.

Eleanor blew again, then settled into a state of meditative hyperawareness, as if she were preparing for an Aikido practice session. An automatic count ticked on just below her consciousness, and every ninety seconds or so, she sounded the whistle three times.

She had done everything she could. Sooner or later, someone would come.

TWENTY-FIVE

Megan had studied the six-inch map pretty thoroughly while sending out her team. The direct route from the cars to the deadly bog was reasonably straightforward. Once Scumble had given her permission, on the grounds that only she could identify the villains, she had jogged most of the way. Biking to work every day, downhill there but uphill all the way home, kept her fit.

She reached the spot just after DC Dawson gave up trying to revive the corpse. Or rather, after he had told the uniformed men to give up—he himself had not actually touched the revolting object.

"Wouldn't want to get so mucky that I couldn't handle evidence," he said to Megan, showing her his clean hands.

"I'm sure that was your only reason." She thanked the filthy constables and told them to stand by. "You said my aunt found him. Where is she?"

"I dunno, Sarge. Must've left when I was busy."

Megan sighed. "I hope she knows what she's doing."

"She found him, didn't she?"

"True. Let me have a look." She eyed the prone body, its head turned to one side.

"He's all yours, Sarge." Dawson's torch beam lit on the mask of mud that had once been a face.

"Wait, here's Sergeant Nayak."

"He already came and went! Dog lost the scent, Sergeant?"

"What's up, Jay?"

"Kali is confused. I am sorry, Megan; I cannot read her mind. But in the van were the smells of several people, I understand? So Dawson told me. And here, this man"—the Indian gestured—"the mud also adds its own scent."

"*Scent* isn't the word I'd use!" Dawson exclaimed. "Sorry, Sarge."

"You are correct; it has a stink that changes the smell of the man. So does death. Also, she is told to note this smell and to seek, yet here is that which she seeks. The trail I want her to follow is older, fainter, and without the odours stirred up from the stagnant water."

"Small wonder she's confused," said Megan.

"It is, perhaps, the most difficult task she is asked to do, to find not a person or an object, but where that person or object came from."

"The reverse of the usual search."

"Add that some or all of the others from the van may have followed the same path—"

"And the job becomes impossible."

"Oh no, just complicated and requiring patience. Kali will try again."

Kali, who had been sniffing the body, came back to Jay and whined.

"What's she saying?" asked Dawson. "'Look, here he is, you daft buggers'?"

Jay smiled. "She says, 'I am ready. Let's go.'"

"Just a minute. I've got to make sure of the identification, if possible; then I'll go with you."

"You will be welcome, Megan, but you must stay behind us, so as not to confuse the scent."

"You're in charge."

She stepped closer to the body, turned her torch on the face, and bent over it. The grotesque mud mask resembled a facial beauty treatment, except that the man's eyes and mouth were covered, his nostrils plugged. Drowned or suffocated? Not that it mattered. He was dead.

Insofar as she could make out the features, the face was Stone's, and the burly body-type matched his.

"The Sandman." The torch beam moved down his back. "That looks as if it could be a footprint. You know how to use one of these, Dawson?" She handed him the mini-camera.

"Sure, Sarge."

Her light swept over the bog, stopped, and moved back to a rock on the edge. A polythene bag was draped over it, held down by several smaller stones. "Dawson?"

"I reckoned maybe it tripped him, so I took a look. There's a sort of scuff mark that could be leather from his boots, and part of a footprint. Thought it'd better be protected for SOCO."

"Well done. Take some snaps of that, too. All right, when you're done with the photography, leave a man here on guard and report to the guv'nor. Tell him I'll be in touch on the two-way. The rest of you, get back to your search areas as best you can. All right, Jay."

He brought the harnessed dog to take another sniff at the body, to refresh her memory, then commanded, "Track."

Kali set off with apparent confidence, tail held high, making Jay trot after her. Megan followed about twenty feet behind.

They were in a shallow valley, gently sloping up, the bog being in the lowest part. The going was smooth. In the fog, Stone had probably had little idea where he was going, so he took the easiest path leading downhill. With the van out of commission, he must have hoped to reach the road sooner or later. She could think of only one reason for his having come this way in the opposite direction.

The dog began to cast about, as though she had lost the scent. Jay let out the line she was on, giving her more freedom of movement. He watched her intently. She raised her head, sniffing the air, then stopped and looked back at him.

"From the way she moves, I think the trail splits here, Megan. She does not know which branch to choose." He pointed straight up the valley, then diagonally to the right, where the hillside rose comparatively steeply. "Have you a preference?"

"I wish she could talk! I wish I had some idea what they were doing, and whether they had Nick and Freeth with them. I just don't understand what was going through their minds."

"Nor I."

"Does Kali show the slightest preference for one way over the other?"

"Straight up the valley, if anything. Perhaps the scent hangs in the air longer down here than up on the hillside. Or perhaps the scent is that of the dead man, the most recent she was introduced to."

"Any reason is better than none. We'll go straight ahead."

"Straight ahead it is. Heel." Jay gathered up the long leash as Kali came to his side. When he started walking, the dog moved with him as if her nose were glued to his leg.

As she started to go after them, keeping her station twenty feet behind, Megan was suddenly aware of motion behind her. Why hadn't Kali alerted them to someone following? One-track mind, perhaps: When tracking, she tracked, and had no attention to spare for her surroundings. Turning swiftly, Megan was about to shout for Jay and his dog.

A long, narrow shadow stretched from her feet, leading straight towards the moon. It took a moment to realise that the last couple of yards of the black stripe were not shadow, but Tariro.

"What the hell are you doing here? You were supposed to go back to the cars."

"You can't send me back now, on my own. I might get lost. What would Sir Edward say? Besides, I've never before had an opportunity to watch a police dog at work."

"How long— Were you lurking down there?" She gestured in the direction of the fatal bog.

"The body? Yes. I didn't get too close."

"Did you see my aunt?"

"I did, though my attention was on DC Dawson and the bobbies when she left, so I didn't see which way she went. I haven't spoken to her since you sent me to show PC Johnson the way to the van."

Reminded that she herself had involved Tariro in the business, Megan didn't question what she felt was a somewhat evasive reply. "All right, come along. Just don't for pity's sake get in the way, or I swear you'll go back by yourself, Sir Edward or no Sir Edward."

He laughed. "So much for Sir Edward."

Jay and Kali were at the head of the valley. As Megan and Tariro hurried after them, Jay took off the dog's collar. She dashed over the brow of the hill and disappeared. Jay looked back.

"Come on," he called. "She is now certain of the trail." He plunged over the ridge.

Tariro overtook Megan, running with long, loping strides. "Cross-country team," he said consolingly as he passed.

She redoubled her efforts to stay at his heels. At the top, she had to stop for a moment to relieve a stitch in her side. From here, she could see that the land continued rising on her right, up to the Cheesewring tors. Lit by the moon, they stood out against the starry sky. The fog and clouds were gone.

The chilly breeze that had cleared them was welcome, hot as she was from running.

The hillside below her was dark. She switched on her torch and, breath regained, started downward after the men. Ahead, she saw their bobbing torch beams, both moving slower now, more cautiously.

Suddenly Kali barked, and went on barking.

Jay's torch found her. She was on a more or less level stretch of ground, grassy, with patches of bracken, new green beginning to spring through the old, withered brown. What interested Kali was a dark blotch nearly surrounded by bracken, with a leafless bush on one side. About a third of the circumference was grass. Here the barking dog danced sideways back and forth, facing the dark patch, her attention focussed on something in the middle invisible to Megan.

As Megan reached the level ground, she could tell that Kali was looking downward. Jay a step ahead, he and Tariro approached her together.

"Sit!" Jay commanded.

Kali obeyed, and stopped barking, but she continued to stare down into what appeared to be a hole. The two men both shone their torches into it. Jay spat out what sounded like a curse in his own language.

"Megan, it is Nicholas. And another man."

"Dead?" She forced the word past the lump in her throat.

Two more steps took her to his side. They stood on the brink of a cup-shaped hollow, six or eight feet deep and about a dozen wide, a sink-hole or perhaps an aborted mine shaft. It was half-full of bracken, with a small, bent hawthorn tree—what Megan had taken for a bush—on the far side. A few blood-red berries still clung to the sheltered lower branches, among the pale nubs of leaf buds.

Megan made herself look down. The bottom of the bowl was grassy, not bog or water, thank goodness.

Nick lay curled up on his side. Freeth was sprawled on his back. Both faces were deadly pale in the torchlight, but their eyes were closed, not open in the fixed, blank stare of death.

Which didn't mean they were alive. Instinct screamed at Megan to rush down and do whatever she could to help them. Training urged caution, learning as much as she could from observation before she jumped in and perhaps destroyed evidence.

She handed her two-way radio to Jay. "Report to Dawson, please. Two stretcher parties, as fast as they can get here, and a doctor if possible. Lend your torch to Tariro for the moment."

With three torch beams directed into the dell, it was well lit. Megan could see that Nick's ankles were still tied with gauze bandage. His wrists were free, though. A tangle of white gauze lay beside him, suggesting that he had freed himself after arriving here. So he was alive! Or he had been when dumped in this spot.

Freeth had a cut on his cheekbone that had bled freely. *Sprawled* was the wrong word for him. He was still trussed at both wrists and ankles, so he lay quite neatly, except that his head was bent at an angle that would give him a bad crick if he stayed long in that position. His neck was not twisted enough to be broken, Megan assured herself. But it could be.

"I'm going down." She felt in her pocket. "Damn, I left my pen-knife in my bag in the car. Either of you have one?"

Jay, the radio to his ear, put his other hand in his pocket and produced a Swiss Army knife.

"Thanks."

"Shall I come?" Tariro asked.

"Not yet. There isn't much room."

Jay handed her the radio. "Dr. Prthnavi just arrived. DC Dawson will put him on."

"Thanks, Jay." The radio joined the knife in her pocket. She sat down on the edge and let herself go. It wasn't so much a drop as a slither down the steep grass-grown side.

Landing, she knelt between the two men. Finding Nick's pulse took only a moment. Its beat was strong and regular. She let out the breath she hadn't realised she'd been holding and turned to Freeth.

Jay's knife slashed through the string binding the lawyer's wrists. Moving his arms as little as possible, in case his neck actually was injured, Megan searched for a pulse. She gave up on the wrist and tried for the carotid artery. She couldn't feel it. She moved her hand to try again, and again, concentrating fiercely. Was that it? Wishful thinking? The echo of her own heartbeat? No, her own heart hammered in her chest, faster than usual but strong and steady, nothing like the weak, erratic flutter beneath her finger-tips.

She sat back on her heels and took out the radio. "DS Pencarrow here. Dr. Prthnavi?"

"Prthnavi speaking. Tell me what you see, Miss Pencarrow."

"Mr. Freeth—he's unconscious, and his pulse seems to me very weak and uneven. What should I do?"

"Is he bleeding?"

"Not that I can see. His head, his neck is at an angle, but his neck is not broken, I'd guess."

"Do not move him. The most important thing is to keep him warm, as warm as you possibly can. Coats, jackets, whatever you have."

"Okay. Hold on a minute, Doctor. Jay, Tariro, I need your coats for Freeth."

She set down the radio and torch and took off her own jacket in the near darkness as the men's torches were also laid down. A moment later, their coats landed next to her, along with Jay's scarf and gloves. Light restored, she swathed them over and around Freeth, easing the gloves onto his hands as gently as she could.

"Megan, Kali is trained to lie quietly close to a person in trouble such as this. I remember, you see, that what my cousin needed most when you pulled him from the sea was warmth."

Megan hesitated. The big dog might scare Freeth to death if he came round—but her warmth might make the difference between life and death. "All right, send her down. Doctor, we've done what we can for him. Nick, Nicholas Gresham—" She glanced at him as she said his name. His eyes were open.

"Megan," he whispered, and gave her a twisted smile.

"Oh Nick!" She leaned over and kissed him very softly on the mouth. "Doctor, Nick is conscious now. His pulse is strong."

"Check his pupils."

"Right. You heard, Nick? I'm going to turn the torch on your face. Try to keep your eyes open for a moment. . . . Doctor, they're odd. Uneven. I mean, unequal, not the same size. Concussion?"

"So it would seem. He, too, should stay still."

"May he talk?"

"If he chooses. The stretcher parties are here. If you have no more questions, I shall be on my way to join you."

"Thank you, sir. Be careful, please! The last thing we need is for you to break an ankle."

"Pencarrow?" Scumble's voice.

"Sir."

"Dawson's guiding the medics, as he knows at least how to get to the bog. Can you send Sergeant Nayak back there to show them the rest of the way, or do you need him?"

Megan explained that the dog was sharing her body warmth with Freeth. "I'd rather not withdraw that, sir, and I think her handler should stay near her. I can send Ta—the other person with me. Or go myself," which she emphatically did not want to do.

A long, windy sigh came through the radio. "Him! I don't know what the super is going to say. But there's the lawyer to consider, as well as Sir Edward. Beggars can't be choosers. If he's willing, go ahead."

Megan looked up at Tariro, almost invisible behind his torch. "You heard?"

"At your orders, baas."

"He's willing, sir."

"Convey my thanks. Gresham's able to answer questions?"

"A few, at least."

"I'll leave it to you, Pencarrow."

"Yes, sir." She pocketed the radio and took out Jay's knife. "Nick, I'm going to cut the bandage round your ankles."

"Bandage!" His voice seemed a little stronger. "Is that what they used? I undid the one round my wrists with my teeth, and I couldn't make out what the hell it was."

She sliced through the gauze. "Don't move your legs."

"I doubt I could if I tried."

"Well, don't try." She cut Freeth's ankles free and turned back to Nick. "Are they very painful?"

"They? My legs? I don't know. I hurt like hell all over. How is Freeth?"

"Not good."

"The bloody bastards left us tied and unconscious rolling about loose in the back of the van. I came round—I have a very hard head. When I played rugger at school, I took several hard hits, and they were always surprised I wasn't concussed. In the van, I could protect myself a bit, but Freeth was out and I couldn't do much for him. Have you nabbed them yet?"

"One of them is dead."

"Good! You know they killed Mrs. Mason?"

"We know."

"I suppose you don't happen to have any water with you?"

"Nick," said Jay from above, "I carry water for Kali. I pour it into her mouth, but I cannot swear she has not touched the neck of the bottle."

"What's a little dog slobber between friends? Pass it down."

Jay knelt and reached down, and Megan took the metal bottle from him. As she unscrewed the cap, attached by a short chain, she tried to work out how to give Nick a drink without choking him, given that he wasn't supposed to move. He raised his head an inch or two and she hastily moved to support it.

"If you can do that, your spine seems not to be injured."

"It hurts to breathe."

"More likely ribs than spine. Shall I raise you a little more, or would you rather I just pour and hope not to drown you?"

"It's not the drowning; it's getting wet. I'm already bloody frozen."

Cautiously, slowly, Megan raised his head a little farther. He managed to sip some water.

"Enough?"

"Thanks. Thanks, Jay, but before your next rescue, teach the dog to drink hot tea and carry a thermos!"

He gave a slight moan as Megan carefully lowered his head to the cold, damp ground. "We took quite a beating, one way and another. Is Freeth going to be all right?"

"I don't know, Nick. Dr. Prthnavi and the ambulance men are on their way." She felt for Freeth's pulse. It hadn't changed, but his skin felt slightly less icy. Kali, stretched out alongside him, was putting out a good deal of warmth. Megan turned back to Nick and held his hand as they waited. His eyes were closed again, so she didn't speak to him.

Where were the medics? Had Tariro lost his way?

It seemed a long time before Kali growled to announce their approach. A word from Jay brought the dog scrambling from the hole. Megan dropped a kiss on Nick's forehead. Tariro appeared, and he and Jay together hauled Megan out of the hole as Dr. Prthnavi came up, the stretcher party close behind him.

Megan moved back to give them room. Jay and Tariro helped the little doctor safely down into the hole and handed down his black bag. He bent over Nick and Freeth, muttering to himself, then started to issue orders to the stretcher-bearers.

Megan was taking out the radio to report their arrival when it suddenly called for attention.

"Pencarrow!" Scumble, not Dawson.

"Sir?"

"The doctor arrived yet?"

"Yes, sir, I was on the point of calling in."

"I thought you might be interested in a report that's just come in."

"Sir?"

"Someone is up at the top of the quarry blowing a whistle. And as whistles are not standard police issue these days, the only person on this bit of moor known to possess one is your auntie."

TWENTY-SIX

At last! Eleanor was getting chilly. She had been sitting still, blowing her whistle at intervals, for what seemed a very long time; at last it looked as if someone had heard and worked out roughly where the sound was coming from. Two of the torch beams that had been bobbing around down below were now directed at the cliff-top. More joined them.

She wondered how she could show herself without giving her captive a chance to jump while her attention was elsewhere. Alternatively, despondent and penitent as he seemed, he might regain his nerve and decide to shove her over the edge.

Ever since she had pulled him back from that edge, he had lain meekly where she had deposited him. And most of the time, he had been talking.

All Eleanor had wanted was a clarification.

"You said you killed 'him.' Do you mean the man known as the Sandman?"

"The Sandman. Victor Stone. I told you there were too many stones, but now there's one less. My brother-in-law."

"Good gracious! Mrs. Mason was really Mrs. Stone?"

"She changed her name when she ran away. She could at least have switched back to Carpenter—that's the family name. I'd have had half a chance of finding her. It's been deuced inconvenient not knowing where she was. Not that I blame her for getting away while she could. He's—he was a nasty man."

"He was sent to prison?"

"Yes. She seized her chance while he was in quod. Plenty of time for the trail to go cold. He got fifteen years."

"For manslaughter?"

"He was lucky; he got a soft jury. But there were several counts of GBH, too."

"GBH?"

"Grievous bodily harm. He was a muscle-man—"

"A bodybuilder?"

"He had plenty of actual muscle, though he didn't need it often because he got to be expert with the sandbag." Carpenter's disapproving tone turned to admiration.

It dawned on Eleanor that she was learning some of the ins and outs of criminal activity from a man with a public school accent very like Nick's. How odd!

He went on: "The Sandman knew exactly where to hit and how hard to lay out the opposition for a couple of hours without doing too much damage. The only thing he was ever any good at, but he was really good. The most successful burglary and holdup gangs don't want anyone killed, you know. They sometimes get away with robbery, but when it's a matter of murder, the coppers descend like a horde of locusts. Especially if it's a copper who's killed."

"Stone had a gang?"

"Not him. Nowhere near bright enough. He worked for anyone who needed muscle, for a share of the loot. He always did pretty well, but I don't know how much work he'd have got after killing that bloke. Not that he meant to."

"What do you mean? He killed a man by accident?"

"He had a thin skull, apparently, poor chap. Vic meant to knock him out, like the rest, but of course if you deliberately hit someone over the head and he dies, it's murder. He had a sharp brief, though—"

"Brief?"

"Lawyer. A smart lawyer my father recommended. He persuaded Vic to confess to a couple of other jobs he'd done where he'd given a few people headaches. It set a pattern and made the jury believe that he hadn't intended to kill anyone. So, as I said, he got sent down for manslaughter, with several counts of GBH added on. That's why he was put away for a good long stretch."

"Are you saying he didn't mean to kill Mrs. Mason?"

"That's right. He lost his temper and slapped her. Rosie offered to pay him everything Dad owed him, on the spot, but he wanted to rummage through her things. She tried to stop him, and it made him suspect she was hiding something more valuable. That's when he sandbagged her, just to put her out for a couple of minutes. Or so he claimed. And what if she *was* hiding valuables? That was my business, not his. Dad left everything to her so Vic wouldn't get his filthy paws on it."

"Your father left you nothing?"

"Not a penny. I was livid all right, but Rosie promised me an allowance, and she always sent it, spot on, once a month. I'm not saying I didn't come down here with Vic to cadge a bit extra, as well as just to see her."

"Why did your father cut you off?" It was none of her business, but the more information she was able to pass on to the police, the better, and besides, she was curious.

He was in a confessional mood. "Because I'd have lost it all at roulette. It's his fault. He sent me to a public school to learn the lingo and then to Monte Carlo to get in with the nobs. It's easy to meet people casually there. He wanted me to make friends and be invited to stately homes. The trouble was, I could fit in nicely in Monte, but staying at a country house wasn't at all the same thing. It was hellish."

"He wanted you to rise in the world," Eleanor said encouragingly. She was so fascinated, she suddenly realised the automatic count in her head had reached a hundred and twenty. She blew her whistle vigorously.

"He wanted me to find out where they kept their valuables."

"Oh dear! Was *he* a burglar too?"

"What do you mean, 'too'?" In his indignation, Carpenter started to push himself up. Teazle yipped and Eleanor tightened her grip on his wrist. He subsided again, limp as a dead fish. "I never burgled a house in my life. Nor did Dad, come to that. As far as I know. I didn't do anything illegal, not then. You can't blame me for how my father used the information I gave him."

"Did he pay you for it?"

"Not exactly. He bought me a couple of new outfits and a ticket to the Riviera, and told me it was time I proved I could make my own way. Well, I did. You'd be surprised how many well-off widows and divorcées like to gamble but feel uncomfortable placing their own bets. They'll happily give a presentable young man half the winnings to do it for them."

"And the losses?"

"Most of them are sporting old birds who know the odds favour the house. You learn to steer clear of the others. The trouble starts when you have a run of bad luck. Word gets round, and soon no one wants you touching their money. You just have to move on.

At that point, you can recoup. It's when you can't resist betting with your own money that the end is in sight. To pay my debts, I had to pawn my signet ring and—"

"You had a signet ring?"

"Solid gold, with a crest." With a pitiful remnant of pride, he boasted, "It was a brilliant idea. Only for Americans; I didn't try it on the English."

"I don't understand. Try what?"

"That's just it: I didn't try anything. I waited until they asked me—they always did in the end. Then I told the sad story of how my father was the black sheep of a noble family and this was the sole memento that remained to him. He'd passed it on to me as my only inheritance, on condition that I never mentioned the name of the noble family. They lapped it up, I can tell you, all sympathy and unsatisfied curiosity."

"Misrepresenting your family origins isn't a criminal offence, though, is it? Unless you try to extort money from the family you're pretending to descend from."

"Certainly not."

"But you said you didn't do anything illegal *then*, implying that you did at another time."

"I don't see why I should tell you," Carpenter said fretfully, and proceeded to do just that. "If you must know, I forged a cheque. They can't get me for that again. I served my time. I'm freezing, and I'm getting a crick in my neck. Can't I turn over on my back?"

Eleanor blew the whistle while she considered his request. She, too, was cold and getting stiff. She wouldn't at all mind standing up and stretching. He didn't seem to be suicidal still. If she was on her feet, she could counter any attack he might attempt. He was not at all fit, as she had discovered when she tackled him.

"All right. Move slowly."

"I can barely move at all," he whined. The public school accent was fading in favour of what Eleanor thought might be the forces of South London. "Tell the dog to get off me."

"She'll jump off as soon as you stir."

Teazle gave a warning bark as she hopped off his back—unless it was a complaint that she had lost her warm spot.

"Hey, dog, she said I could!"

"It's all right, girl."

With a great deal of effort and a groan or two, Carpenter pushed himself up on hands and knees. "Do I have to lie down? The ground's cold."

"Yes, you do. You should have considered the possible consequences before you embarked on this venture."

"It's not my fault." With more groans, he turned over and subsided on his back. Teazle sniffed at him suspiciously, then decided he'd do equally well as a cushion in this new position. She sprang up onto his abdomen, eliciting a grunt, and settled on his stomach.

Carpenter continued to justify himself. "All I wanted was to talk to Rosie, explain that she wasn't sending me enough to live on, with inflation sky-high. She had plenty; she would have agreed. And even if she hadn't, I would never have harmed her. She's— she was my sister. We grew up together."

"Assuming for the moment that you're telling the truth, why on earth did you take the Sandman with you? You knew he was violent."

"Me take him with me—that's a laugh! I didn't know where she was, did I. I wrote to her bank, but she never wrote back. I even went there once. God, how humiliating, begging a stuffed-shirt bank manager to give me my own sister's address! Vic had contacts who could find her, and did. He didn't need my help, except as a driver."

"You did all the driving?"

"After the years inside, he wasn't too sure about driving. But he could have found someone else. He didn't depend on me. And after all, it was him she was hiding from in the middle of nowhere."

To Eleanor, it sounded as if poor Rosie Mason had been hiding from her cadging, whining brother as well as from her brutal husband. She was beginning to understand a lot of things, but a lot was still obscure. "Do you honestly believe Stone didn't mean to kill her when he hit her with his sandbag?"

"Dunno. It's not as if I could have stopped him. Even if I was strong enough, he moved fast. She was off-balance, went over backwards and hit her head on the hearth. It must have cracked her skull." He covered his face with his hands. "It was horrible, horrible!"

Eleanor nearly told him that his sister had been seriously ill and might have died from the shock of being hit. She decided the knowledge might abate his horror and guilt, and he deserved to suffer both. If he was really feeling those emotions, she didn't want to ease them by so much as a jot. He'd find out soon enough—at the inquest, if not before.

She wondered if he felt any remorse for Nick's and Freeth's predicament—or deaths. How could she have let her curiosity about other matters make her forget them even for a moment? They weren't dead, she told herself. Why tie them up if they were dead?

"What about the two you kidnapped? Did Stone sandbag them?"

"They barged in and saw Rosie," he said sullenly. "He hit them both in just a couple of seconds and they both went down like logs. He only wanted to put them out for a couple of hours, but he couldn't be sure if he'd hit 'em hard enough and in the right spot, being out of practice. That's why we had to tie them up and bring them with us, in case they came round before we'd got away."

"So that they wouldn't give the alarm too soon?"

"Yeah. The idea was to head straight back to the Smoke, dropping them off halfway, somewhere in the country. Vic would give 'em another tap on the head to keep them quiet, and we'd untie them and dump them. It's easy to lie low in London."

"But this isn't anywhere near halfway to London. We can't be more than twenty miles from Tintagel as the crow flies."

"Didn't have much choice, did we. The car chasing us had to be coppers; then we saw the blue light on and off in the distance, getting closer. You can see them a long way off. Vic panicked and said we had to get rid of the evidence in a hurry."

"Get rid . . . ?" Eleanor's voice quavered. "You killed them?"

"No, that would be murder." Carpenter sounded indignant. "Vic reckoned he had a chance of another manslaughter verdict for hitting Rosie. Fat chance. I wouldn't have let him get away with it."

"You'd have testified against him?"

"I knocked him off, didn't I? I should've known better than to go along with any plan of Vic's in the first place. He reckoned the fog was a bit of luck, but that was what did for us. There's a reason he was always hired muscle, following orders. He couldn't plan his way out of a cardboard box," Carpenter said bitterly.

"He must have had some redeeming qualities. Your sister married him."

"He was a business crony of Dad's. I don't know the details. He never told me anything."

"What on earth was your father's business? You said he wasn't a burglar."

"He had a pretty successful antique shop, but the real money came from fencing."

"Fencing?" she said dubiously. Building fences didn't sound like the kind of business that would lead to violence. Not by a competitor, at least, though the Ramblers Association were sometimes a bit stroppy in defence of ancient rights-of-way.

"Buying and selling stolen goods. That's why he wanted me to cosy up to the nobs. He'd pass on the gen I collected and they'd offer him first choice of the best of the loot. A high-class operation. And somehow he managed to keep it completely separate from the antiques. He was a fly one, my pa."

"Was your sister involved in the . . . the fencing business?"

"Never. She helped out in the shop now and then, but that was legit, like I told you. She never even knew Pa was a fence, not till—" He grunted as Teazle stood up, whining, on his stomach and launched herself into the air with a volley of furious barks. She scurried off behind the tor.

"Teazle, hush. You remember Kali." Megan appeared with the little dog in her arms. "Aunt Nell? What on earth are you doing here?"

The big Alsatian followed them, then Jay, holding her leash. Kali nosed at Carpenter. She gave a short, sharp bark and stood leaning over him. She had found her quarry, who lay rigid with terror. "Good girl! Hello, Mrs. Trewynn."

"Mrs. Trewynn!" That was Tariro. "What minnow have you caught here?"

Eleanor sat down, suddenly aware of how weary she was. "I'm very glad to see you all, though I still have several questions for Mr. Carpenter that I haven't had time to put to him."

"He's been talking?" Megan sounded astonished.

"Like anything, dear."

"Confession and absolution," pronounced Tariro in mock solemnity.

"No absolution for this one." Megan nudged the captive with her toe. "You, get up. What's your name? Your *real* name?"

"Don't let it bite me!"

"She's not going to bite you," said Jay disgustedly. "Unless you misbehave. Answer the sergeant."

"F-F-Frederick Carpenter," he stammered, scrambling stiffly to his feet.

"Frederick Carpenter, you are under arrest." Megan gave him the judges' warning. "You'll be informed of the charges later, but they may include assault causing grievous bodily harm, and homicide."

Eleanor's heart stood still. "Megan, Nick's not dead?"

"No, it looks as if he'll be all right. Alan Freeth is in pretty bad shape, though. The doc isn't sure he'll make it."

TWENTY-SEVEN

Megan, Jay, and Kali escorted Carpenter down from the Cheese-wring, leaving Tariro to give Eleanor a hand. Her tiredness was more emotional than physical, she decided, the aftereffect of listening to Carpenter's horror story. Being cold didn't help. The southeast wind funnelled between the tors had thoroughly chilled her.

Whatever the cause, she was happy to accept Tariro's support over the steep and rocky bits she had managed perfectly well earlier. Teazle, after her warm nap, scampered ahead.

Exercise warmed Eleanor, but she was glad to get out of the wind when Tariro suggested she should sit in Megan's deserted car while he went to find out what was going on. Especially as the alternative was to join Megan, who was reporting to DCI Scumble. Sooner or later, she knew, she'd have to face him and listen to just what he thought of her "interference" with police matters. Give him time to cool down!

She would have liked a word with Nick, but the ambulance had already left.

Tariro solicitously draped the tartan rug over her. Teazle,

unfazed by all the unorthodox activity, jumped up on her lap, turned round three times, and went to sleep. Eleanor rested her head against the seat back and started to drowse off.

She dreamed Nick was standing on top of a huge tor, about to jump off. Eleanor, at the bottom, was desperately trying to work out how to stop him, when a massive, hideous figure plastered with mud materialised behind him, arms outstretched to push.

"Aunt Nell!" said the mud man, whereupon she woke up and saw Megan's face. "Sorry to disturb you, but the guv'nor wants to talk to you."

"Mr. Scumble? Can't he wait till tomorrow, when I've got my thoughts together?"

"He'd prefer to hear what Carpenter told you before he questions him." She opened the door and Eleanor followed Teazle out. They walked down along the queue of cars.

"Is he furious?"

"Furious? Good lord no, happy as a sandboy. We've bagged two villains, though it's a pity one is dead, and we've found the hostages alive. It's only a few hours since Mrs. Mason was killed. Murder cases more complicated than simple domestics are rarely cleared up so fast."

"I'm afraid it actually was a 'simple domestic,' though dressed up with a lot of frills."

"What?"

"Didn't he tell you?"

"He said he'd explain everything, but not till he has a solicitor present. Here, you're going to have to tell Mr. Scumble. I've got to go back to Tintagel with Tariro. Apparently Sir Edward is having kittens."

"Good luck, dear. I presume someone will take me back?"

"If you want to."

"I think I'd better. And is someone going to ring up to tell Mr. Bulwer about Alan Freeth?"

"He's not next of kin, Aunt Nell. Officially, we're not responsible for notifying him."

"Oh rubbish! Well, if you can't ring him, can you ring Joce, as the vicar's wife? Ask her to tell Mr. Bulwer."

"We-e-ell . . . Yes, all right."

"Thank you, dear. Hello, Mr. Scumble."

Megan softly and silently faded away.

"Mrs. Trewynn." His voice was carefully neutral. "I gather the man we have detained spoke to you at some length. If you wouldn't mind joining me in the car, Dawson will take notes so that a statement can be prepared for you to sign."

Dawson opened the rear door of the chief inspector's Land Rover and winked at her encouragingly as she climbed in. The step was on the high side for Teazle. He picked her up and handed her to Eleanor. Scumble got in the other side, and Dawson took the front passenger seat. Meanwhile, Eleanor was desperately trying to make a coherent narrative of her "rescue" of Carpenter and the bits and pieces he had told her.

She gave up. It would probably be better for Scumble's blood pressure if he didn't know she had pulled the villain back from the brink. And Carpenter's story had emerged in response to her random questions; coherence was not possible without time to think.

"Well?"

"Oh! The first thing he said was that he'd murdered the Sandman."

"Just like that? Out of the blue, when you walked up to him?" Scumble sounded exceedingly sceptical, and she couldn't very well blame him.

CAROLA DUNN

"Not exactly." Inspiration struck. "He seemed to have a sort of phobia about dogs. You can ask Jay—DS Nayak. He was terrified of Kali."

Dawson snickered.

"Do you mean to tell me, Mrs. Trewynn, that a self-confessed murderer was afraid of Teazle?"

"I couldn't swear to it, but when she jumped onto him and did her tramping-about thing— They say it's to make sure there're no snakes in the bed, but if you ask me, if there were a snake, trampling on it would make it bite. Anyway, Teazle did it, and Carpenter didn't utter so much as a squeak. She went to sleep on his back. Which was good, because I knew she'd warn me if he moved to get up."

"He was lying on his—? No, never mind! Could you possibly put your mind to recalling his exact words when he confessed to murdering Stone?"

Eleanor thought back to the moment when she had come round the tor and seen the man standing on the brink of the quarry. He had told her he was going to throw himself over. But she didn't want to get into that with Scumble.

"The moonlight was bright by then. He must have known you were close on his heels. I said something—I can't remember what—and he said, he'd killed Stone. Then: he said, 'He deserved it, the dirty rotten bastard.'"

"He didn't mention how he killed him?"

"Oh yes. Apparently Stone tripped over a rock and fell in the mud. Carpenter said, 'I put my foot on his back and held him down'—let's see—'held him down till he stopped moving.' Something horrible like that."

"No reason given?"

"He told me Stone had killed his sister."

"His sister!"

"So he said. And her name is—was really Rosie Stone. She was married to Victor Stone. But I'm sure you know that already."

"Not exactly. DI Eliot found hints to that effect in her house. Let's not worry about what I know already, just go on with what Carpenter told you."

Eleanor did her best. When she thought she had wrung her memory dry, Scumble prompted her with painfully patient questions, and more details emerged. At last, he gave up hope of further revelations. Eleanor's relief was tempered by a niggling feeling she had forgotten something important.

"Thank you, Mrs. Trewynn." He leaned forward as if eager to move on. "You've been tremendously helpful. It was a lucky accident that you happened to come across Carpenter—"

"Accident! That's what I was trying to remember to tell you."

Scumble leaned back with a sigh. "Go on. What accident?"

"Carpenter insisted that Stone didn't mean to kill his wife. He hit her because he was angry—no wonder she hid from him!—and she happened to knock her head on the raised hearth. It's just dawned on me: As her husband, he would inherit from her if she died intestate. Isn't there some law to that effect? Or is that immaterial now that he's dead?"

"Not really. Having helped her into the other world, he couldn't profit from her death anyway. Her estate would probably go to her brother. But then her brother murdered her husband. . . . All I can say is that it's going to give the lawyers a lot of work."

"Freeth and Bulwer, I expect. But perhaps she didn't die intestate? If Alan Freeth was there to draw up a will for her, it would explain his presence, though not why he was there for several days. I suppose it might have been complicated—but still, he was only a few miles from home and his office, so why—"

"A waste of time speculating, Mrs. Trewynn. Let's hope he'll be able to inform us. I don't see why I shouldn't tell you that Eliot found burnt papers in the grate that could well have been a will."

"Aha! I still want to know—"

"There are plenty of questions unanswered, but you've pointed me in the right direction to start, even if you should never have been here in the first place."

"I didn't have a great deal of choice, Mr. Scumble. And before you go blaming Megan, nor did she. If we hadn't followed immediately, there'd have been little or no chance of catching them before they disappeared in London."

"I know, I know. She's done an excellent job under difficult circumstance, and I'll try to remember to tell her so. It should ease her recovery from whatever Sir Edward Bellowe's going to be saying to her. Again, my thanks, Mrs. Trewynn. If you think of anything else before you sign the statement tomorrow, please let me or Dawson know. He's going to drive you home now."

"Thank you."

"Dawson, kindly restrain your urge to break the land speed record while you have Mrs. Trewynn in your car. When you've delivered her safely, go back to the nick and type up your report."

"Of this conversation, sir?"

"From the moment you joined in the bloody—beg pardon, Mrs. Trewynn—chase, including this conversation. But for pity's sake, leave the African laddie out of it!"

"Right, sir. Uh, sir, it's not going to be that easy getting my car out of here. It's the second in line, after DS Pencarrow's."

"Well, she's already left, so there must be a way. At least, she hasn't come back to say she's stuck. Go and look."

Dawson got out, opened the door, and held it for Eleanor. Teazle jumped down. Reminded of the high step of the vehicle, he offered Eleanor his arm. In his eyes, all too obviously, she was a frail little old lady, in spite of having apprehended a murderer single-handed.

Ah well, his heart was in the right place. Accepting his help, she said, "I'm pretty sure I know how to get back to the road. If you just go straight ahead along the old railway, we'll come to the quarry, and the main track from the car park ends up there, too."

"Makes sense." They trudged up the row of cars and found Megan's gone. "Looks as if Sarge got out somehow. Hope she hasn't come to grief like the van."

"The van went astray trying to hide off the beaten path." Seated in Dawson's patrol car and once again jolting over the stone sleepers, Eleanor went on, "Carpenter said their plan—the Sand-man's plan—was to drop off their hostages halfway to London, but with Megan closing in from one side and you from the other, they had to get rid of the evidence fast. Not very clever, either of them."

"I wouldn't call it very clever of Carpenter to blab to you. What on earth possessed him?"

"I suspect he was simply in a state of shock. He'd seen his sister killed in front of his eyes and been coerced into kidnapping and abandoning two strangers to their fate. He's no saint, but he isn't a thoroughgoing villain like Stone. Weak and selfish and not very scrupulous. He was horrified by what he'd got into and would have babbled to anyone, the first person he saw."

"'A waste of time speculating,' as the guv'nor would say. Ah, here we are. You were dead right, Mrs. Trewynn. As nice a turnaround as you could ask for."

"We're in the quarry. The railway was built to move the granite." Dawson peered up at the top of the cliff. "I see the tors up there.

So that's where you found Carpenter?" He drove on down the slope towards the car park.

"Yes." She wasn't sure whether he was questioning her or just chatting.

"What took you up there?"

"I wasn't sure where I was. The fog was beginning to break up, so I thought if I just climbed as high as I could, I'd be able to see the cars, or the village, or some landmark. Even a glimpse of Rough Tor would have told me which direction was which. Mr. Dawson, could you possibly take me to the hospital before we go to Tintagel? I badly want to see how Nick—Nick Gresham—and Alan Freeth are, and you know how impossible it is to persuade hospitals to give information on the phone."

"Course, why not? Bodmin they were taken to, so it's on the way for you, and it makes no odds to me."

"It's very kind of you."

"Not really. The guv'nor's done for my plans for the evening, and I like driving."

"So I've heard."

"Not to worry." He sounded as if he were grinning. They reached the road and he turned right. "The guv'nor said to take it easy, and I will."

"In the normal way, I wouldn't mind a bit of speed," Eleanor said apologetically, "but after racing through the lanes earlier, round blind corners and flying off humpback bridges, and watching you nearly collide with the van on the old aerodrome . . ."

"That was a bit of fun, that was! We don't often get the chance of a real car chase hereabouts."

"I imagine not." And a very good thing too; in Eleanor's opinion, the best place for car chases was in James Bond films.

"You have to be behind the wheel, though. It sounds as if those poor buggers rolling about in the back of the van got pretty badly bashed up."

"I do hope they'll be all right."

"Gresham's a neighbour of yours, isn't he?"

"Next-door neighbour. And it's my fault he was there to be kidnapped. My car broke down, so he took me to Tintagel, and he couldn't get home again because of that dreadful storm."

"Blame the storm, not yourself, Mrs. Trewynn. Or better, blame the Sandman. What I heard is, Gresham's not too bad; it's the solicitor who's in bad shape, and him being there was nothing to do with you. Lucky for him that Sarge happened to be on the lookout for him when he was kidnapped, else he wouldn't've been found so soon."

"Poor Mr. Freeth! I wonder whether they'll send him to the Plymouth hospital, like Kalith."

Jay Nayak's young cousin Kalith had been too ill for the local cottage hospital's facilities, but he had been suffering from exposure and pneumonia as well as concussion. Alan Freeth hadn't been lying out on the moor, exposed to cold and damp, for very long, thanks to Jay's dog.

Concussion alone could be very serious, though. Eleanor hoped Megan had remembered to ring up Jocelyn and ask her to break the news to Roland Bulwer.

TWENTY-EIGHT

Megan and Tariro had reached the parking lot in time to see the ambulance carrying Nick and Freeth turn right into Minions village.

"Damn," said Megan, "that means they'll be taken to the hospital in Bodmin. Makes it more difficult for me to visit. What's more, the Bodmin coppers won't like cooperating when one of us goes to take statements from them. Still, that's for the super to worry about." She turned left.

"We're not going back the same way?" Tariro asked.

"You can't get there from here."

"Huh?"

"The moor's in the way. Only the A30 crosses it, and it runs northeast to southwest. We want to go northwest. I think it's slightly shorter going round the north side, which is pretty much the way we came, but without all the van's diversions in their effort to lose us."

Tariro checked his watch. "It's still surprisingly early. It felt as if we were being 'diverted' and then tramping about for ages, but with luck we'll get back in time for dinner. There's a phone box," he added as they drove into Alton. "You said you promised Mrs. Trewynn to ring the vicar's wife."

"If it's functioning . . ." Megan pulled up next to the red box. Its light was on; phones in villages were vandalised much less often than in towns and cities. It even had a directory for North Cornwall, including Port Mabyn. And no one had torn out the one page she wanted. She found the Stearnses' number.

The disadvantage of a rural phone was old-fashioned equipment that took only old coinage. Megan had nothing but new pence in her purse. She pushed open the door and called, "Tariro!" He rolled down the window. "Have you got any old pennies or sixpences, by any chance?"

"A couple of sixpences. One is George the Sixth. I was going to keep them as souvenirs."

"I'll replace them, promise, King George and all."

He handed over his treasures. She returned to the phone, shoved the Elizabeth II coin in the slot, dialled the number, and listened to it ringing: *Brr-brr, brr-brr* . . . If no one answered, she'd have to stop again on the way to Tintagel.

"Hello?" said a tentative male voice.

Megan pressed button A. "Mr. Stearns? This is Megan Pencarrow. Mrs. Trewynn's niece."

"The detective." The vicar sounded pleased with himself for remembering. "What can I do for you, my dear?"

She was about to tell him, when she recalled that Aunt Nell had specified his wife, though he was the obvious person to lend aid and comfort to Freeth's partner. "May I speak to Mrs. Stearns, please, if she's available."

She heard him calling, "It's for you, dear. That nice detective . . ."

"Megan? Megan, I hope you're going to explain—"

"Mrs. Stearns, sorry to interrupt, but I'm using a public phone and my time is running out. Please listen. Mr. Freeth—Alan Freeth—has been seriously injured. He's been taken to Bodmin Cottage Hospital. I'm passing on a plea from Aunt Nell asking you to inform Mr. Bulwer. This is not an official request, but I hope you—"

"Of course, Megan. Timothy and I will go to him at once and ring the hospital from his house. I hope Eleanor is not in any trouble?"

"She's fine. I'd better let her tell you all about it herself."

"Whatever happened to Alan Freeth? A car crash?"

"I'm sorry, I can't talk about it. Thank you, Mrs. Stearns. I must go. Good-bye."

She managed to escape further questions. Hanging up, she automatically pressed button B, though she supposed as a police officer she probably shouldn't. Tariro's sixpence did not reappear in the little cup.

Returning to the car, she gave him five pee. "That's to pay for the call. I didn't have to use the George sixpence—here you are—but I'll replace the other, honestly."

"That's all right, there are plenty of Queen Elizabeth coins still in circulation. Did you get through?"

"Yes." She drove on through Alton. "I'm sure Jocelyn Stearns will do everything that's necessary. She's a formidable woman."

"So," said Tariro, "is your aunt."

"She is. Fluffy and sweet and formidable. I wonder what really happened up there above the quarry. Did she tell you, as you were walking down together?"

"She said you wouldn't like her to talk about it, and Detective Inspector Scumble would wax mighty wroth. All I know is what she told us when we found them. The way he was lying, though, flat on his back— He seemed to be scared stiff. I wish she were going to be there at the hotel to protect me from Sir Edward!"

"I don't think you need worry about that," Megan said drily, "as the whole aim of the meeting is to conciliate and win you over, isn't it? I'm the one who's going to get it in the neck."

Tariro laughed. "I expect I can protect you from that. I can witness that you had no choice but to follow the van, and I absolutely refused to be left behind. I would have refused, if you'd had time to offer to drop me off. In fact, he ought to be grateful to you. You've given me a new appreciation of the British police."

"Favourable, I hope."

"But of course. And of the English countryside, also. I've always thought it a bit tame, compared to Africa, but our country walk today could hardly have been more exciting had we unexpectedly met a lion or an elephant."

"Very funny."

"I have to admit I enjoyed the expedition, though I'm sorry your boyfriend and the lawyer were hurt."

"He's not— Oh, all right, I suppose he is. Sort of."

"I don't understand how he—how either of them got mixed up in the murder of Mrs. Mason."

"Nick was just spending a couple of nights there as a bed-and-breakfaster. They both seem to have arrived at her house at just the wrong moment. That's about all I know."

"It's all very well for you," Tariro grumbled. "You're bound to find out all the details sooner or later, when you read the reports or whatever. I'll probably never find out."

"Don't worry, it'll be in the press. The *North Cornwall Times*, for sure. Their reporter, David Skan, adores Aunt Nell. I'd be surprised if it doesn't make the nationals, too."

"Send me a copy of the *North Cornwall Times*, will you? Care of my college, Brasenose, will reach me."

"Without your surname? Yes, I daresay it would. Can't be too many Tariros studying there. If you weren't so damned incognito, you'd probably be called to testify at Carpenter's trial."

"Really? Damn! But I suppose I'd better not offer myself as a witness. Sir Edward would blow a fuse. Speaking of which, I hope you intend to go in with me to help me explain my absence."

"Scaredy-cat? I don't believe it. I'm not supposed to use the outside door—"

"You're not supposed to have taken me on a car chase and a hunt for killers in the fog on the moor."

"True, but all the same . . . Don't tell him too much. No names. Otherwise, I'll leave it to your discretion, and I'll give you time to butter him up before I make my appearance through the correct entrance."

"You don't think suppressing his irritation with me will bring his blood to the boil in time for your— Oh lord! I've just thought! How am I going to explain Mrs. Trewynn's absence? Shall I say she's been detained by the police? Helping them with their enquiries?"

"Don't you dare say anything of the sort!"

"Right, baas," said Tariro, laughing. "I'd better just let that formidable lady deal with it herself."

They crossed the A39 and plunged again into the lanes. "Nearly there. And nearly dinner-time. If you're lucky, Lady Bellowe will make Sir Edward wait until after eating to blast you to smithereens. I definitely need to fortify myself before facing him."

The clouds still hung over the coast, so it was pitch-dark when Megan drove round the hotel and dropped Tariro at the tower entrance. She waited a moment to make sure the door was opened to him, then sped off round to the front.

The receptionist's shocked stare suggested that her wanderings on the moor had not left her appearance unscathed. She hurried upstairs and knocked on Ken's door.

She heard hasty strides crossing the room. The door opened. "Megan, where the hell have you . . . Good lord, what have you been up to? You look like something the cat dragged in. Are you all right?"

"I'm fine. But—"

"You've missed all the excitement."

"I have? What excitement?"

"What we came for, of course. Spies." He stood aside. "Come in and I'll tell you."

"You've caught a spy?"

"*Ssshh.* Come on, come in. We can't talk about it here."

Right then, Megan didn't give a hoot about spies. But it was easier to go in than to argue. She sank into the only chair, avoiding looking at the mirror. She didn't want to see what it would show her. "Well? You're serious? A nosy Chinese restaurant proprietor turned up?"

Ken sat on the bed. "No, a couple of Germans."

"Germans? But—"

"Almost certainly East German, and the Russians get the DDR to do some of their dirty work for them. They don't stick out like sore thumbs in the West, as Soviets tend to. Or perhaps they have interests of their own in Africa, who knows."

"Who cares? What makes you think they aren't perfectly ordinary West German tourists?"

"Who've been misinformed about the Cornish climate? Come

off it! No, it was Nontando who gave me the tip-off. We were sitting in the car in the parking lot—"

"Snogging."

"MYOB. At least *I* was here and keeping my eyes open."

Megan could think of a rude response or two to that. She kept her mouth shut. The last thing she wanted was for him to think she was jealous. Which she wasn't. Her mind flew back to Nick . . . but she'd better listen.

"A couple with rucksacks came up the drive," Ken went on. "Nontando recognised the woman at once. She's a postgrad at LSE, in the English department."

"Sounds perfectly respectable."

"Good cover. The odd part is that she's been sucking up to Nontando and a couple of other Zimbabwean students, although—and Nontando isn't very specific about this. It must be painful. I gather she has a strong impression that the woman is uncomfortable around dark-skinned people."

"Perhaps she's trying to overcome—"

"Will you just listen, Megan, or we're not going to get anywhere! In spite of the efforts that have been made to keep this bloody conference secret, it's possible something about it and its location has leaked out. It's possible—grant me this!—that the powers vying to gain influence in Zimbabwe are interested; otherwise you and I wouldn't be here. It's possible the woman and her companion are East German and have been sent to find out what they can. Right?"

"I suppose so. Why are they all so desperate to control a country that's nothing but tobacco farms?"

"Because the tobacco farms are sitting on top of huge mineral deposits. Or next door anyway."

"Oh! Tariro never mentioned that!"

"Nontando did."

"You didn't already know?"

"I don't keep tabs on the economies of all our ex-colonies."

"Good. That makes me feel better. So what did you do about Nontando's German and her friend? Even if you knew for certain they're spies, you couldn't arrest them. And warning them off would just convince them they're right."

"Obviously. As soon as they'd disappeared into the hotel, I drove Nontando round to the back and immured her in her tower with dire threats about staying hidden. She doesn't really care whether Sir Edward's machinations are kept secret, and she doesn't take to being told what to do, so I can only hope she'll be sensible."

"Didn't someone say she favours the Chinese version of communism? They're even worse than the Soviets for telling people what to do."

Ken laughed. "She expects to be one of those telling other people what to do, à la Madame Mao. She made me climb over to the castle this afternoon."

"No, did she really? I must remember to congratulate her."

"I think she'll behave herself, though, at least as long as Sir Edward is her host. Once I'd stowed her away to the best of my ability, I went to have a chat with your barman pal. He couldn't tell me much, because the Germans hadn't been into the bar. They just arrived this afternoon, while we were out—"

"Ken," Megan interrupted, noticing the time, "can you cut it short, or you'll have to tell me the rest later. I really must go and make myself decent and report to Sir Edward. It's quarter of an hour since I dropped off Tariro."

"All right, long story short: Later on, I met them in the bar. We got matey and in the course of a friendly chat I mentioned that

I'd come to Cornwall for a weekend with my girlfriend. We don't see much of each other, I told them, since you had transferred down here to the Cornish police to be near your family but I stayed in town because I was happy working at Scotland Yard. They pricked up their ears at *police* and almost cringed at *Scotland Yard*. You should have seen their faces."

"Ken . . ."

"I'm getting there. Inge suddenly remembered having promised to ring the aunt she's living with, who's not well. I suspect they'll be leaving in the morning."

"And how did you explain your girlfriend's absence?"

"Lying down with a queasy tum after lunch. Another induce-ment to depart. I just had to hope if you came in, I'd be able to warn you before you blew it. Which brings us back to where were you?" He grinned. "And what are you going to tell Sir Edward to excuse your dereliction of duty? And taking whatsisname with you, into the bargain?"

"Nothing but the truth." Megan stood up wearily. "I was hunt-ing down a couple of murderers—acquaintances of ours, as it happens—and rescuing their hostages. Tariro was a great help."

She left him speechless.

TWENTY-NINE

"I'm sorry, Mrs. Trewynn," Dawson said apologetically as they drove through the outskirts of Bodmin, "I've been racking my brains to think of an excuse to drive you to Plymouth, but the guv'nor would go through the roof."

"Good heavens no. I wouldn't dream of asking you. Besides, I hope neither Nick nor Alan Freeth will be sent there. I wonder why they were brought to Bodmin?"

"The ambulance came from here, the one that picked them up. The other was from Launceston. That'll be for the body, when the SOCO's had a go at it and it's brought down off the moor."

"But Rajendra practises at Launceston hospital."

"Dr. Prthnavi? He went with them in the ambulance. I'm sure he'll hand them over to the best doc available."

"Yes, of course, but . . ."

"I'll tell you what, while you're at the hospital waiting to find out what's what, I'll go and get us takeaway. You'll feel better after eating something. At least, I know I will."

"I am hungry. I hadn't realised. That sounds like a good idea."

"Chinese? Or there's a nice little Indian place in Bodmin. I bet you like Indian?"

"I do, but if we're going to eat in the hospital waiting room—if they let us—it had better be Chinese. Not everyone is keen on the smell of curry."

"More fools them. The dog must be peckish, too. Does she like Indian?"

"If it's edible, she'll eat it."

"Right, then, Indian it is. I've given myself a craving, talking about it. We'll eat in the car."

The very thought of food heartened Eleanor. When they reached Bodmin Cottage Hospital, she was ready to do battle for information if necessary.

Dawson stopped in front of the hospital. "I'll wait for a few minutes in case they say there's no news yet, or something. If you have to wait, we might as well go and eat in comfort and come back after."

Telling Teazle to stay, Eleanor went through the swinging glass door into the lobby. The girl at the reception desk was on the phone. She smiled and nodded but put her finger to her lips.

"Dr. Vine, I have Mr. Coates for you on line one." She pressed a couple of buttons on the phone; then her voice came over the intercom. "Dr. Prthnavi, there's an urgent call for you on line two. Please respond ASAP. Dr. Prthnavi, emergency, line two." She pressed another button and turned her attention to Eleanor. "Visiting hours seven to eight, madam."

Eleanor glanced at the clock above the girl's head. It was ten past eight already. "I just wanted to enquire—"

"All the medical staff are busy. We just had a couple of patients arrive in A & E, so—"

"They're the ones I want to enquire about."

"The doctors are still evaluating them. You can wait, but unless you're next of kin, you'd do better to phone in the morning."

Eleanor had to admit that she was not next of kin. She was trying to decide whether to wait or rush out in hopes that Dawson was still there, when Dr. Prthnavi appeared, struggling into his overcoat. Eleanor went to help him.

He greeted her with unexpected enthusiasm. "*Namaste*, Eleanor. Is it possible you are able to assist me? A patient of mine is about to give birth. A nervous young woman, and there are complications. I came by police car and ambulance, so I have no means to reach her. If you could drive me—"

"I came by police car, too." As she spoke, Eleanor hustled him towards the door. "If we're lucky, he'll still be— Yes! Mr. Dawson, Dr. Prthnavi has an urgent case and no transport. Would you mind taking him—"

"Launceston way? Right, hop in, Doc."

"There you go, Rajendra, you couldn't be in better hands." Faster hands, anyway.

"You coming along, Mrs. Trewynn? Or I can come back for you."

Eleanor hesitated, but she was desperately anxious to know about Nick and Freeth. "I think I'll stay, then. Thanks so much, Mr. Dawson."

She waved them off, then realised they'd left in such a hurry that the dog was still in the car. "Oh dear!" she exclaimed aloud. Teazle would be worried but safe, she assured herself. Dawson wouldn't be gone long, with an emergency giving him an excuse to drive fast. Thank goodness the fog had cleared.

Meanwhile, she might as well pop along to the Indian restaurant and have a bite to eat. She really was extremely hungry.

Some forty minutes later, she returned to the hospital feeling much better and more hopeful. The receptionist was typing now.

She looked up, not at all pleased to see Eleanor back, but she said, "I told Dr. Vine you're a friend of Dr. Prthnavi. He said he'd have a word with you if you returned. Could I have your name, please? I'll let him know you're here."

"Mrs. Trewynn. Thank you."

Eleanor took a seat in one of the excruciatingly uncomfortable plastic chairs lined up against the wall. The people—men, no doubt—who designed such things without regard to human anatomy ought to be forced to sit in them for a few hours before they started mass production.

After five minutes, her back hurt, which it rarely did, regardless of her age. She got up and strolled over to look out of the glass door, wondering how long Dr. Vine would keep her waiting and how long it would be before Dawson came to pick her up. A vaguely familiar car pulled up just in front of the hospital.

From it the tall, stooped form of Roland Bulwer extricated itself, not without difficulty. He went round to the other side to open the driver's door, and Jocelyn Stearns stepped out.

She was wearing a beautiful tapestry coat that Eleanor hadn't seen before. Though dressed almost entirely from the LonStar shop, Joce was undoubtedly the best-dressed vicar's wife in Cornwall. To be fair, she always had one of the other volunteers price clothes she wanted to buy, though she did have the advantage of making her choice before they were moved from storeroom to shop.

She advised Eleanor on her purchases, too, but Eleanor just didn't have the right figure for elegance.

As Eleanor opened the glass door to go and greet her and Mr. Bulwer, the rear car door opened and a plaintive voice said, "Jocelyn, my dear, I'm afraid I can't undo the safety belt." The vicar had come with them. Timothy Stearns's usual transport was a

Vespa. On it he tootled happily and accident-free round his parishes, but somehow he still hadn't managed to master the intricacies of the newfangled seat belts.

"Coming, dear. Eleanor! I didn't expect to see you here."

"It's a long story, Joce. Mr. Bulwer, I'm so sorry Alan was hurt." She offered him both her hands and he took them in a convulsive grasp. His hands were icy. "I was just waiting for the doctor to come and tell me how he's doing, and Nick. Come inside."

Ever courteous, he gave her his arm and opened the door for her, though he was much more in need of support. As the door swung to behind the Stearnses, the receptionist rose to her feet and began a flustered protest, and a large, pink, harassed man in a white coat, stethoscope round his neck, arrived from the rear. His face was rosy as a baby's, and thinning white hair with the scalp showing through added to the overall impression of pinkness.

He frowned at the four intruders and asked, "Mrs. Trewynn?"

"I'm Eleanor Trewynn. Dr. Vine, I presume. I've come to ask after your two A & E patients, Nicholas Gresham and Alan Freeth."

"I'm afraid I can give information only to close relatives."

"That's all right. I'm Nick's aunt." At least he wasn't insisting on next of kin, unlike the receptionist. "Aunt" was a permissible fib, Eleanor considered, in anticipation—or at least in hope—of becoming his aunt by marriage one of these days. Joce gave her a shocked look.

"And I, Doctor," said Timothy in his gentle manner, "I am the vicar of Port Mabyn. Both Mr. Gresham and Mr. Freeth are my parishioners." He patted Jocelyn's shoulder. "This is my wife and my right hand, Mrs. Stearns."

"Very well. And . . . ?" Vine turned to Roland Bulwer.

"I'm a lawyer." His voice was tightly controlled. "The name is Bulwer. Alan—Alan Freeth—is my partner, and I hold his power of attorney."

"It's most unorthodox," the doctor complained. He hummed as he considered his options in the face of such unorthodoxy. "You'd better all come through here."

They followed him into a small office walled with grey metal filing cabinets. Seating himself behind the desk, he waved the ladies to a pair of the nasty plastic chairs in front of it, leaving the men to stand.

"Yes, well." After this unilluminating beginning, Vine took a pair of rimless spectacles from his breast pocket, put them on, and peered over them at his audience. Then he straightened some papers on the desk and set them aside with neat precision. He ran his hands through what was left of his hair.

"Doctor, please!" burst from Bulwer.

"Hm. I daresay the police have informed you that my patients' injuries are the result of some sort of criminal activity."

"Dear me," said the vicar, "this is very shocking and most distressing."

Dr. Vine ignored him. "As a result, I have to be more than usually cautious in what I say, so as not to compromise their investigation. I can tell you that both have severe contusions over their entire bodies. Mr. Gresham says both were hit on the head with a blunt instrument. My colleague, Dr. Prthnavi—an acquaintance of yours, I gather, Mrs. Trewynn?"

"Yes, indeed. A good friend."

"Dr. Prthnavi has found indications that such is the case. He's better versed in these fine distinctions than I, being a police surgeon. If it is so, then Mr. Freeth appears to have been hit considerably harder than Mr. Gresham. In Dr. Prthnavi's expert opinion. The significance of the difference, if any, is a matter for the police."

" 'Out of practice,' " Eleanor murmured, "because of being in prison."

"What? What's that?"

"Just something I ought to tell the police, if I didn't already."

"Never mind that," cried Bulwer. "How badly is he—are they hurt?"

"Gresham is badly bruised, has a cracked rib or two, both shoulders wrenched, with a possible torn tendon, and what appears to be a mild concussion. He should be out of here in twenty-four to forty-eight hours. He spoke of someone called Megan. I'm not sure who . . ." He looked at them interrogatively.

"Megan is my niece," said Eleanor. "I'll see her tomorrow, if not tonight, and I'll pass on any message."

"Perhaps I'd better write it down." He took a prescription pad from his pocket and scribbled a few words. Eleanor hoped they were more legible than the majority of prescriptions.

He didn't fold the paper and, his writing being surprisingly clear, she couldn't help reading it as he passed it to her. "Give Megan my love." She had to suppress a smile as the doctor continued.

"Freeth, I'm afraid, is not so lucky. Besides even worse bruising, his concussion is severe. I would prefer that he be in a hospital with more facilities, but I believe moving him is a worse choice. I have requested the advice of a brain specialist from Plymouth. He's on his way."

Bulwer buried his head in his hands. "Oh lord, oh lord, oh lord!" He raised a haggard face. "May I see him?"

"No point. He's unconscious, and the less disturbance, the better."

It was Jocelyn who put into words what Eleanor did not choose to voice. "Doctor, is his life in danger?"

"Brain injuries are unpredictable, Mrs. Stearns. I can give no assurance that he will recover."

THIRTY

The Stearnses left to take Roland Bulwer home to Port Mabyn. He was going to get his own car and come back to Bodmin. Shortly after their departure, Teazle returned unscathed from her unexpected trip to Launceston.

"She slept most of the way," DC Dawson reported. "On the doctor's knees on the way, and on mine on the way back."

"Didn't she get in your way, driving? I never let her do that."

"Better hope she won't expect to now. I let her out for a moment when we got there, so we can leave right away if you're ready."

Having been refused permission to see Nick, Eleanor was ready. She reckoned Megan and Tariro must have reached Tintagel long since and explained their disappearance to Sir Edward, so she wouldn't have to. Just as well, as the more she considered the events of the day, the more questions she had.

Many of them were questions DI Scumble had asked her, which she hadn't been able to answer. At least that meant a possibility that he would find out the answers, and with luck Megan would pass them on. She decided to start making a list.

With Dawson at the wheel, the return to Tintagel was accomplished in record time. Eleanor directed him round to the tower door, feeling in the pocket of her slacks for the key. She was sure she'd put it there, but she couldn't find it, nor in any other pocket, and she hadn't carried a bag for a walk on the cliffs, the original aim of the expedition. Either she hadn't brought the key, taking for granted that Tariro or Megan would have one, or it had fallen out at some point in her subsequent adventures.

By then, Dawson had opened the car door for her and was waiting patiently, and Teazle had already hopped down. She thanked Dawson warmly for his chauffeuring and his patience, then went to ring the doorbell. He got back into the car but stayed watching until Norton opened the door for her. She looked back and waved as she stepped inside. Dawson zoomed off, far too fast for a car park.

"Her ladyship will be relieved to hear you're back safely, madam. I shall inform her while you—"

"Thank you, Norton, I'll tell her myself. I know I'm not fit to be seen in company, but if I go to my room, I'll probably have a bath and go straight to bed."

"Very good, madam. May I bring you a hot drink?" He surveyed her with his impassive gaze. "Or a brandy, perhaps?"

"A brandy would be most welcome. And Teazle hasn't been fed yet."

"I shall see to it at once, madam."

Eleanor went up to the sitting room.

Tariro was the first to see her. He jumped up, grinning, looking very cock-a-hoop. "Mrs. Trewynn!"

Gina welcomed her back with open arms. "My dear, you must be exhausted! Come and sit down. Have you eaten? I held dinner back for half an hour, but we had no idea when you would get here, so we went ahead and ate."

"I'm sorry, I should have rung up from the hospital. It's been such a . . . a *confusing* few hours."

"You were hurt?"

"No, not at all."

Tariro became solemn. "You went to the hospital they took Megan's Nick and the other poor chap to? How are they?"

Eleanor gave them a brief report. Sir Edward and Nontando stopped what appeared to be an acrimonious dispute to listen. The secretary, Payne, murmured something in Sir Edward's ear. Sir Edward nodded, looking resigned, and came over to offer his sympathies.

"Friends of yours, I gather, Mrs. Trewynn. A very shocking thing to happen. I must admit I could scarcely believe my ears when Tariro and your niece told me the story."

"I doubt they told you the half of it."

"We didn't," Tariro said regretfully. "Megan warned me not to, and she left out lots that she said could compromise the case." He gave Eleanor a meaningful look, which she interpreted as a warning not to talk about her part in arresting Carpenter.

Norton came in with a tray of drinks, followed by Teazle. Eleanor gladly abandoned the subject that had occupied her thoughts to the exclusion of all else for the past several hours.

Gina, as always, had plenty of anodyne chat to supplant touchy topics, at least until Eleanor had taken her last sip of cognac and declared her intent to take a hot bath and go to bed. "I'll go up with you," Gina said, "and get you a couple of aspirin in case you have trouble sleeping."

The door closed behind them. "A transparent ruse," said Eleanor. "I never have trouble sleeping. What did you want to tell me?"

"Oh, just about the sliver of excitement we had here while you were off doing your derring-do. And incidentally, Tariro won't breathe a word about whatever it was you did, but he's full of admiration."

"He's a nice boy. Now tell. Is it secret from your husband?"

"Not at all. It's just that I didn't want to set him off again, him and Nontando. He's not happy, poor dear. She and DS Faraday between them have convinced him a German couple staying here are East Germans spying for the Russians. Mr. Faraday seems to think he's scared them off without letting them know there's actually anything going on that they might be interested in."

"How clever. I expect he's right. Megan says he's a good policeman."

"But Edward says the very fact that they're here shows there's been a leak and renders the whole business null and void. And Nontando, who favours the Chinese, seems to think Edward could have them arrested and charged if he tried. She's annoyed with DS Faraday, too. I suspect, if she ever attains a position of power, she's not going to be terribly scrupulous about the rule of law. Like Madame Mao, she'll make her own."

"Heavens above! What a lot of drama. Is Sir Edward abandoning the whole idea?"

"The idea of secrecy. Not the idea of getting to know and hoping to influence the younger generation. He's thinking of approaching them singly, though. Tariro and Nontando are not a happy combination, in spite of your noble efforts, for which I thank you. Good night, my dear, sleep well."

After her bath, Eleanor had intended to start a written list of her questions arising from the day's events. She was too sleepy. Drowsing in bed, she found one in particular circling in her head. What was Freeth's relationship to Rosie Mason/Stone? At first, she had thought they might be brother and sister, perhaps estranged when she found out he was gay. But she had been Rosie Carpenter before marrying Stone, it seemed—unless Carpenter was as fake a name as the egregious Adrian Arbuthnot.

Or were Freeth and Rosie cousins? Against that, against their being any sort of close relatives, was the fact that Carpenter/Arbuthnot had not, apparently, recognised Alan Freeth. Or perhaps he had, but had some inscrutable reason for not admitting it. . . .

Eleanor fell asleep.

The following day, the tower party broke up. Saying good-bye to Tariro, Eleanor invited him to come and stay if ever he felt like a holiday in Cornwall. Sir Edward sent him and Payne to Launceston station in his Bentley, driven by Norton, as Megan was otherwise occupied. Nontando and Ken Faraday left together, to all appearances reconciled. When the Bentley returned from Launceston, the Bellowes gave Eleanor a lift to Port Mabyn on their way to the Scillies.

Eleanor wished them good weather for the crossing.

Two days later, Nick came home, as promised. Megan brought him from the hospital in an unmarked police car. She had to take an official statement, she explained to Eleanor.

Later, Eleanor told Jocelyn, who was driving her to pick up Nick's car, just released from police custody. With some trepidation, she added, "And she moved in with him because he needs looking after until he's fully recovered,"

The vicar's wife was scandalised. "That's no excuse."

"His shoulders are still very painful. He's not allowed to paint, though the doctor says he may draw, as long as he takes frequent breaks. But he's not supposed to lift anything heavier than a cup of tea. He can't manage on his own."

"Megan is away at work most of the day."

CAROLA DUNN

"During the day, I can look in now and then," Eleanor countered. "It's no good making a fuss about it. That's the way young people do things these days."

"They're both in their thirties," Jocelyn said stringently. "Quite old enough to make a proper commitment to each other, if that's how they feel."

"Commitment is in the mind and heart, don't you think?"

"Not in the eyes of the Church or the law."

"Just consider the divorce rate."

"That's what Timothy says. Really, sometimes I don't know where he gets his odd notions!"

They reached Mrs. Mason's house, already looking forlorn and deserted, with police barriers surrounding it. The three cars—Freeth's Range Rover, Nick's Traveller, and another that must have been Rosie Mason's—were each individually barricaded, but Megan had told Eleanor to go ahead and move the barriers round Nick's.

Teazle hopped out as soon as Eleanor opened the door. She wanted a walk. It was a beautiful day, windy but sunny.

"I'll just take her up to St. Materiana's," said Eleanor, having thanked Joce for the lift. "Do you want to come with us?"

Jocelyn hadn't brought any suitable shoes, so Eleanor and Teazle enjoyed a walk free of theological debate.

Eleanor also enjoyed the drive home to Port Mabyn in a car that barely rattled at all. Nick wasn't allowed to drive for at least a week, so she was to have the loan of the Traveller while the Incorruptible was in the shop for a new starter and rust repair.

Nick was cheerful, in spite of his aches and pains and the fact that his envisioned painting of King Arthur's castle had gone wonky on him, as he put it. Megan had retrieved his sketches from

Mrs. Mason's house; the drawings of the kitchen now absorbed him and he could talk of little but angles and planes.

Things were otherwise with his fellow kidnap victim. Alan Freeth still drifted between life and death.

The brain surgeon had decided that moving him would surely kill him, and had instead operated in Bodmin in less than ideal conditions to relieve pressure on his brain.

Roland Bulwer, growing visibly more haggard, spent every day working like a demon to serve his partner's clients as well as his own. The first two nights, he had spent in fitful sleep in a hideously uncomfortable plastic chair in the bleak hospital waiting room.

Eleanor and Jocelyn persuaded him to take a hotel room near the hospital, where he could easily reach Freeth's bedside in a few minutes if there were any change in his condition. The matron had been unwilling to recognise his right to information and access, but in the end she couldn't resist Timothy Stearns's dog collar and gentle persistence.

Megan was sent up to London for a couple of days to consult Scotland Yard's records and make other enquiries about Stone, Carpenter, Rosie Mason, and the father of the last two.

When she came back to Cornwall, Megan also returned to Nick's, bringing many of her possessions with her, although he was getting about very well on his own now. So there she was, living right next door to Eleanor, but she still wouldn't answer any of her aunt's questions. It was infuriating.

Eleanor attended the inquests on Rosie Mason and Victor Stone, as a prospective witness. Both were adjourned for three weeks after medical evidence was taken. She didn't have to testify, and she learned nothing new except that Stone was considered to have suffocated rather than drowned. However, the pathologist

CAROLA DUNN

couldn't state with any certainty whether Mrs. Mason had died of a heart attack or head trauma. Both had occurred virtually simultaneously.

But Alan Freeth lived. Another few days passed before he was declared out of danger, as Jocelyn reported to Eleanor.

"Mr. Bulwer says they're as sure as they can be at this stage that there's no significant brain damage. He's still in serious condition, of course. Roland's visits are limited to fifteen minutes, but at least Alan is awake, alert, and able to talk."

"What a relief! No other visitors?"

"Not yet. Not even Timothy. The police are going to be allowed to question him for a few minutes at a time, as long as they don't upset him."

Megan, as CaRaDoC's only woman detective, was chosen as least upsetting. After a week of regular visits, she admitted to Eleanor, "He's filled in practically all the gaps in our investigation. But sorry, Aunt Nell, I'm still not allowed to discuss it with you. And the guv'nor said to warn you again not to talk to the press. If David Skan turns up on your doorstep, tell him he'll just have to wait till after the resumed inquest. Freeth will be home soon. Then I'll be able to take a full statement from him, in time for the inquest."

Eleanor sighed. "I suppose at the inquest I'll find out as much as I'm ever likely to find out."

"I wouldn't say that. There'll be the trial after that, and much more comes out at a trial than at an inquest."

"A trial? Even though Carpenter has confessed?"

"One reason I can't talk to you about the case is that Carpenter may have confessed to you, but he's clammed up, on the advice of his solicitor. He hasn't said a word to the purpose since he was arrested. He's not making things easy by pleading guilty. Your evidence is going to be extremely important."

A couple of days after Alan Freeth came home from the hospital, Eleanor received an invitation to drinks before lunch on Saturday, three days hence. As Sunday was a more usual day for such occasions, she assumed the day had been chosen with an eye to the Stearnses' Sabbath duties.

It wasn't one of Jocelyn's days for the LonStar shop, so Eleanor went next door first to Nick's to see what he made of it, and whether Megan had had a hand in it.

Nick was completely recovered except that his shoulders were still painful at times. Eleanor and Teazle found him in the studio behind his gallery, painting flower miniatures. Along with his Cornish landscapes, they were his bread and butter. The jam was provided by the abstract and semi-abstract paintings that sold occasionally for quite astonishing sums.

"I can do these without moving my arms too much," he explained, adding delicate touches of bright yellow to the blue Dutch iris blooming on the small rectangle of canvas.

"Whatever happened to make such a mess of your shoulders?" A question she hadn't thought of before.

"I was unconscious part of the time, and I'd rather not dwell on the rest."

"Sorry, Nick, I shouldn't have . . . I came to ask, did you get an invitation from Messrs. Freeth and Bulwer?"

"Yes, two. At least, I got one, and there's a similar envelope addressed to DS Megan Pencarrow. I'm not certain that's what it is, since she had already left for work when the post came."

"It's jolly lucky Mr. Scumble's letting her use a police car to drive back and forth."

"She's in his good books at the moment. Clearing up the Stone murder so fast looks good on his record, as well as hers. His benevolence has already lasted longer than we expected."

"It's not a quality he's noted for."

"So far, he's found some sort of work for her to do over in this direction most days. Yesterday, she took Alan Freeth's official statement, and this morning she got the typed copy signed before heading to Launceston. She's keeping on her room there for bad weather or working late."

"Sensible." Eleanor was itching to ask whether marriage had entered the picture yet. She managed to hold her tongue.

"Besides, there's not enough room here for all her stuff as well as mine. As it is, I've got her blouses hanging over in that corner."

They both glanced round the studio, crammed with art, art equipment, and art supplies. If they married, they'd probably move. The thought dismayed Eleanor.

Nick added, "Not trusting in Scumble's continuing benevolence, we were going to go prospecting for a car for her on Saturday."

"You won't be accepting Alan and Roland's invitation, then?"

"I can't answer for Megan, if that's what hers is. I'll be there. Freeth and I are practically blood brothers, now, after all."

"I'm glad he's feeling well enough to celebrate. I dropped in yesterday to enquire and Mrs. Raleigh said he's already doing some work upstairs in the morning. Not seeing clients yet, though, and in need of an afternoon nap, and early to bed."

"Poor devil." Nick frowned at his iris and picked up a paintbrush.

"I'll leave you in peace," Eleanor said. "Come on, Teazle."

They started up the hill towards the vicarage, only to meet Jocelyn on her way down with a shopping basket. Joce was far too proper to enquire about an invitation that Eleanor might not have received, so Eleanor asked her.

"Yes, I'll be there. Timothy wants to go, but at that time on a Saturday, he's usually struggling with his sermon. I believe he has some parish visits scheduled at St. Endellion in the afternoon. It's no picnic covering three parishes, I can tell you, not when you're as conscientious as Timothy is."

"I'm sure no one could do more than he does," Eleanor said soothingly. Pastoral visits were the vicar's forte, and often used as an excuse for avoiding social visits, which left him floundering. "He was magnificent when Roland needed his help. They'll understand if he can't make it to celebrate with them."

"Celebrate? Is that what you're expecting? I was rather hoping for an explanation, myself."

"Who knows, perhaps we'll get that, too, though I hardly think they owe us any explanation."

"Not *owe*, no. However . . . I wouldn't admit this to anyone else, Eleanor, but I, for one, am simply dying to know the story behind all your melodramatic goings-on. And that unfortunate woman . . . Don't tell me you aren't curious."

"Of course I am. I've got a list of questions as long as your arm. Megan won't answer them and I can't possibly put them to Alan, so I'm hoping he'll tell us without prompting. Hmm, Megan's invited, though. She may stop him revealing all, if there's a chance it'd compromise the case. Anyway, if it's just a celebration, I'm ready to celebrate."

THIRTY-ONE

Saturday was a perfect April morning, warm and sunny. Black-thorn and gorse were in full bloom outside the back door, sweetly scenting the air. Crookmoyle Lighthouse stood out against the cloudless sky, with gulls soaring round it in the currents created by the cliffs. Down at the harbour, frills of foam rolled in and broke in sparkling froth against the quay.

Eleanor took Teazle for a walk through the opes and up the little stream that now and then rose and flooded the meadow. She might miss the shops, but the bakery at least would stay open all day now that the tourist season was getting under way. She could have a pasty for dinner today, and baked beans or chicken noodle soup tomorrow. She always had a few cans in the cupboard for emergencies. There was always toasted cheese or scrambled eggs, too.

Returning home later than intended, she hastily changed into a respectable dress and shoes, then went round to Nick's—or Nick and Megan's, as she was beginning to think of it.

She took Teazle with her, after some havering. The dog hadn't been specifically invited, but nor had she been specifically disin-vited. Alan Freeth had welcomed her into his office. She was a good girl and might even serve to lighten the atmosphere if things got over-emotional.

Nick wore paint-free jeans and a blue shirt with only a single small splotch of purple on one cuff. Megan, in a plain dark dress and jacket, looked as if she wasn't sure whether to be a police officer or just a guest.

"I hope it's a purely social occasion," she said forebodingly. "I don't want to have to butt in to break up the party to prevent things being said that we want kept quiet for the moment. Nor to have to whip out my notebook and start taking notes."

"Don't borrow trouble, dear. Surely they wouldn't have invited you if Alan intended to reveal anything problematic. Are you ready to go? Here are the Stearnses."

The bell on the street door of the gallery jangled as Jocelyn came in alone. "Timothy's had to cry off, as I expected," she said. "Sunday's sermon is in its usual Saturday muddle. Shall we go?"

What with shoppers and the early-tourist traffic, they had to go single file on the narrow pavement. A breeze had started up and tiny puffs of white cloud were scudding in from the west. Eleanor was glad she'd walked Teazle earlier. When they reached the lawyers', Roland Bulwer came down in response to the doorbell. He ushered them up to the sitting room.

Alan Freeth pushed aside the ottoman he'd had his feet on and stood up to greet them. Pale and thin, he couldn't be said to look in the pink of health, but considering he'd been at death's door not so long ago, Eleanor thought he was making a remarkable recovery.

Jocelyn apologised for the vicar's absence. Everyone sat down except Roland, who bustled about pouring drinks, sherry for Eleanor and Jocelyn, bitter lemon for Megan—in case she had to consider herself on duty at some point—beer for Nick.

"Top up your brandy, Alan?"

"No, thanks." Alan visibly braced himself. "I . . . I had a speech prepared, but in the end, all I want is to tell you about Rosie. You were all caught up, one way or another, in the"—he took a deep, shuddering breath—"in the horrible events—"

"Alan!" Roland put out a shaking hand. "You don't have to do this."

"I owe them an explanation. I owe it to Rosie's memory. I can't let her remain in the minds of my friends—I hope, my friends—"

Eleanor joined in a murmur of assent. She was afraid Megan had not.

"I don't want you remembering her as a shadowy figure somehow associated with vicious criminals, not when I owe her so much." Alan stopped, and seemed to be trying to reassemble his thoughts.

"Start at the beginning," suggested his logical lawyer partner with a sigh.

"The beginning. Yes. Roland and I were articled to the same firm in London. I'm a Londoner. He's a West Country man. When he qualified, a year ahead of me, he joined this practice, just one elderly man looking for someone to take some of the burden off his shoulders. Roland wanted me to join him when I had taken my articles." He fell silent.

"Alan, you don't have to—"

"I do. I want everything out in the open at last. I'm tired of living in ambiguous shadows, pretending, wondering whether people know who—what I am, whether they'll mind if they find out. I'm sorry, but I do have to."

With a nod, Roland raised one hand to his brow and bowed his head, concealing his eyes.

Alan turned back to his rapt audience. "You must understand, things were different then, the law, people's attitudes. Not that it's all smooth sailing today. I didn't want to admit, to myself or anyone else, that I'm gay, as they say nowadays. Gay! Not a word I'd have chosen. Be that as it may, Roland came down here and I stayed in London and a year later went to work for another firm. I did all right, started collecting clients, including George Carpenter, an extremely prosperous dealer in objets d'art, as he called himself."

"Mr. Freeth," Megan interjected, "I trust you don't intend to—"

"I'm telling my personal story, Sergeant. Miss Pencarrow. What I have to say will not impinge on current police investigations, you have my word."

"Thank you." Megan subsided, though she remained alert.

"Carpenter invited me to his house, and there I met Rosie. Much as I wished to prove myself 'normal,' I don't suppose the notion of marrying would have crossed my mind if he hadn't pushed us together."

Married! thought Eleanor. So that was the elusive connection between the two. She hadn't even considered the possibility.

"He gave me more work," Alan continued, "encouraged me to take Rosie out for a stroll, to tea, to the cinema, and finally dinner and dancing. I didn't mind. She was very sweet. Her mother had died some years earlier, and her father had doted on her and sheltered her. It never seemed to occur to her not to follow his orders, couched as gentle suggestions."

"What about her brother?" Eleanor asked. Freddy Carpenter had shown no signs of having recognised Alan, hadn't even said he looked familiar.

Megan frowned at her. "He's very much part of a current case, Aunt Nell."

"But we're talking about long ago."

Megan made a resigned gesture.

"I never met him," said Alan. "He was abroad, carrying out some shady business or other for his father. I didn't discover until Rosie and I were married that George Carpenter was a crook. I assume I can say that, Miss Pencarrow, as he's dead? He expected that once she was my wife, I'd be his tame solicitor, dealing discreetly with his breaches of the law and advising him how to skirt it."

He glanced at Megan, who looked grim but didn't stop him. George Carpenter was beyond the reach of the law.

"I refused to involve myself in skirting the letter of the law. That was part of the reason I couldn't stay with Rosie. She loved her father. She had no idea then that he was a criminal. He kept his legitimate business well separated from the crooked. I couldn't disillusion her and remove her from his influence. Or so I told myself."

Jocelyn was incredulous. "She must have suspected something was wrong."

"Not as regards her father's business ethics, and I never said a word against him. But innocent as she was, she could hardly help knowing there was something wrong with our marriage, even though we were . . . very fond of each other. The truth is, I couldn't go on living the pretence, and I realised how much I loved and missed Roland."

His partner raised his head with a faint smile.

Alan didn't appear to notice. His faraway look was focussed on the past. "My poor Rosie, all along the line she got the short end of the stick. I told her to divorce me, promised I wouldn't contest anything she said. She had my bank's address if she needed to get in touch, to get papers signed, or if she needed money, but I didn't tell her where I was going. I had to make a clean break, more with her father than with her. I didn't hear from her again till last month."

"She didn't ask for money?" Nick asked.

"Not a penny. She went back to her father, as I'd assumed she would."

"No papers to sign?" The vicar's wife was still—or again—incredulous. "In a divorce, there are always papers to sign."

"How do you know, Joce? You've never—"

"I've held the hands of weeping parishioners while they signed. The Church does not approve of divorce, but straying sheep are the more in need of shepherding."

"There are always papers to be signed," Roland confirmed, "though in the case of desertion, where the deserting party cannot be found, they are not always signed. But Alan left a forwarding address."

Alan and Megan exchanged a glance. He shrugged and gestured to her to proceed.

"There's no record of a divorce," she confirmed. "But there is of her second marriage, in the name of Carpenter, to Victor Stone."

"So Rosie is—was still your wife, Alan?" Bigamy, Eleanor supposed, frowned upon by law, religion, and culture. She continued her thoughts aloud. "In Nepal, polyandry is customary, and of course polygamy is common all over the world."

"Really, Eleanor!"

"Saying 'really' doesn't change the facts, Joce."

"The fact is, Aunt Nell, bigamy is against the law in Britain. However, it's not likely it would ever have come to our attention if Mrs. . . . Freeth had not been murdered. The lack of a divorce was at least in part responsible for her death."

"It's not the fact that's important," Alan said impatiently. "It's her reason. It was for my sake Rosie didn't divorce me. She was afraid that what came out might wreck my career, or even land me in gaol. She didn't tell her father why I left her, and let him assume she had got a divorce. When he decided she should remarry, she didn't dare explain."

"You say he loved her," Nick objected. "I can see why he might want her to remarry, but why pick a monster like Stone?"

"The Yard did some research for us," said Megan. "At the time, he needed a hard man, or thought he did. He'd crossed a competitor and he wanted a bodyguard he could count on. We reckon he felt a son-in-law was more reliable than a hired man. I can't comment on whether he loved his daughter, but his own skin was certainly more precious to him."

"What about her brother?" Eleanor asked. "He cared for her, or at least that was his excuse for—"

"Aunt Nell!"

"Oh, sorry. He probably didn't have much influence with their father anyway."

"It wasn't long after the wedding that Freddy did time—in prison," Megan elucidated for Jocelyn's sake. "For fraud. He was never a bullyboy. And he wasn't present to see how Stone treated her."

"According to Rosie," said Alan, "that was when her father more or less kicked him out of the family. He said he didn't mind whether Freddy was straight or crooked as long as he was competent at it. That was what opened her eyes to his own unlawful activities, and to his using her to keep Stone's allegiance."

"He may have bought his son-in-law's allegiance," Megan said sceptically, "but the Sandman went on taking outside jobs. They'd only been married a couple of years when he was arrested for murder, though convicted of manslaughter, I'm sorry to say. He got out a couple of months ago. And the present case begins at that point, so I can't tell you anything more."

"You're ahead of me, Sergeant. I'll go back to Rosie's story. A couple years after her husband was incarcerated, her father died, leaving a large fortune to her and not a penny to Freddy. That was when she came to Cornwall, not knowing I was here."

"Did she say why she chose Cornwall?" Eleanor asked.

"She wanted to be far away from London. She'd heard that many people retire here, because of the climate, so she wouldn't stick out like a sore thumb. She bought the house, using the 'Mason' alias. She didn't want anything to do with her brother, straight or crooked, but she made him an allowance, knowing that if she gave him a share of the inheritance, he'd just lose it gambling and come begging. And she was afraid of Stone."

"With good reason," said Nick, rubbing his shoulders.

"Nick!"

"Sorry, darling."

"Rosie had covered her tracks," Alan said, "but when Stone was due to be released—"

"How did she find out?" Jocelyn asked.

"She knew how long his sentence was, Mrs. Stearns. She was afraid he'd find her in spite of her efforts at concealment."

"How right she was!"

"She decided to consult a lawyer, and when she asked her bank for advice, one of the names they suggested was mine."

"Sir, I think that's far enough."

"Not quite, Sergeant. There's one more thing I want everyone to know about. It's a public document, so I don't believe there can be any objection."

"Not until after probate." Megan sighed. "All right, but Nick, Aunt Nell, Mrs. Stearns, *please* keep quiet about it till after the inquest. If you talk, the guv'nor will have my head."

"I do not gossip, Megan," Jocelyn said stiffly.

"Her will, of course," said Nick. "I saw the envelope when she sent me to her drawer for sketching paper. Stone found it, presumably. Is that why—"

"Nick, shut up! If Freeth insists on telling us about it, that's one thing. Speculating about Stone's motive is out of bounds."

"She had never made a will. When I urged her to do so, the two points she was clear on were that she wanted her brother provided for and she didn't want Stone to inherit as her presumed husband. The will I drew up cut him out in definitive terms, denying that their marriage was valid."

"No wonder he— All right, Megan, I won't say it."

"Further, it acknowledged that she and I were still husband and wife. I tried to persuade her against that, but in the end she was adamant. The most time-consuming part was setting up a trust for her brother. She kept changing her mind about the terms, the main reason the whole business took several days. It was complicated, too, as she wanted to ensure his being able to access the principal to pay for lawyers if he got into trouble again."

"Still more complicated now," said Roland. "The law prohibits his profiting by her death if he caused it, which is a moot question until after the trial." He noticed Megan's scowl. "My apologies, Miss Pencarrow. I must also apologise for having troubled the police with a report that Alan was missing. I was unaware of his marriage, you see, let alone that his . . . wife was in the vicinity. That's why he didn't let me know. . . ."

"It's a very good job you called us in, sir. If you hadn't, I wouldn't have been on the spot to witness . . . events." Megan turned back to Alan. "Are you finished with the terms of the will, sir? Because, if so—"

"Not quite. It's a large estate. Wisely, she'd kept her father's very sound investments and lived almost entirely on half the interest and dividends, added to what she made with the bed-and-breakfast business. The other half paid Freddy's allowance. That will go into the trust, whatever becomes of it. Her half, though I argued strenuously against it, comes outright to me."

"Good lord," said Nick, "assuming Stone found the will—"

"He did," said Megan. "DI Eliot says he burned it in her fireplace."

Eleanor was puzzled. "But if it was destroyed . . ."

"I'd already posted a second signed copy to myself here."

"If he'd known who you were, sir, it's unlikely you'd have come out of the adventure alive."

"Believe me, I know I'm lucky to have survived."

"I doubt you would have," Megan said flatly, "if Nick hadn't hung on to you in the van."

"So that's what strained your shoulders, Nick?" Eleanor guessed.

"Megan, I asked you not to tell!"

"I didn't. Aunt Nell did."

"Don't squabble, children," said Eleanor. "Alan, you were saying? About the will? Won't you go on? Rosie left you half the estate?"

Alan and Roland were gazing at Nick as if they'd never seen him before. Alan pulled himself together.

"I can't keep it, of course. Apart from other considerations, most of it is probably the fruit of ill-gotten gains. There appears to be no way to make restitution. So I've decided—Roland and I have decided—to give it to LonStar."

Eleanor was flabbergasted. So, judging by her face, was Jocelyn.

Jocelyn recovered first. "Ill-gotten or not, on behalf of LonStar, we are extremely grateful, and you may be sure it will be put to good use."

Eleanor added her thanks. "How very, very generous."

"You have all been more than kind to us," said Roland. "Gresham, I can't express—"

"Then please don't," Nick begged. "Honestly, it was not an enjoyable exploit and I never want to hear another word about it."

Jocelyn tactfully intervened. "The vicar asked me to tell you he's most concerned about your arrangements for Mrs. . . . Freeth's funeral service. He's very willing to officiate if you wish, unless . . . Did she have a church affiliation in London, perhaps?"

"My dear Mrs. Stearns," said Alan, "I'm much obliged to the vicar, but I won't need to trouble him. Rosie was a Londoner, born and bred, but she wanted to be buried at St. Materiana's, in Tintagel. The church was good enough to grant her request. The service will be on Monday, if any of you would like to attend. Roland arranged everything. You see, Rosie made us joint executors." His voice wavered. "She said she wanted to show she didn't hold a grudge against either of us." He broke down in tears.

Roland Bulwer crossed the room to sit on the arm of his partner's chair and put his arm round his shoulders. Their guests quickly finished their drinks and departed amid muttered goodbyes, thanks, and promises to attend the service.

Outside, as she clipped on Teazle's lead, Eleanor said, "I wish I'd had a chance to get to know Rosie properly. I found her very pleasant."

"She was," Nick agreed.

"And she sounds like a good person, in spite of everything."

"We all have our faults," said Jocelyn with unwonted tolerance.

"The reverse goes for her brother," Megan said. "No one could call him a good person. In fact, he was a rat. But he avenged her in the end and he deserves kudos for that. If I wasn't sworn to uphold the law, I'd be inclined to shake his hand. All the same, I'm damn glad you collared him, Aunt Nell."

"I beg your pardon?" Jocelyn exclaimed.

"Sorry, Mrs. Stearns."

"Not the '*damn*.' " The vicar's wife flushed. "The '*collared*.' "

Eleanor caught Megan's eye. "I'm not allowed to tell you about that before I tell the coroner," she said virtuously. And she had no intention whatsoever of telling even him the whole story.

Emotionally drained, she turned down Jocelyn's offer of lunch. After a brief stop at home to change, she took Teazle out through the back door and up the footpath behind the cottages to the clifftop walk north of the village.

The ever-restless sea reflected the grey clouds. A brisk, chilly breeze encouraged Eleanor to walk fast. No one else was about.

She quickly reached her favourite spot on this stretch of the cliffs. A wooden bench set back a few yards from the edge gave a magnificent view from Tintagel Head to The Mouls, and behind it was a flat area of turf perfect for her exercises.

The grass was wet, so she sat on the bench. After a few deep breaths, she noticed the scent of thyme and gorse in the air. She closed her eyes and heard a skylark singing, the cries of seagulls, the distant, intermittent roar of waves breaking on the rocks at the foot of the cliff. The stress of the morning ebbed.

Calm and focussed, she began her exercises. After all, even here in peaceful Cornwall, her skills sometimes came in handy.

HISTORICAL NOTES

Launceston station was axed by Dr. Beeching in 1966. For the purposes of this story, I have axed Dr. Beeching.

Sanctions forced Ian Smith and his supporters into a peace agreement with the African freedom fighters in 1980, and universal franchise was established.